W9-CPF-119

DISCARD

TRAVEL TEAM

TRAVEL TEAM

MIKE LUPICA

Thorndike Press • Waterville, Maine

Recommended for Middle Readers.

Published in 2005 by arrangement with
Philomel Books, a member of Penguin Group (USA) Inc.

Thorndike Press® Large Print The Literacy Bridge.

The tree indicium is a trademark of Thorndike Press.

The text of this Large Print edition is unabridged.
Other aspects of the book may vary from the original edition.

Set in 16 pt. Plantin by Ramona Watson.

Printed in the United States on permanent paper.

Library of Congress Cataloging-in-Publication Data

Lupica, Mike.
    Travel team / by Mike Lupica.
       p. cm.
    Summary: After he is cut from his travel basketball team
— the very same team that his father once led to national
prominence — twelve-year-old Danny Walker forms his own
team of cast-offs that might have a shot at victory.
    ISBN 0-7862-7415-8 (lg. print : hc : alk. paper)
    1. Large type books. [1. Basketball — Fiction.
2. Fathers and sons — Fiction. 3. Schools — Fiction.
4. Large type books.] I. Title.
PZ7.L97914Tr 2005
  [Fic]—dc22   2005000621

For my sons,
Christopher and Alex and Zach,
who always play bigger.

This book is for them,
and any kid in any sport ever told he,
or she, wasn't big enough.
Or good enough.

And, as always, for Taylor.

ACKNOWLEDGMENTS

One last time,
my thanks and gratitude go to
my pal Jerry Hartnett,
to Coach Keith Wright,
and to one travel team I will never forget:
The 2002–03 Rebels.

He knew he was small.

He just didn't *think* he was small.

Big difference.

Danny had known his whole life how small he was compared to everybody in his grade, from the first grade on. How he had been put in the front row, front and center, of every class picture taken. Been in the front of every line marching into every school assembly, first one through the door. Sat in the front of every classroom. Hey, little man. Hey, little guy. He was used to it by now. They'd been studying DNA in science lately; being small was in his DNA. He'd show up for soccer, or Little League baseball tryouts, or basketball, when he'd first started going to basketball tryouts at the Y, and there'd always be one of those clipboard dads who didn't know him, or his mom. Or his dad.

Asking him: "Are you sure you're with the right group, little guy?"

Meaning the right *age* group.

7

It happened the first time when he was eight, back when he still had to put the ball up on his shoulder and give it a heave just to get it up to a ten-foot rim. When he'd already taught himself how to lean into the bigger kid guarding him, just because there was always a bigger kid guarding him, and then step back so he could get his dopey shot off.

This was way back before he'd even tried any fancy stuff, including the crossover.

He just told the clipboard dad that he was eight, that he was little, that this was his right group, and could he have his number, please? When he told his mom about it later, she just smiled and said, "You know what you should hear when people start talking about your size? Blah blah blah."

He smiled back at her and said that he was pretty sure he would be able to remember that.

"How did you play?" she said that day, when she couldn't wait any longer for him to tell.

"I did okay."

"I have a feeling you did more than that," she said, hugging him to her. "My streak of light."

Sometimes she'd tell him how small his

dad had been when he was Danny's age.

Sometimes not.

But here was the deal, when he added it all up: His height had always been much more of a stinking issue for other people, including his mom, than it was for him.

He tried not to sweat the small stuff, basically, the way grownups always told you.

He knew he was faster than everybody else at St. Patrick's School. And at Springs School, for that matter. Nobody on either side of town could get in front of him. He was the best passer his age, even better than Ty Ross, who was better at everything in sports than just about anybody. He knew that when it was just kids — which is the way kids always liked it in sports — and the parents were out of the gym or off the playground and you got to just play without a whistle blowing every ten seconds or somebody yelling out more instructions, he was always one of the first picked, because the other guys on his team, the shooters especially, knew he'd get them the ball.

Most kids, his dad told him one time, know something about basketball that even most grown-ups never figure out.

One good passer changes everything.

Danny could pass, which is why he'd always made the team.

Almost always.

But no matter what was happening with any team he'd ever played on, no matter how tired he would be after practice, no matter how much homework he still had left, this driveway was still his special place. Like a special club with a membership of one, the place where he could come out at this time of night and imagine it up good, imagine it big and bright, even with just the one floodlight over the backboard and the other light, smaller, over the back door. His mother had done everything she could to make the driveway wider back here, even cutting into what little backyard they had the summer before last. "I told them you needed more room in the corners," she said. "The men from the paving company. They just nodded at me, like corners were some sort of crucial guy thing."

"Right up there with the remote control switcher for the TV," Danny said. "And leaving wet towels on the bathroom floor."

"How are the corners now?"

"Perfect," he said. "Like at the Garden."

He had just enough room in the corners now mostly for shooting. He didn't feel as if he was trying to make a drive to the basket in his closet. Or an elevator car. He had room to *maneuver*, pretend he really *was* at the real Garden, that he was one of the small fast guys who'd made it all the way there. Like Muggsy Bogues, somebody he'd read up on when one of his coaches told him to, who was only 5-3 and made it to the NBA. Like Tiny Archibald and Bobby Hurley and Earl Boykins, a 5-5 guy who came out of the basketball minor leagues, another streak of light who showed everybody that more than size mattered, even in hoops.

And, of course, Richie Walker.

Middletown's own.

Danny would put chairs out there and dribble through them like he was dribbling out the clock at the end of the game. Some nights he would borrow a pair of his mother's old sunglasses and tape the bottom part of the lens so he couldn't see the ball unless he looked straight down at it. This was back when he was first trying to perfect the double crossover, before he even had a chance to do it right, his hands being too little and his arms not being nearly long enough.

Sometimes he'd be so dog tired when he finished — though he would never cop to that with his mom — he'd fall into bed with his clothes on and nearly fall asleep that way.

"You done?" she'd say when she came in to say good night.

"I finally got bored," he'd say, and she'd say with a smile, "I always worry about that, you getting bored by basketball."

Everybody he'd ever read up on, short or tall, had talked about how they outworked everybody else. Magic Johnson, he knew, won the championship his rookie season with the Lakers, scored forty-two points in the final game of the championship series when he had to play center because Kareem Abdul-Jabbar was hurt, then went back to East Lansing, Michigan, where he was from, in the summer and worked on his outside shooting because he'd decided it wasn't good enough.

Tonight, Danny had worked past the time when his mom usually called him in, not even noticing how cold it had gotten for October. Worked underneath the new backboard she'd gotten for him at the end of the summer. Not the only kid in his class with divorced parents now. Not the smallest kid on the court now. Just the only one. He'd drive to the basket and then hit one of the chairs with one of his lookaway passes. Or he'd step back and make a shot from the outside. Sometimes, breathing hard, like it was a real game, he'd step to the free throw line he'd drawn with chalk and make two free throws for the championship of something.

Just him and the ball and the feel of it in his hands and the whoosh of it going through the net and the sound one of the old wooden school chairs would make when he tipped it over with another bounce pass. He knew he was wearing out another pair of sneakers his mom called "old school," which to Danny always meant "on sale." Or that she had found his size at either the Nike store or the Reebok store at the factory outlet mall about forty-five minutes from Middletown, both of them knowing she couldn't afford what Athlete's Foot or Foot Locker was charging for the new Kobe sneakers from Nike, or Iverson's, or McGrady's. Or the cool new LeBron James kicks that so many of the Springs School kids were wearing this year.

He finished the way he always did, trying to cleanly execute the crossover-and-back five times in a row, low enough to the ground to be like a rock he was skipping across Taylor Lake. Five times usually making it an official good night out here.

Except.

Except this was as far from a good night as he'd ever known.

Basically, this was the worst night of his whole life.

Danny's mother, Ali, watched him from his bedroom window on the second floor, standing to the side of the window in the dark room, trying not to let him see her up here, even though she could see him sneaking a look occasionally, especially when he'd do something fine down on the court, sink a long one or make a left-handed layup or execute that tricky dribble he was always working on.

Sometimes he'd do it right and come right out of it and be on his way to the basket, so fast she thought he should leave a puff of smoke like one of those old Road Runner cartoons.

God, you're getting old, she thought. Did kids even know who the Road Runner was anymore?

"Nice work with that double dribble," she'd tell him sometimes when he finally came in the house, tired even if he'd never admit that to her.

"Mom, you *know* it's not a double dribble. *This*" — showing her on the kitchen floor with the ball that was on its way up to his

14

room with him — "is a double *crossover*."

"Whatever it is," she'd say, "don't do it in the kitchen."

That would get a smile out of her boy sometimes.

The boy who had cried when he told her his news tonight.

He was twelve now. And never let her see him cry unless he took a bad spill in a game or in the driveway, or got himself all tied up because he was afraid he was going to fail some test, even though he never did.

But tonight her son cried in the living room and let her hug him as she told him she hoped this was the worst thing that ever happened to him.

"If it is," she said, "you're going to have an even happier life than I imagined for you."

She pushed back a little and smoothed out some of his blond hair, spikey now because he'd been wearing one of his four thousand baseball caps while he played.

"What do I always tell you?" she said.

Without looking up at her, reciting it like she was helping him learn his part in a school play, Danny said, "Nobody imagines up things better than you do."

"There you go."

Another one of their games.

Except on this night he suddenly said,

15

"So how come you can't imagine a happier life for us *now?*"

Then got up from the couch and ran out of the room and the next thing she heard was the bounce of the ball in the driveway. Like the real beat of his heart.

Or their lives.

She waited a while, cleaned up their dinner dishes, even though that never took long with just the two of them, finished correcting some test papers. Then she went up to his room and watched him try to play through this, the twelve-year-old who went through life being asked if he was ten, or nine, or eight.

Ali saw what she always saw, even tonight, when he was out here with the fierce expression on his face, hardly ever smiling, even as he dreamed his dreams, imagining for himself now, imagining up a happy life for himself, one where he wasn't always the smallest. One where all people saw was the size of his talent, all that speed, all the magic things he could do with a basketball in either hand.

No matter how much she tried not to, she saw all his father in him.

He was all the way past the house, on his way to making the right on Cleveland

Avenue, when he saw the light at the end of the driveway, and saw the little boy back there.

He stopped the car.

Or maybe it stopped itself.

He was good at blaming, why not blame the car?

What was that old movie where Jack Nicholson played the retired astronaut? He couldn't remember the name, just that Shirley MacLaine was in it, too, and she was going around with Jack, and then her daughter got sick and the whole thing turned into a major chick flick.

There was this scene where Nicholson was trying to leave town, but the daughter was sick, and even though he didn't care about too much other than having fun, he couldn't leave because Shirley MacLaine needed him.

You think old Jack is out of there, adios, and then he shows up at the door, that smile on his face, and says, "Almost a clean getaway."

He used to think his life was a movie. Enough people used to tell him that it was.

He parked near the corner of Cleveland and Earl, then walked halfway back up the block, across the street from 422 Earl, still wondering what he was doing on this street tonight, cruising this neighborhood, in this stupid small small-minded town.

Watching this kid play ball.

Mesmerized, watching the way this kid, about as tall as his bad hip, could handle a basketball.

Watching him shoot his funny shot, pushing the ball off his shoulder like he was pushing a buddy over a fence. He seemed to miss as many shots as he made. But he *never* missed the folding chairs he was obviously using as imaginary teammates, whether he was looking at them when he fired one of his passes. Or not.

Watching the kid stop after a while, rearrange the chairs now, turning them into defenders, dribbling through them, controlling the ball better with his right hand than his left, keeping the ball low, only struggling when he tried to get tricky and double up on a crossover move.

The kid stopping sometimes, breathing hard, going through his little routine before making a couple of free throws. Like it was all some complicated game being played inside the kid's head.

He hadn't heard anybody coming, so he nearly jumped out of his skin when she tapped him on the shoulder, jumping back a little until he saw who it was.

"Why don't you go over?" Ali said.

"You shouldn't sneak up on people that way."

"No," she said, "*you* shouldn't sneak up on people that way."

"I was going to call tomorrow," he said.

"Boy," she said, "I don't think I've ever heard that one before."

Ali said, "You can catch me up later on the fascinating comings and goings of your life. Right now, this is one of those nights in his life when he needs his father, Rich. To go with about a thousand others."

Richie Walker noticed she wasn't looking at him, she was facing across the street the way he was, watching Danny.

"Why tonight in particular?"

"He didn't make travel team," she said now on the quiet, dark street. "*Your* travel team."

"Look at him play. How could he not make travel?"

"They told him he was too small."

2

Just like that — like always, really — it was as if his dad had appeared out of nowhere.

Danny sometimes thought he should come with one of those popping noises that came with the pop-ups on the videos.

Pop-Up Richie Walker.

"Hey," his dad said.

"Hey."

This was one of those times Danny always carried around inside his head, where his dad would get down into a crouch, like one of those TV dads coming home from work, and put his arms out, and Danny would run into them.

Only it never seemed to happen that way. It happened like this: Both of them keeping their distance and neither one of them knowing exactly what to say.

Or how to act.

Richie Walker had never been a hugger. It was actually a joke with them, Richie having taught Danny when he was five or six what he called the "guy hug" from sports, one without any actual physical contact, one where you leaned in one way and the other guy leaned in the other way and then you both backed off almost immediately and did a lot of head nodding.

"In the perfect guy hug," his dad had said, "you sort of look like you're trying to guard somebody, just not too close."

Like them: Close, but not too close.

Neither one of them said anything now. At least that way, Danny thought, they were picking right up where they left off.

His dad said, "How you doing?"

"I'm okay." Danny put the ball on his hip. "What're you doing here?"

All his dad could do with that one was to give a little shrug.

"You see Mom?"

"Just now."

"You want to go inside?"

"I always liked it out here better."

Danny thought about passing him the ball, knowing they'd always been able to at least talk basketball with each other. Instead, he turned and shot it.

Missed.

"You call that a *jump* shot?" his dad said. "Looks more like a *sling* shot to me."

His dad, Danny knew, had always been more comfortable giving him a little dig than having a real conversation with him. His mom once said that the only time Richie Walker had ever been happy was when he was one of the boys. So all he knew how to do was treat Danny like one of the boys.

Except sometimes Danny didn't know whether he was being sarcastic when he picked at him. Or just mean.

"No," Danny said, retrieving the ball. "On account of, I can't jump."

Richie Walker said, "You need to work on your release. Or you're gonna get stuffed every time."

Danny thinking: *Tell* me about getting stuffed.

Danny dribbled back to the outside now, desperate to make one in front of him, like this was some test he needed to pass right away, barely looked at the basket before he turned and swished one.

"That better?"

"Not better form," Richie said. "Better on account of, it went in."

His dad moved out of the shadows from the back door then. Danny thought his dad could still pass for an older kid himself, with his white T-shirt hanging out of his jeans, low-cut white Iverson sneakers, untied. And, Danny could see he still had those sad, sad eyes going for him, as if he weren't watching the world with them, just some sad old movie.

Same old, same old, Danny thought.

Richie was limping slightly, just because he'd limped slightly for Danny's whole life. Moving like an old man, not just because of his knees, but because of the plate in his shoulder, and his rebuilt hip, the one he used to tell Danny the doctors made for him out of Legos, and all the rest of it.

"Anything new with you?" his dad said.

And just by the way he said it, trying to make it sound casual, like he was making an effort to start a conversation, Danny knew his mom must have told him about travel.

Danny stood there, twirling the ball, wanting to hug the non-hugger, and then he couldn't help himself.

He started crying all over again.

The tears seemed to throw his dad off, like Danny had thrown a pass he wasn't expecting.

Even then, Richie Walker wanted to talk about basketball.

They sat in two of the folding chairs.

His dad said, "You still do the one I showed you?"

"The one where I tape the bottom of my sunglasses and try to dribble through everything without looking down?"

"Yeah."

"I raised the bar a little," Danny said. "Sometimes I put a do-rag over my eyes and try to do it completely blindfolded."

He actually saw his dad smiling then. Though Richie Walker could manage to do that without anything different happening with his eyes.

"So did I," Richie said. "Except we didn't call them do-rags, we called them bandanas."

He picked up the ball in his big hands. Danny was always fascinated by his father's hands, just because they didn't seem to go with the rest of him. Like somebody with a tiny head and Dumbo's ears.

Big hands. Huge hands. And those long arms that the writers used to say Richie Walker had borrowed from somebody 6-6 or 6-7; in one of the old stories he'd read, Danny couldn't remember where, one of his dad's old teammates with the Warriors had said, "Richie Walker is the only little 5-10 white man had to reach *up* to zipper his pants."

He had been listed at 5-10 in his playing days, anyway.

But his dad had said that was only if you counted the lifts in his sneakers.

Danny watched as his dad — without even trying, almost not aware he was doing it, like somebody not knowing they were cracking their knuckles — dribbled the ball on the right side of his chair, took the ball behind him, keeping the low dribble, picking it up with his left hand on the other side, finishing the routine by spinning the ball on his left index finger before putting it back in his lap.

"Your mom already told me what happened," he said.

Danny said, "I figured."

"They still do the tryouts the way they did in the old days — two nights?"

Danny nodded. "The dads running the twelves can't have one of their own sons trying out. There were, like, six of them doing the evaluation. Mr. Ross didn't get to do any evaluating because of Ty, but he was in the gym the whole time."

"Just in case they needed somebody to explain basketball," Richie said.

Jeffrey Ross was the president of the Middletown Savings Bank. President of the Middletown Chamber of Commerce. President of Middletown Basketball. Danny had always wondered if his son, Ty

— the best twelve-year-old basketball player in their town, or any town nearby — was required to call his father Mr. President, or if he could get by with Dad.

"He still act as if somebody should stop and give him the game ball if he actually remembers your first name?" Richie said.

"Some of the other kids were saying that you don't have to worry about him blowing his whistle, because somebody already stuck it up his you-know-what."

Richie Walker said, "It was the same way when he was your age." He gave Danny a long look now and said, "He say anything to you?"

"Not until tonight, really, when he called to tell me how sorry he was that I didn't make it. He said he didn't want me to find out in a letter."

"Right," Richie said.

"The only other time I actually heard him say anything was when he welcomed us all the first night."

"He thinks he's the mayor."

"Mom says that in his mind, it would be a step down, from his current position as king."

"That's all you ever got out of him? That he was sorry?"

Danny said, "There was the one other

thing, as we were breaking up into groups the first night. He was talking to a couple of the evaluators — you know, the clipboard guys? — and he told them, 'Remember, I want us to get bigger this year, last year we were too small and we couldn't even get out of the sectionals.' "

"He said that he wanted the twelve-year-old travel team from Middletown to get *bigger?*"

Danny nodded.

"What," Richie said, "so we can match up better with the Lakers?"

Danny told him the rest of it.

How the travel teams in town still went from fifth grade through eighth, but that seventh grade was still the glamour team in Middletown, in any sport.

Richie: "So that hasn't changed."

Danny: "You guys were the ones who changed it, remember?"

Richie: "Nobody ever lets me forget."

This year there were thirty kids trying out for twelve spots. The first night, Danny heard one of the moms in the parking lot saying that none of the other age groups had even close to that many boys trying out. Last year, Danny told his dad, they'd only had to cut seven kids when he'd made the sixth-grade team.

"This is all about the chance to get to the nationals," Richie said, "and be on television. Parents probably think it's the peewee basketball version of one of those *Idol* shows. Or one of those talented-kid deals. Think Dick Vitale or somebody is going to discover their little Bobby as a future all-America."

"That's what happened with you guys," Danny said.

"Yeah, and the town never got over it."

His dad didn't usually like to talk about what he called back-in-the-day things. Or talk about anything else, really. Tonight was different, and Danny didn't know why. He just knew it was the two of them, sitting here.

The way Danny had always thought things were *supposed* to be.

"Back to you," Richie Walker said.

Like passing him the ball.

Okay, Danny said, first night they all did some basic drills, shooting and dribbling and fast breaks and passing and one-on-one defending; they broke up the big guys and little guys as evenly as they could and scrimmaged for the second hour, while the evaluators sat in the gym at Middletown High School, carrying those clipboards.

Evaluating their butts off.

Richie said, "How'd you do?"

"I thought I was flying," Danny said. "I mean, I knew I was going to look better because I had Ty Ross on my team. But when I got home, I told Mom that I didn't want to get ahead of myself or anything, but I thought I'd made the team."

"He's that good? The Ross boy?"

"Better than good. He's someone for me to pass the ball to."

The second night, the one that killed him, they scrimmaged the whole night. When Mr. Ross called to give him the bad news, he said that what they'd tried to do, in the interest of fairness, was have the kids on the bubble spend the most time on the court.

Richie said, "He actually used those words? On the bubble?"

"His exact words."

"The whole goddamn world is watching too much sports on television, and don't rat me out to your mother for swearing."

"The second night," Danny said, "I didn't have anybody big who could catch, or shoot."

"Out of all those bubble boys."

Danny said, "They had this new kid from Colorado guarding me."

"How big?"

Danny looked down at his old white Air Force Ones, high-tops, noticed a new hole near his right toe. "Big enough."

He didn't know anything that night about being on some stupid bubble, he told Richie Walker now. He could just tell that everything got real serious toward the end; that he would look up sometimes when he made a good play, when he made a good pass or got past the Colorado kid — Andy Mayne — and got to the basket, hoping to see some reaction from the clipboard dads.

"Guys like that," Richie said, "they're too busy getting ready to agree with each other."

"Anyway," Danny said, "the last fifteen minutes or so I played like crap, I didn't need anybody to tell me that afterward. I was just hoping then that they hadn't forgotten how good I thought I looked the night before."

"They tell you they'd send out letters telling you whether you'd made it or not?"

Danny nodded. "We'd all filled out the envelopes with our addresses on them when we checked in."

"But Jeff Ross called you personally."

"Because you and Mom and him are old friends."

"What a guy."

They sat there in the cool night, listening to the sounds of Earl Avenue, up and down the block, an occasional car passing, the Malones' cocker spaniel yapping away, rap music coming from somebody's bedroom window, Danny content to sit here like this until morning.

Danny finally said, "You haven't told me yet what you're doing here."

Richie Walker grinned at his son, and did what he'd do sometimes, put a little street in his voice.

"Doing the same thing I have my whole life, dog," he said. "You know, chillin' and lookin' for a game."

He took the ball out of his lap and handed it to Danny. "Shoot for it."

"Winners out."

"You feeling any better?"

Danny had already decided something: He wasn't going to cry about this ever again. Not in front of his parents, not in front of him*self*.

No more crying in basketball.

"I'll feel better when I beat the great Richie Walker in a game of one-on-one."

He dribbled to the foul line, getting fancy, crossing over with his right hand to his left, wanting to come right back with the ball and go straight into his shot.

"Don't take this the wrong way, junior," his dad said. "But that move needs work."

Danny said to his dad, "Yeah, yeah, yeah, you want to talk or you want to play?"

3

Sometimes Danny would Google up his dad's name when he was online, Google being the Internet version of going through the scrapbooks that his mom still kept down in the basement.

Even if you practically needed a treasure map to find the scrapbooks.

He did it now with the two of them downstairs in the kitchen, drinking the coffee his mom had made, telling him they were going to catch up a little, his dad saying he'd come upstairs to say good night before he left.

Good *night*, Danny noticed.

Not good-bye.

His parents were acting friendly with each other when they left the room, smiling at him, at each other, as if nobody in the room had a care in the world. Danny loved it when adults tried to put a smiley face on something, thinking they were putting something over on you.

It made Danny want to yell "Busted!" sometimes.

Oh, sure. There was a definite kind of smile you'd get from your parents, your teachers, your coaches. Danny thought it should come with some kind of warning siren. Most of the time it meant they were pissed, but still getting to it. Pissed at you, about something you did, or something you said.

Or in this case, pissed at each other.

He couldn't remember a time when his mom wasn't mad at his dad for leaving them.

It was more complicated with his dad, who had been mad at everything and everybody for as long as Danny could remember.

Now they were downstairs, catching up on all that, probably trying to see who could say the meanest things without either one of them ever raising their voice. His mom, he knew, would do most of the talking, wanting to know what he was doing in town and how come he hadn't been sending enough money from Las Vegas, where he'd been working for the Amazing Grace casino the past few years, how long he was going to be in Middletown before he left and — her version of things — broke his son's heart all over again.

Only it didn't break his heart, that was the thing he could never get her to understand.

There were plenty of things that bothered him, sure. His father hardly ever called, start there. Never wrote. Are you joking? And wouldn't learn how to use a computer, which meant e-mail was out of the question. Maybe that was why tonight felt like the longest conversation they'd had in a long time. Or maybe the longest they'd ever had.

You want to know what came closest to breaking his heart? That Danny had to look up all the things about Richie Walker's basketball career, from Middletown on, that Richie Walker could have told him himself.

Basically, though, Danny had just decided his dad was who he was. Like some sort of broken and put-back-together version of who he used to be. He was who he was and their relationship was what it was, and Danny couldn't see that changing anytime soon. And maybe not ever. He'd never describe it to his mom this way, but he'd worked it out for himself. It went all the way back to something she'd told him once about heart, and how you could divide it up any way you wanted to.

So, cool, he'd set aside this place in his heart for his dad, and what his dad could give him. Wanting more but not expecting more, happy when his dad would show up, even unexpected, the way he did tonight, sad when he left.

You got used to stuff, that's the way he looked at it.

Even divorce.

He would never say this to his mom, but he always thought he'd gotten used to divorce a lot better than Ali Walker ever had. Or ever would.

He just didn't go out of his way trying to put a fake smiley face on it the way they did, at least when he was still in the room.

So now he was in front of the Compaq his mom had gotten him from CompUSA for Christmas, Googling away. He had typed in "Richie Walker," knowing the first page of what the search engine would spit back at him, the list of Web sites, knowing that the one he wanted was at the top of the second page.

ChildSportsStars.Com.

He clicked on *W,* knowing his dad's was there at the top of the list, Tiger Woods's down a bit lower. And Kerry Wood, the Cubs pitcher, even though Danny didn't exactly think you were a child because you made the big leagues when you were nineteen or twenty.

Then he clicked on his dad.

"The biggest little kid from the biggest little town in the world," the headline read.

And proceeded to tell you all about Richie Walker, the dazzling point guard from the tiny town in Eastern Long Island who took his twelve-year-old travel team all the way to the finals of the nationals — what was now known as the Little League Basketball World Series — and about the Middletown Vikings' last upset victory in their amazing upset run to the title over a heavily favored team from Los Angeles.

On national television.

Danny felt as if all of it had been tattooed to his memory, the way you wished you could tattoo homework to your memory sometimes.

He knew almost all of it by heart, including the stuff in the little box on the side that told you about how ESPN was just starting out in those days and was putting just about anything on the air; how they decided to give the full treatment to the twelve-year-old nationals once they realized what kind of story they had with Richie Walker and his team.

The bio in ChildSportsStars.Com said:

". . . and so Richie Walker and his teammates became a Disney movie even before Disney owned ESPN, the travel-team version of *The Bad News Bears*. There would even be the suggestion later that it was the story of the Middletown Vikings that had at least partially inspired the *Mighty Ducks* movies that would come later, the one about a ragtag hockey team from nowhere always finding a way. . . .

"But every movie like this needs the right star. The right kid. And Middletown had one in Richie Walker, the sandy-haired point guard with what the commentators and sportswriters of the day described as all the Harlem Globetrotters in his suburban game. . . ."

By the time Middletown had pulled off its first huge upset, over a heavily favored team from Toledo, Ohio, ESPN had fallen in love with Richie Walker and the Vikings. By the second week of the tournament, the whole thing had picked up enough momentum in the middle of February, the dead time in sports between the Super Bowl and the start of the NCAA basketball tournament, that ABC came in and made a deal to put the finals on *Wide World of Sports*, just because ESPN wasn't getting into enough households in those days, cable television not being nearly the force it is now.

Or so it said on ChildSportsStars.Com, and anywhere else they gave you a detailed account of the life and times of Richie Walker.

Middletown's own.

He had heard so many people say it that way, his whole life, that he sometimes felt as if the last part, Middletown's own, was part of his dad's name.

The son an expert on the town's favorite son.

Before it was all over, there would be a small picture of his dad's face on the cover of *Sports Illustrated*, not the main part of the cover, but up in a corner. His dad would end up on *The Today Show*, too.

Even people who didn't watch the Middletown–L.A. final on a Saturday afternoon had managed to see the highlights of the last minute of the one-point game.

Most of which involved Middletown's little point guard, Richie Walker, dribbling out the clock all by himself.

Going between his legs a couple of times.

Crossing over in the last ten seconds and even pushing the ball through one of the defender's legs when it looked as if L.A.

had finally trapped him in a double-team, while their coach kept waving his arms in the background and telling them to foul him.

Problem was, they couldn't foul what they couldn't catch.

You could watch the last minute by clicking on the video at ChildSportsStars.Com.

Danny had watched it what felt like a thousand times. Watched his dad and felt like he was watching himself, that's how much alike they looked (and how many times had people in town told him *that*, like it was breaking news?). Watched him with that old blue-and-white jersey hanging out of his shorts, dribbling. Finally being carried around the court at Market Square Arena in Indianapolis when it was all over and Middletown had won, 40–39.

They had that picture on the Web site, too.

The rest of it told how Richie Walker went on to become a high school all-America at Middletown High. A second-team all-America at Syracuse University and one of the first real stars who helped make the Big East a major draw on ESPN. First-round draft choice of the Golden State Warriors.

Finally a member of the NBA's All-Rookie Team, even though his rookie season was cut short by the famous car accident on the San Francisco side of the Bay Bridge after a Warriors-Spurs game.

Pictures of that, too: What was left of the Jeep Cherokee Richie Walker had bought before the season with some of his bonus money, the one they had to use the Jaws of Life to get him out of that night.

Danny knew the pictures the way he knew everything else about his dad's basketball career. . . .

"Hey sport," Richie Walker said now from behind Danny. "What you looking at there?"

Danny executed the essential kid laptop move, clicking off and folding down the screen, as slick as anything he could do on the court.

He gave his standard answer, no matter which parent was the one who'd suddenly appeared in the doorway.

"Nothing," he said.

He and his mom were in the kitchen having breakfast, both of them already dressed for school, him for the seventh grade at St. Patrick's, his mom for her eighth-grade teaching schedule there. He went there because she taught there. They could afford Danny going there because she taught there, and his tuition was free.

His mom used to joke that it was usually private-school people that were supposed to be snobs, but that somehow they'd tipped that on its head in Middletown, and it was the parochial school kids, the ones who *didn't* go to Springs, that were supposed to be from the wrong side of the tracks.

"Even though we don't really have any tracks," she'd say.

He had *SportsCenter* on the small counter television set, sound muted. It was part of their morning deal, just understood. Sound on until she came into the room, then sound off.

If there was some important news story going on, they watched *Today*.

Danny said, "Did he tell you why he's here?"

"He says he's not sure, exactly."

Ali Walker stuffed one last folder into an already-stuffed leather shoulder bag, one that looked older to Danny than she did.

She turned and looked at him, hand on hip.

Giving him her smiley-face, even with his dad nowhere to be found.

"Sometimes he can't figure out why he's here until he's not here anymore," she said. "Part of your father's charm."

"I didn't mean to make you mad."

"Look at me," she said. "Do I look mad?"

Danny knew enough to know there was nothing for him with an honest answer to that. "No," he said.

"I'm not mad," Ali said, "I'm just making an observation."

"Right."

Aw, man, he thought. Where did that come from?

Rookie mistake, Walker.

"What does that mean?" she said. *"Right?"*

Danny took a deep breath, let it out nice and slow, trying to be careful now. Trying to make his way across a patch of ice. "It just seems to me, sometimes, no big deal, that he seems to make you as mad when he is around as when he's not around. Is all."

She started to say something right back, stopped herself with a wave of her hand.

"You're pretty smart for a guy who's really only interested in perfecting the double dribble."

"Crossover dribble."

"What*ever,*" she said, as if impersonating one of the girls in his class.

"Hey," he said, "that's a code violation."

Another one of their deals. There were strict rules of conversation at 422 Earl Avenue. No cursing of any kind, not even in the privacy of his own driveway. No *"duh."* And, under penalty of loss of video privileges for the night, no "what*ever.*"

Ever.

Ali Walker taught English. And was constantly telling her son that in at least one classroom — hers — and one home — theirs — the English language was not going to sound as if they were communicating by instant-message.

"I was just making a joke," she said. "Trying to sound like one of the dear, ditzhead girls in one of my classes."

"Well," he said, imitating her now, "I'm going to let it go just this one time."

She laughed and came over with her coffee and sat across from him at the table, close enough that he could smell the smell of her, which was always like soap. She looked pretty great for somebody's mom, the way she always did, even before she started fussing with her hair and doing some fast makeup deal and getting ready for the day. Danny knowing that his mom

44

was the prettiest woman in their school and probably in Middletown. Occasionally even described as "hot" by the high school boys at St. Pat's, something he wasn't sure should bother him or not. He just decided it was the ultimate guy compliment and left it at that.

This morning his mom wore the new blue dress she'd bought for herself last week at the Miller's fall sale.

Because Ali Walker was, in her own words, the "queen of sales."

As moms went, from his own limited experience with them, Danny believed you couldn't be much cooler than his was, even considering all the things she didn't know about guys.

Despite all she *thought* she knew.

"Straight talk?" she said.

He knew what was coming, just because sometimes he did, sometimes he got into her brain the way she got into his. Maybe because it was just the two of them.

"You have to be strong today, you know that, right?" she said.

Danny said, "I'd have to be strong at Springs. I don't even think anybody from St. Patrick's made the team."

"Are you sure? Did Jeff Ross tell you that?"

Danny pushed Waffle Crisp cereal around in his bowl. "I'm the best at St. Pat's," he said.

"Your friends are still going to ask you about it. And they're going to want to talk about it. Because that's what kids do, they talk dramas like this to death."

He was still staring down at what was left of his cereal, as if there were a clue in there somewhere.

Or a code he was trying to crack.

"Them asking me can't be worse than him telling me," he said in a quiet voice.

"Hey," she said, "is that true? The whole team is going to be from Springs this year?"

"Last year we only had three from St. Pat's. Me. Matt Fitzgerald. And Bren. Bren didn't even try out this year, he said he heard they thought he was too small to have made it last year."

Bren Darcy had been an inch taller than Danny since first grade, an inch Danny kept thinking he could make up on him but never did.

"But what about Matt?" his mom said. "He's the tallest seventh grader in this town. God, his sneakers look like life rafts. If the mission statement is to get quote *bigger* unquote, how does he not make the team?"

"The only reason he made it last year was because he is so big. But he really doesn't know how to play basketball yet, and I don't think anybody's ever really taught him. His dad's a hockey guy, and I still think he's pis . . . mad that Matt didn't want to be the world's tallest defenseman."

"Your father always said you can't teach tall."

"Matt had just made up his mind that he was lucky to make it last year and wasn't going to make it this year. Like the opposite of Bren. And that's pretty much the way he played in tryouts."

"A self-fulfilling prophecy."

Danny looked up at her. "Like you telling me how hard today is going to be at school."

"I'm just being realistic," she said. "You know some of your friends are going to know, I'm sure the news has been instant-messaged through just about every neighborhood in Middletown, USA, who made the team and who didn't."

"Mr. Ross said the letters won't arrive until today's mail."

"Right. And everybody in this town is soooooo good at keeping secrets."

"Mom," he said. "I'm okay. Okay?"

"Look out for the ones who bring it up

first, like they want to commiserate."

He was pretty sure what she meant, just by the way she said it. The rule was, if he didn't know what a word meant, he was supposed to ask.

She said, "You know what I'm saying here?"

"They'll act like they feel bad, but they really won't?"

"They'll be the ones who are happiest that you didn't make it."

"I get it."

"And you'll get through this, kiddo," she said. "It's like I always tell you: Everything's always better in the light of day. Especially for my streak of light."

"Yeah."

"Danny?"

"Yes, I'll get through it. And everything *is* better in the light of day."

Ali Walker said, "I don't have to tell you about Michael Jordan again, do I?"

"Every time I go out for anything, you tell me about how he got cut from his junior high school team."

"There'll be other teams," she said. "There were for Michael Jordan and there will be for you."

He thought: Just not this team.

Not the one that'll probably be the first

one to make the World Series since his dad's.

"Are you ready to rock and roll?" she said.

Danny took his bowl over to the sink — good boy, Walker — and rinsed it and placed it on the bottom rack of the dishwasher.

" 'Rock and roll' is so incredibly lame," he said. "You need to know that."

"Rock and roll is here to stay," his mom said. "And will *never* die."

"You tell me that about as often as you tell me about Jordan getting cut."

She shut off the television, and the kitchen lights, made sure the back door would lock behind them when they left.

"I get with a good thing," she said, "I stay with it."

"I forgot to ask before," Danny said. "Is *he* staying?"

Ali Walker went out the door first, saying, "He actually mentioned that he might hang around for a while."

Danny made one of those looping undercuts like Tiger Woods made after sinking a long putt.

Without turning around, his mom said, "I saw that."

4

As soon as he walked in the side door at St. Patrick's, the side facing the baseball and soccer fields, Danny knew that everybody knew.

As if somehow his classmates had all Googled up "Danny Walker" and there was a place you could go to read all about how he hadn't made seventh-grade travel. How being a small, flashy point guard in Middletown wasn't nearly as big a deal as it used to be.

How Richie Walker's kid hadn't made the team.

He walked down the long hall to his locker, eyes straight ahead, imagining they were all watching him and they all knew.

Even the girls.

Tess Hewitt, who he really liked — though he was quick to point out to Will that didn't necessarily mean *liked* liked, and to please shut up — was standing next to his locker when he got there about ten after eight, five minutes before first period.

So was the red-haired witch, Emma Carson.

Danny believed that Emma got to St. Patrick's every morning by taking the bus from hell.

Emma had started liking Danny in fifth grade, and had continued liking him right up until it was clear that not only did he not feel the same way about her, he was never going to feel the same way, he didn't even want her on his e-mail buddy list. That was when she apparently made a decision to torture him any chance she got.

Which meant today was going to be the closest thing for her to a school holiday.

Or a national holiday.

"Any word yet on travel?" she said.

Tess gave her a look and poked her with an elbow at the same time. Tess was taller than Emma, taller than Danny, too, by a head, with long blond hair that stretched past her shoulders, and long legs, and blue eyes.

Next to her, Emma Carson looked like a fire hydrant.

She wasn't as pretty as Tess, as nice, as smart. As skinny. Even at the age of twelve, Danny Walker knew that Emma going through middle school and maybe even high school standing next to someone who looked like Tess Hewitt wasn't the most brilliant idea in the whole world.

Danny tossed his backpack, the one his mom said was heavier than he was, into his locker, grabbed his algebra book; he'd done his homework in study hall the day before, knowing he wasn't going to be much interested in cracking any school books later if he happened to find out early that he hadn't made the team.

"I didn't make it," Danny said, his words landing harder in his locker than the backpack had.

He turned to face Emma. "But you knew that already, didn't you, M and M?"

Danny knew she hated that nickname, whether the other kids were talking about the rapper Eminem or the candy. Probably the candy more, since it was generally acknowledged by the male population at St. Patrick's School that Emma Carson could stand to lose a few.

"I didn't do anything, Daniel Walker," she said. "You're the one who didn't make travel."

"Well, you got me there," he said.

Tess said, "I'm sorry, Danny."

He wasn't sure whether this was technically commiserating from Tess or not, since Emma was the one who'd originally brought up the subject of travel, and him not making it. He was sure of this, though: He wanted to talk to Tess about this in the worst way; he'd even thought about going online last night to see if she had her own computer up and running and open for business.

It was a lot easier to talk about stuff like this online. To talk about almost anything, actually.

It's why he wished his dad would get a computer. Maybe then they could have a real conversation.

Maybe then they could talk.

"Whatever," he said.

Emma said, "I heard the whole team is from Springs."

Danny said, "Boy, you have all the sports news of the day, don't you? Tell me, Emma, have you ever considered a career in broadcasting?" And then before she could say some smart-mouth thing back to him, Danny said, "Wait a second, considering how you spread news around this place, you've started your career in broadcasting already, haven't you?"

"C'mon, Tess," she said. "I guess it must be *our* fault he won't be playing travel basketball this season."

Tess looked as if she wanted to stay, but knew that would be violating some code of girl friendship. So the two of them walked away from him down the hall.

Before they turned the corner, Tess quickly wheeled around, made a typing motion with her fingers without Emma seeing, and mouthed the word "Later."

Danny nodded at her, and then she was gone.

If yesterday was the worst day of his whole life, you had to say that today was at least going to be in the picture.

His best friend at St. Pat's was Will Stoddard, whose main claim to sports fame in Middletown was that his uncle was the old baseball pitcher Charlie Stoddard, who'd been a phenom with the Mets once and then made this amazing comeback a few years ago with the Red Sox, pitching on the same team with his son, Tom, Will's cousin.

Will's other claim to fame, much more meaningful to all those who knew and loved him — or just knew him — was this:

He could talk the way fish could swim.

He talked from the moment he woke up in the morning — this Danny knew from sleepovers — until he went to bed, and then he talked in his sleep after that. He talked in class, in the halls, in study halls, on the practice field, in the car when Ali Walker would drive him to St. Pat's, on the computer. When Danny would go to Will's house, he would watch in amazement as Will would carry on one conversation with him, another on the phone, and have four instant-message boxes going on his computer screen at the same time.

Knowing that he was going to have to listen to Will go on about travel basketball for the entire school day wasn't the most exciting prospect for Danny, but he'd caught a break when Will didn't show up at the locker next to his before the bell for first period; didn't, in fact, show up for algebra until about two minutes after Mr. Moriarty had everybody in their seats and pulling out their homework assignments.

When Will came bursting through the door, red-faced as always, his thick dark curly hair looking as if it had been piled on top of his head in scoops, Mr. Moriarty looked over the top of his reading glasses and said, "So nice of you to join us, Mr. Stoddard."

At which point Will stopped in front of the class and theatrically produced a note from the pocket of his St. Pat's–required khaki pants, like it was a "Get Out of Jail Free" card he'd saved from Monopoly.

"From my mother, sir," he said. "Car trouble. We had to drop the Suburban off at Tully Chevrolet this morning, and pick up a loaner, which turned out to be a piece of cra . . . junk, which meant we had to turn around and go back and get another one when we were halfway here. Plus, my father is out of town, and the car conked out at the end of the driveway. . . ."

"If it's just the same with you, Mr. Stoddard, I'll wait for the movie to find out the rest of it."

As he walked past Danny's desk at the front of the classroom, Will said, "Does this suck, or what?"

Danny knowing he meant travel, not being late for class.

Will had tried out for travel even though he knew he wasn't going to make it the way he hadn't made it last year or the year before. He had more heart than anybody Danny knew, more heart than Danny himself, he had always tried out, had always spent more time diving for loose balls than anybody in the gym.

But knowing the whole time he wasn't good enough.

Sometimes Danny thought that the only reason Will was even there was to cheer him on, to watch his back.

That kind of friend.

Now he was the friend saying "suck" too loud in Mr. Moriarty's classroom.

Mr. Moriarty said, "I don't believe I quite caught that, Mr. Stoddard."

Will stopped where he was, turned to face the music.

"I *said*," Will said, "that being late for a great class like yours, sir, really *stinks*."

There were some stifled laughs from behind Danny. When they subsided, Mr. Moriarty said, "Why don't we just say it now, and get it over with."

To the rest of the class, Will Stoddard said, "You've been a great audience, don't forget to tip your waitresses."

It was his favorite line from some old *Saved by the Bell* rerun.

As always, there was a brief round of applause. Mr. Moriarty was older than water and liked to carry himself like a bit of a stiff, but he was a good guy. One who seemed to get it.

Or most of it, anyway.

Will was definitely right about one thing, though:

This did suck.

Even for a streak of light, even in the light of stinking day.

5

Even when the week should have been over, at the end of school on Friday, it wasn't over.

Because the Middletown Vikings were going to have their first practice, at five-thirty sharp, in the gym at St. Pat's.

Danny's mom had told him at lunch. The new basketball floor they'd put down in the Springs gym had suddenly turned lumpier than a bowl of Quaker oatmeal, and they were talking about tearing it up and starting all over again. And the high school gym was booked and there was an art fair at the Y.

And St. Pat's was always looking for any new ways to raise money and now they had this exciting moneymaking opportunity from the Middletown Basketball Travel Team.

Starting today.

"Figured you ought to hear it from me, sport," she said.

"They're coming to *my* school?" he said. "*My* gym? What's the next thing I'm going to find out, they expect me to ball boy for them?"

"Why don't you go with Will after school today instead of playing ball?" she said. "Or take the bus and I'll meet you at home?"

His mom usually had teacher conferences after school on Friday, and Danny would get the gym to himself.

He shook his head no, closing his eyes good and tight.

No crying in basketball.

"I'm staying until they come," he said.

"But I'm going to be late today."

Danny said, "I'm staying."

Will tried to get Danny to take the town bus with him after school. Or take the bus he took to the Flats, on the north side of town where he lived, a few blocks from Danny, and play his new *NCAA Football 2005* video game.

"My dad *played* college football," Will said. "He says *NCAA 2005* is better."

Will Stoddard basically said Danny should do anything except be anywhere near the St. Pat's gym when the "Springers" — it's what he called Springs School kids, in honor of *The Jerry Springer Show* — showed up for their first practice.

But Danny kept shaking his head every time Will came at him with a new alternative plan, even after they'd started playing one-on-one in the gym, and all the St. Pat's buses, including Tess's, were long gone.

Occasionally Will would whip out his cell phone, which he kept in his baggy white North Carolina shorts even when playing basketball. There was a part of Will, Danny knew, that believed that cell phones could even make sick people better.

"I'll call my brother," he said. "He got his license yesterday. He's *looking* for reasons to ride around. He *wants* to come get us, and he usually doesn't want anything to do with either one of us."

Danny shook his head from side to side, more slowly than before, trying to get through to him. "This is my day to have the gym to myself," he said. "I'm not going to go hide in my locker."

They had finished their first game of one-on-one, Danny winning, 10–7. The game was only that close because Danny had given Will his usual spot of five baskets. Sometimes he'd given him seven baskets in a game of ten and still beat him.

Will always took the points and always

acted as if he was the one doing Danny the favor.

But then Danny would watch with great admiration sometimes as Will would borrow money off one of their other classmates and make the other kid feel as if this was his lucky day, that handing over five bucks to Will Stoddard was somehow exactly the same as the other kid winning the lottery.

Danny had just scored the winning basket by pushing the ball between Will's legs, flashing around him to collect it, and banking a combination hook-layup high off the backboard.

"Where'd you get that one?" Will said.

"My dad showed me."

"I've been meaning to ask you all day — is he still in town?"

They had finished playing now, were sitting on the stage, still sweaty, legs dangling over the side. Danny bounced the ball on St. Pat's floor. "Unless he left while I was in school today."

"You haven't seen him since . . . ?"

"No," Danny said. "But no biggie. You know how my dad is." He turned to look at Will and shrugged. "Sometimes he's as hard to cover as ever."

"Yeah," Will said. "I know what you mean."

Danny thinking: But how could you know, really? Danny knew how most people in Middletown were still obsessed with Richie Walker's comings and goings, how the Town Biddies still loved to gossip up a storm about the biggest star to ever come out of here, the kid who put Middletown on the map because of travel basketball, the kid who finally made it to the NBA, then left his wife and child not too long after the car accident that ended his career.

They didn't really know anything about his dad, any more than people who'd only ever seen him play on television or read about him in the newspapers knew about his dad.

Of course Danny felt the exact same way sometimes, not that he was going to put an ad in the *Middletown Dispatch* about that.

Danny said, "You don't have to stay until they come."

Will, whose hair looked even more like steel wool when he'd start to sweat, the Bob Marley T-shirt his parents had brought him back from Jamaica looking as wet as if he'd just gone swimming in it off Main Beach, said, "Correction: *You* don't have to stay."

"They're going to be practicing here for

a couple of months," Danny said. "I'm going to have to see them around here eventually. I might as well get it out of the way today."

He hopped off the stage. "Like I said, I'm not running away, dude."

Will sighed, the sound like air coming out of a balloon. "No, why do something like that when you can get your butt run *over* by the Springers instead?"

"Don't take this the wrong way," Danny said. "But I don't remember asking for your opinion about any of this."

"Let me ask *you* something," Will said. "When have I ever cared whether you asked for my opinion or not?"

"You want me to spot you seven this time?"

Will said, "I don't want your pity. Make it six."

They were finishing that game when Ty Ross showed up. The first of the Middletown Vikings.

Ty Ross had gotten both taller and skinnier during the summer, which Danny knew from the tryouts.

He also knew Ty was still great.

Could still dribble with either hand, shoot with either hand when he got close in to the basket, see the whole court as if he had two sets of eyes going for him. He would pass the ball if somebody else even remotely had a better shot than he did *every single time.* Sometimes he would just give it up because in addition to all his other qualities as a ballplayer, Ty Ross was completely unselfish, sometimes to a fault. He wasn't the fastest kid in town, wasn't nearly as fast as Danny was, but he knew when to drive to the basket, when to step back and make one from the outside, from as far away as the three-point arc in the gym at Middletown High, when to pull the ball down and just set the offense all over again.

As far as Danny was concerned, Ty knew as much about the way the game should be played as he did. The two of them just seemed to know stuff that other kids their age didn't. Ty had been that way when they played fifth-grade travel together, and when they'd played sixth-grade travel together. He didn't just know more about basketball than the rest of the players, he knew more than the coaches, too.

He sure knew more than any parent yelling at them to do this or that from the stands.

All in the name of being good sports parents, of course.

That even went for Ty's dad, who, according to *Danny*'s dad, acted as if he'd invented basketball, not Dr. James Naismith.

"You know those Peach baskets Dr. Naismith used for the first basketball games?" Richie Walker had said one time. "Jeff Ross thinks he invented those, too."

On top of everything else, Ty Ross was such a nice kid that Will Stoddard said it made him physically ill.

He had dark hair, like his father, almost black, cut short this school year, his summer buzz still not having grown all the way out. He was wearing his own baggy basketball shorts, looking even baggier on him because his legs were so skinny they looked like stick-figure legs somebody had drawn on him. He was wearing a maroon Williams College T-shirt that looked to be about three sizes too big. Williams, Danny knew, was where Mr. Ross had gone to school.

Ali Walker had told Danny once that Ty was the player his father had always wanted to be. That he'd been the second-best player on the Vikings team that had won the World Series, behind Richie Walker, and that it had been pretty much the same way in high school. Danny's dad had then selected Syracuse — and the chance to play in front of thirty or forty thousand people every night in the Carrier Dome — after passing on most of the big ACC schools and even schools as far away as UCLA.

Mr. Ross, who had the grades, thought he'd have a better chance to play at a small school like Williams. Only he didn't, his mom said, never getting off the bench there before quitting the team his senior year.

"You know how your father says that the town never got over their team winning the travel-team World Series?" his mom said. "I'm not sure Tyler's dad ever got over being number two to your father during all their growing-up years."

"So," Danny remembered saying to her that night, "Mr. Ross was a real number two guard."

"That's basketball talk, right?"

"Mom," he said. "You know the point guard is called a one, the shooting guard is called a two, the center —"

"Stop," she said, and not for the first time when the subject was basketball, "I'll pay the ransom."

Ty and Danny had been teammates, starters both of them, on the fifth-grade team. Same thing the next year. Just not teammates this year. And maybe not ever again.

Now Danny watched as Ty came walking toward him with that pigeon-toed walk of his, walking straight down the middle of the gym, Danny knowing as he watched him what every kid in town knew already, that for as long as Ty Ross lived in Middletown, he was going to be the best kid walking into *every* gym.

All this time later, Danny thought to himself, it had worked out that a Walker was finally jealous of a Ross when it came to playing basketball.

Ty saw them over by the stage and came over, dribbling his own ball as he did.

"Hey, dude," Danny said to him.

Ty got right to it, not messing around, not even bothering with a greeting of his own.

"You should have made it," he said. "I should have called you as soon as I found out. You can ask my mom, I told her that night that you should have made it ahead of a lot of the guys who did."

It was the closest thing to a speech for him, coming out almost as if he'd rehearsed it.

"Thanks," Danny said, not knowing what else to say.

Wondering if Ty had expressed that same opinion to his dad, even though Ty was probably as intimidated by Mr. Ross as everybody else in town was.

Ty wouldn't let it go, as if this had been bothering him all week as much as it had bothered Danny himself. "You can play rings around some of the guards they picked ahead of you. And you know *how* to play better than *everybody* they picked ahead of you, that's for sure. And the whole thing is stupid and I wanted you to know it."

"Quick heads-up?" Will said. "I wouldn't let any of those other nose pickers who got picked ahead of our boy hear you saying that."

"Will," Danny said in a sharp voice, "I will pay you to shut up."

Will said, "I hate to reduce our relationship to money — but how much?" Then he said he was going to beat the soft drink machine out of a Coke, and did they want anything? Danny and Ty both said no.

Now it was just Danny and Ty in the gym.

Ty said, "You want to shoot around a little?"

"Nah," Danny said. "Will and me have got to be someplace. Maybe next week when you guys are here or something."

You lied enough, it got easier — that had been his experience, though pretty limited.

"Later," he said.

"Later," Ty Ross said.

Danny found Will at the soda machine and told him he was meeting his mom soon, which was technically true, as long as you had a pretty loose definition of the word *soon*.

"I'll call you later," Danny said, "or check you out on the computer."

"Either way," Will said. "You know my motto: We never close."

Then he whipped out his cell phone again to call his brother. The last thing Danny heard as Will walked down the hall was him saying, "Great news, you need to come get me at school." Then Danny saw him nod his head before saying, "You can thank me later."

Danny wasn't meeting his mother anytime soon. She was going to be later than usual on this Friday because she had promised to handle Drama Club rehearsals for Sister Marlene, the drama teacher at St. Pat's who had been out sick for a couple of days. The big first-semester production this year was *Guys and Dolls*, with

Bren Darcy playing one of the lead roles, a gambler named Nathan Detroit.

"Just remember Nate Archibald, one of our all-time faves out of ancient history," Bren had said. "And the Detroit Pistons."

They both loved Nate Archibald because his nickname as a player had been "Tiny."

Ali Walker had said that rehearsal went from four-thirty to six-thirty, which had been just fine with Danny at the time, it meant more gym time for him. It wouldn't have been that way a few years ago, when this auditorium had served as both a gym and a theater at St. Pat's. But since then, the Annual Fund drive had raised enough money and the kids had chipped in with money of their own and now Drama Club kids held both rehearsals and the plays themselves in the brand-new theater that had been built next to the lower school.

Only now he couldn't make himself leave the gym.

He knew he was better off going over and sneaking into the theater, up in the top row, watching Bren try to sing so he could bust his chops to the high heavens on Monday.

Except.

Except here he was, like he was nailed to the spot on the old stage at St. Pat's. Here

70

he was in what used to be the wings, stage right, peering through the sliding panel some St. Pat's kids had fashioned in the old days, like a sliding door, so on the night of the school play the kids could look out when they weren't on the stage trying to remember their lines, watching the audience while the audience watched them.

That was where Danny was watching the Middletown Vikings as they began their first practice.

In the past, the Middletown Basketball Association had hired outside coaches, usually young, to coach the various travel teams in town, boys' and girls', from fifth grade until the travel program ended in eighth. Danny had loved his coach of the last two years, a cool black guy in his twenties named Kelvin Norris, who'd thought nothing of making the two-hour car ride out from Queens twice a week, sometimes three times a week, for travel practices and games. Sometimes during the season, when there had been a Friday night game followed by a Saturday morning game, Coach Kel would stay over at the Walkers' house, or the Darcys', to the point where most of the travel-team parents considered him part of the family.

After coaching fifth grade his first year and sixth grade the next, moving up with them to the next level, everybody had just assumed that Coach Kel would move up again this season and work with the seventh graders. But then over the summer, Mr. Ross had called up Coach Kel at the summer camp he ran in the Catskills and told him that he, Mr. Ross, planned to coach the seventh graders himself this season.

Coach Kel had called Danny when it happened, wanting him to know, saying, "I think Mr. Ross's first choice to coach Ty all the way into the national spotlight was Phil Jackson. Obviously his second choice was himself."

"But everybody wants to play for you," Danny said. "Including Ty. *Especially Ty.* I don't think he's crazy about having his dad as his *dad.* Having him as a coach will probably just make him crazy."

That was when it still mattered to Danny who was going to coach the Vikings this season.

"Before I get too much older," Coach Kel said, "I've got to get as good at kissing butt as I am with those *X*'s and *O*'s and that passion-for-the-game stuff."

Mr. Ross said Middletown Basketball

loved Coach Kel's enthusiasm so much that he wanted him to drop back and work with the fifth graders. Coach Kel turned him down, saying he wanted to work with older kids, not younger kids.

Danny didn't know what Coach Kel was doing now, whether he was coaching somewhere or just teaching phys ed at Christ the King High School. Danny just knew that kneeling at the middle of the court with all the players around him, speaking in such a low voice that Danny couldn't hear what he was saying from his hiding place, was Mr. Ross.

Coach Mr. Ross, that's what he'd probably have them call him.

Danny could see all of the usual suspects out there, trying to act as if they were fascinated by whatever pep talk — or sermon — Ty's dad was giving them:

There was Ty's best friend, Teddy Moran, who was going to be one of the point guards on the team, along with the kid from Colorado, Andy Mayne. Danny noticed that Andy, who'd had long hair almost down to his shoulders for the tryouts, now looked as if he'd gotten his hair buzzed to look like Ty's. He was also wearing the same McGrady sneakers as Ty. Top of the line, a hundred bucks, maybe more. Andy's hair and sneakers at least made Danny smile. A lot of kids who grew up in Middletown tried to copy Ty Ross. Now the new kid from Colorado was the latest to run with the crowd.

Danny saw the two black kids on the team, two of the coolest kids in the whole town, Alex Aaron and Daryll Mullins, both of them as long and skinny as Ty.

Towering above everybody was Jack Harty, star tight end on Middletown's twelve-year-old travel football team. Jack, with his dark complexion, looking big and wide like some dark-colored Hummer H2, was a born rebounder, stronger than everybody else his age, one who had a way of finding the ball once the people around him stopped flying off in different directions, like characters he'd just terminated in a blood-gore video game.

Jack Harty was also famous in Middletown for being the only seventh grader who had already started shaving.

Huge deal.

So there they all were. Ty and Teddy. Alex and Daryll and Jack and the rest of them, Mr. Ross reaching into the big bag he had next to him and passing out *practice* jerseys, the guys trying those on before Mr. Ross went into the bag and came out with more goodies: long-sleeved navy-blue shooting shirts you could wear over your jersey while you were warming up.

Great, Danny thought. What did Tess and her friends call it when they went girlie-girl shopping?

Accessorizing?

Now they were even doing that with travel basketball.

"First class for you guys all the way," Mr. Ross said when he was done passing everything out. He was walking toward the stage now, where he'd left his bag of basketballs, walking straight at Danny as if he'd noticed the narrow hole in the wall. "First class all the way for a team that's going all the way this season."

He was a little taller than Danny's dad. Danny was always struck first by how tall somebody was, was always playing off this adult's height against somebody else's. He did the same with kids, like he was comparison shopping, never really knowing how tall other kids were in feet and inches, even if he knew exactly what he was on a daily basis, exactly fifty-five inches — no sneakers — by his last check in the door frame of his room.

Fifty-five.

The speed limit.

He kept looking through the narrow

space, feeling as if he were on the wrong side of a fence.

"One ball," Mr. Ross said, taking a single ball, brand-new, out of the bag. "Three lines at the other end. Big guys — and there's more size on this team than ever, and not by accident — in the middle. I want you to bounce the ball off the backboard, grab it like it's a rebound, make an outlet pass to the guard on your right. Then guards, you pass it to the guy cutting to the middle from the other wing. Cut behind your passes. And make sure to get the lead out of those Hefty-bag shorts you all like to wear."

He threw the ball to the other end of the court and blew the whistle he was wearing around his neck.

Some of these guys love their whistles as much as they do their clipboards, Danny thought.

"I don't want to see that ball touching the floor," Mr. Ross said from underneath the basket closest to the stage, giving another quick blast to his whistle, as if he were using it like punctuation marks. "This is going to be a team that *passes* the ball, not a team that *dribbles* the ball."

The first three-man fast break came right at Danny.

Jack Harty started the play at the other end, wheeling around after he came down with his fake rebound, throwing a hard two-hand chest pass to Teddy, who got it to Ty, cutting toward the middle of the court from the other wing.

Ty gave it back to Jack Harty with so little effort, so quickly, it was as if the ball had never passed through his hands at all.

Jack passed it back to Teddy, who waited a couple of beats too long, hesitated just enough when he fed Ty near the basket — Ty needs *me* passing him the ball, Danny told himself, even in a boring drill like this — that Ty had to go underneath the rim and then twist his body around in the air to make a neat reverse layup.

As soon as those three got out of the way, here came the next three players on the break, Alex and Daryll so fast filling their lanes that they left fat Eric Buford behind, Eric's face already the color of one of the fat tomatoes Ali Walker grew in her backyard garden.

Danny Walker, his hands pressing against the wall above him, watching like he had a hidden camera, felt his knees buckle suddenly, without warning, the way they'd buckle when one of your buddies snuck up behind you and gave them a little karate chop.

Felt his heart sink at the same time.

He slid the board back in place, placed his forehead against it, stayed like that for a minute, listening to the basketball sounds from the other side of the wall, seeing it all with his hole closed up, with his eyes closed.

His gym.

Their team.

Hey little guy, he thought to himself, using the refrain he'd heard his whole life.

You're right back where you started, little guy.

You're with the wrong group again.

6

Danny Walker didn't pick up a basketball for a week, Friday to Friday, a personal best.

Or worst.

He didn't play the weekend after that first Vikings practice at St. Pat's. Or after dinner the first couple of nights of the next week. When his mom finally asked him about it on Tuesday, he shrugged and said, "My knee's been bothering me a little bit, is all."

"An injury?" she said, giving him that raised-eyebrow deal that Danny figured girls must master at, like, the age of ten and then always have in their bag of tricks after that. "To my six-million-dollar bionic boy?"

"Excuse me?"

"Never mind," she said, looking a little embarrassed. "I don't need other people to remind me I'm getting older, I do it to myself. Constantly."

"You're still young," he said, as a mild form of protest.

"Well, not if I'm coming at you with old TV shows like *The Six Million Dollar Man*. It was about this hunky guy who was half-hunky guy and half-superhuman robot."

Danny said, "How big did they make him?"

She acted as if she hadn't heard him.

"Is your knee really hurting you?" she asked. "Should I call Dr. Jim?"

He had muted the Knicks-Timberwolves preseason game he'd been watching when she'd come into the room. Now he pointed the remote at the set and let the voices of Marv Albert and Walt Frazier rejoin them.

"I think I'll just rest it a couple more days," Danny said.

"By the way," she said, "when are the tryouts for Y basketball?"

"Coming up pretty soon," he said, trying to be as vague as possible. "Will mentioned something about that the other day, I think."

"It would be fun if the two of you ended up on the same team."

On television, Frazier was talking about somebody whooping and swooping, then swishing and dishing, but Danny had missed the play.

"*Really* fun," he said. "Fun, fun, fun."

"Is that sarcasm, Daniel Walker?"

"Just kidding," he said.

Always the last line of defense, whether you were kidding or not.

He muted the set again. "Have you seen Dad?"

"At the Candy Kitchen the other day when I ran in to grab a sandwich. He was at the same seat at the counter he's been sitting at since high school. I'm going to petition the town to give it landmark status."

"By himself?" Danny said. "Not doing anything?"

"Yes," his mom said in a voice so soft it surprised him, just because of who they were talking about. "That's exactly what he was doing. Sitting alone. Not talking to anybody. Not doing anything except drinking a cup of coffee."

She came off the couch and knelt next to the easy chair. "Is there something you want to talk about that we're not talking about here? Like this knee of yours, maybe, and how maybe that's not the thing that's keeping you off the court?"

He looked past her to the Knicks game — you had to be careful about eye contact sometimes, eye contact could get you every time — and said, "What would you think if I didn't, like, play basketball this year?"

★ ★ ★

Danny had to give his mom credit. She didn't start yelling about it on the spot, though that didn't actually surprise him, she'd never been one of those parents who felt like she had to pump up the volume every time there was a disagreement in the house, or you stepped out of line.

Even when she got really mad at you about something, she didn't act as if you'd suddenly gone deaf.

Even when you were talking about quitting basketball, at least for the time being.

"You've always played, from the time you were big enough," she said.

Meaning, old enough.

"Maybe I need a break, is all."

"At the age of twelve?"

What she'd do in moments like this was, she'd start straightening up the room. Moving magazines about an inch, one way or the other, on the coffee table. Fluffing up pillows on the couch that didn't need fluffing.

Waiting him out a little bit.

Danny said, "Mr. Fleming has baseball workouts all winter, at the tennis bubble. Just about every weekend."

Danny Walker played second base in baseball, always batted leadoff because of

82

his size. And he was good. Just not as good as he was in basketball. At least as good as he used to think he was in basketball.

"You could do both," she said.

Straightening a picture of her parents on the wall now.

"Like I said, I'm just thinking that maybe I need a little break."

Ali Walker said, "And what other essentials do you plan to take a break from now that travel basketball didn't work out for you — eating and sleeping and bathing regularly?"

Danny tried to lighten the mood in the room a little bit. Fluff things up a little himself.

"Is that sarcasm, Alison Walker?"

She didn't want to play.

"Have you decided that Y ball is some kind of step down?"

"Only on account of, it *is* a step down."

"Not every single good basketball-playing boy in this town is on travel," she said. "And don't say, on account of."

"Sorry," he said. "And, yes, all the good kids in town are on travel, unless they're playing hockey or something."

"You need basketball," she said. Again with the soft voice.

"Well, it sure doesn't need me."

Standoff. They had them sometimes.

"So you're telling me you're quitting."

"Not quitting permanently, Mom. Just for one season."

She had run out of things to move around. So she stood in the middle of the room, between him and the Knicks game, hands on hips. Danny saw that one long piece of hair had somehow gotten loose and had fallen over one eye. She blew it out of the way now, which sounded more like she was blowing off steam.

"I think you need to talk to your father on this one."

They both knew she never called him in. On anything.

Sometimes, when he was in the house, when they were in the kitchen and Danny was upstairs eavesdropping, he would hear her say, "When I want your advice on parenting, I'll send up a flare."

In those moments, Danny wouldn't even recognize his mom's voice, as if it were another person doing the talking down there.

"I was planning to call Dad, actually. So's I could tell him myself."

She walked past him, probably on her way to straighten up the whole kitchen, do the dinner dishes all over again or mop the

84

floor, saying to herself as much as him, "His two specialties, playing ball and quitting things."

Danny had forgotten to shut his computer off, so it was still on when he went up to his room, the screen giving off its spooky glow in the otherwise dark room, like a blue night-light.

He'd also forgotten to go offline.

He went over, sat down at his desk, was about to shut the whole thing down for the night, not even giving one last check to the sports news at ESPN.com, when he heard the goofy instant-message sound — "the old doodlely-doo," his mom called it, "the music of our lives" — come out of it, at the same time a message box appeared in the upper left-hand corner of the screen.

He closed his eyes, knowing he was worn out from talking to Will in real life, and he certainly wasn't in the mood to talk to him electronically, especially at this time of night.

But when he looked closer he saw it wasn't from WillStud, his screen name.

The sender was ConTessa44.

Tess, sitting at her own computer in her second-floor bedroom at 44 Butter Lane.

CONTESSA44: Hey. You there? Hello? Calling Mr. Crossover.

Crossover2 was his screen name. For obvious reasons.

CROSSOVER2: I'm here.

By now Tess knew that Danny wasn't any more chatty in their personal chat room than he was in person. She liked to joke that he had completely mastered the language of instant-messaging, which she called "instant shorthand." She also knew to be patient with him, even when he was only tapping out a couple of words, because he couldn't type nearly as fast as she could. He'd been with her at her computer once while she talked online to Emma, who Tess said was slower than boiling water, and saw how Tess bopped her head from side to side while she waited for Emma to hold up her end of the conversation, occasionally moved from side to side in her chair, like it was sitting-down dancing.

CONTESSA44: What's up?
CROSSOVER2: Just chillin. You know.
CONTESSA44: Oh, I get it. The big hip-hopper.

CROSSOVER2: JK.

More instant shorthand. For "just kidding."

CONTESSA44: I know. You were acting
    weird today. You OK?

He waited a second. And imagined her
waiting for him, doing the head bop, the
side-to-side sway.
He hit the two letters. Then "send."

CROSSOVER2: No
CONTESSA44: What up, dawg?
CROSSOVER2: Now who's the hip-
    hopper?
CONTESSA44: Seriously.

Danny took a deep breath, as a way of
taking his time, telling himself he didn't
need to get into this with her now.
But knowing he wanted to in the worst
way.

CROSSOVER2: I'm thinking about skip-
    ping b-ball this year.

It took so little time for the doodlely-doo
to come right back at him he imagined

their words colliding somewhere over Route 37, the road that divided Middletown in half.

CONTESSA44: NO NO NO NO . . . NO!
CROSSOVER2: Why not?

Now he was the one who waited.

CONTESSA44: Because basketball is who you are. Like taking pictures is for me. It's your gift, DW, no matter what the dumb Basketball Dads say. You can't quit. If you quit, they WIN.
CROSSOVER2: I'm just thinking about it, is all.
CONTESSA44: Stop thinking about it. Right now. That's an order.
CROSSOVER2: You sound like a second mom.
CONTESSA44: Wrong. I'm just your first biggest fan. Talk more tomorrow . . . Love, Tess.
CROSSOVER2: Back at you. With the last part, I mean.

He was reaching for the power button when he heard the goofy sound one more time.

ConTessa44: I know.

Danny always imagined there was some all-seeing, all-knowing Computer God somewhere, up there in microchip hard-drive heaven, monitoring all the computer monitors, checking out all conversations like this. Keeping a Permanent Record like they did at school. Knowing that Tess Hewitt always managed to get the word *love* into the conversation with Danny Walker.

And how he never stopped her, or made a joke about it.

He washed up, brushed his teeth, got into bed, hooked his hands behind his head, stared up at the poster of John Stockton on his ceiling, feeling tired all of a sudden, knowing his eyes weren't going to stay open for long. Still thinking about Tess, though. The tall girl. He didn't know exactly how to describe the feelings he had for her, just knowing that outside of his parents — and ball — he couldn't think of anything or anybody he cared about more.

He smiled to himself, the first time he'd felt like smiling all night, or all week.

Thinking at the same time:

If it wasn't love, for the Twelve-and-Under Division, it was certainly in the picture.

But he was still quitting.

The biggest public park in Middletown, McFeeley Park, was about three blocks from the middle of downtown, and included one regulation baseball diamond, two Little League fields, all the ballfields with lights. There were four lighted tennis courts, a playground for kids, and taking up the whole northeast corner of McFeeley, the part closest to town, was what all the kids called Duck Poop Pond, the kids finding it somewhat less charming than the adults who brought small children there to feed the butt-ugly ducks and little ducklings who resided there.

Up on a hill, past the tennis courts, was Middletown's best outdoor public basketball court, with lights of its own.

In many ways, the downtown area wasn't really the main plaza in Middletown, McFeeley Park was.

Danny sometimes thought that Middletown, even as small as it was, should be broken up into different divisions, the way sports leagues were. There were the Springs School kids, and their parents, and the St. Pat's people. There were the people who lived in the Springs, the nicer section of town, south of Route 37, and the ones who lived on the north side, where Danny and his mom lived, known as the Flats.

"We call it the Flats, anyway," Will Stoddard liked to say. "People in the Springs call it the Pits."

But there was always one day in the fall when the whole town came together, for the McFeeley Fair. It was organized by the Chamber of Commerce to raise money for the upkeep of the pond, the fields, the courts, the playground, all the land donated by the McFeeley family, which had originally owned about half of Middletown.

On the last Saturday in October, McFeeley Park was turned into a combination of amusement park and county fair, with rides and games and booths where you could dunk teachers and coaches, even a local garage band, picked every year in a big Battle of the Bands, providing the music.

Other than maybe an important Middletown High football game, it was the one day of the year when the town actually felt like one town.

"Look," Tess said as she kept training her camera on the people in the crowds, "Middletown being nice to Middletown."

Tess loved taking pictures the way Danny loved basketball. She'd even had a few of them published in the *Dispatch*. Color, black-and-white, it didn't matter. The ones she'd allow Danny to see, when she'd allow him to see her work, were always great. She liked to tell him that the way he liked to play in the dark, she liked to play in a darkroom.

"I think I even saw Mr. Ross looking happy enough to qualify as an actual human being," she said.

"It's some kind of trick," Danny said. "Like you big-time photographers do with lighting and stuff."

Somehow she had been able to ditch Emma. Even more amazingly, Will had decided to *work*, his dad having offered to pay him to handle one of the dunking booths. Will said he needed the money and that you could never go wrong watching a science teacher do what he called the *Finding Nemo* thing.

So it was just Danny and Tess. She had gone through two rolls of film already. He'd won her a stuffed animal by throwing a softball into the top of an old-fashioned milk bucket. After she'd picked out the huge character she instantly named Mr. Bear, she asked the St. Pat's mom running the softball game, Mrs. Damiecki, to take a picture of the two of them.

"C'mon," Tess said when Danny started grumping about it, "it'll take one second."

She was smiling as she said it, Danny could see by looking up at her. It killed him sometimes, having to look up at her.

When Mrs. Damiecki told them to smile, he gave Tess and Mr. Bear a poke and got her laughing so she wouldn't notice him getting up on the balls of his feet and making himself taller.

Now Tess said, "Let's go up to the basketball court, I want to take some shots of the game, in case I want to be a photographer for *Sports Illustrated* someday."

She made it sound casual, but he knew what she was doing. They'd both seen some of the seventh-grade Springers shooting around. There'd be pickup games going on all day at the McFeeley Fair if the weather was nice enough, and it was beautiful today. The crowd around the court had been growing for the last hour, as if people were looking for a diversion from the dunking and Ferris wheel and junky food and garage-band music that sounded like broken electric guitars and overamped speakers.

"Let's go back over to the dunking pool," Danny said. "I'll even give up my body and let you take a picture of me doing my imitation of Leonardo going down for the count in *Titanic*."

"Oh, come up the hill with me," Tess said. In her red plaid shirt and jeans that made her legs look longer than Danny's whole body. In her cute pigtails.

The tall girl, looking like a million bucks.

"You don't have to play," she said. "We'll just watch."

"You want me to play."

"Wherever would you get an idea like that?"

Danny said, "I don't have the right sneaks."

They both looked down at his Air Force Ones, with the hole in the right toe, as if on cue.

"They sure look like basketball shoes to me," Tess said. "Or were something very, very close to basketball shoes at one time."

"Well, they've been bothering me."

"Somehow," she said, "I don't think it's your Nikes bothering you."

"What's that supposed to mean?"

"It means that unless you've come down with some sort of weird virus, you would play ball barefoot if you knew there was a game anywhere near you."

"I thought we were having a good time," he said.

God, he thought, now *you* sound like a girl.

"It's time you started playing ball again," she said.

She had been maneuvering him up the hill as they talked, pushing him along, Danny in front of her. When he turned around, they were nearly eye-to-eye for once.

"Who told you I haven't been playing ball?" he said.

She gave a toss to her hair even though Danny noticed there wasn't any hair in her eyes. Then gave him one of her know-everything looks with that raised eyebrow.

One of those looks that seemed to say:

I know what you had for breakfast, whether or not you remembered to brush your teeth today. And if you're wearing clean underwear.

Danny said, "You talked to my mom."

Tess made a typing motion in the air in front of her.

"Doodlely-doo," she said.

There was a mix of St. Pat's kids and Springs kids laughing and pushing each other at half-court, as Ty and Bren Darcy tried to organize the teams.

They weren't doing it by school, or going from tallest to smallest, Danny saw, just trying to make the best and fairest sides. Jack Harty went with Bren, Daryll Mullins went with Ty, Alex Aaron, wearing an oversized Julius Erving replica jersey from the old New York Nets, went with Bren.

Danny stood next to Tess, who was casually snapping her pictures, and thought to himself: Kids always did the best job making the best game, especially when they took the old Dad Factor out of the equation.

It was Ty Ross who spotted Danny first.

Tess saw, and gave Danny a little nudge with her elbow. "Uh-oh," she said. "You've been made, as they say in the cop shows."

"You don't watch cop shows."

"I try to keep up."

Without even hesitating, Ty said, "I've got Danny."

They all turned to where Danny and Tess were standing.

"Wait a second," Bren said, trying to

sound indignant. "I didn't know he was in the available talent pool."

Daryll Mullins said, "It's the McFeeley Fair, Darcy, not draft day on ESPN."

Ty said, "You in, Walker?"

They were still all looking at him.

Danny looked at Tess, then back at Ty. And smiled. "I'm in."

"These aren't fair sides now," Teddy Moran said. He'd already been picked by Ty and was standing with the rest of his team.

"I'll make them fair," Ty said. "Teddy, you and Andy go with Bren now. We'll take Danny and Matt."

Teddy Moran, career complainer, said, "I don't care about the squirt, but Matt gives you guys too much height."

Daryll Mullins, in that laid-back way he had, said, "But you give them more lip, Moran."

Teddy reluctantly moved over with Bren's guys, trying to give Danny the playground staredown with his small pig eyes as he did. Teddy Moran, every kid in Middletown knew, thought there was something in the Town Charter that said he was always supposed to be on Ty Ross's team.

Ty and Bren sorted out the rest of the

sides. It wasn't quite warm enough for them to play shirts-against-skins; they all just agreed they'd have to know what everybody on their team was wearing.

Right before Ty and Andy shot to see who got the ball, Danny gave a little wave to Tess.

She looked at him without changing expression and snapped his picture, barely focusing it, using one hand, looking like a pro already.

What Richie Walker saw, wearing an old blue Middletown baseball cap, slouched against a tree on the pond side of McFeeley:

He saw his kid and the Ross kid play as if they were Stockton and Malone. Except the Ross kid had more imagination already than Malone ever had with his catch-and-shoot game. Had more of a feel for everything.

Was more interesting to watch.

That's what he saw.

And this: Nobody on the court could guard the Ross kid straight-up and nobody, not even the tiny kid with the freckles who'd helped pick the teams, the one who was like this crazed Mini-Me, could get in front of Danny.

With all the joking around and what he was sure was small-fry trash-talking, all the fake beefs about fouls and who had really knocked the ball out of bounds, with the way the kids in the game kept playing to the kids in the crowd, Richie couldn't take his eyes off Danny and Ty Ross.

They were doing what good, smart players could always do.

Make the game nice.

The word — *nice* — actually made him smile, the way some old song could make you smile if you just heard one lick of it. He'd had a teammate on the Warriors, Raiford Tipton, a forward out of the University of Miami, a dude with the hair rows and the tattoos and the strut. When Richie would hit Raiford Tipton just right on the break, Raiford would run past him when they were getting back on defense and say, "Richie Walker, that was niiiiiicccccce."

Making the word sound like it had three or four syllables in it, making it sound as if what Richie had just done with the ball was practically illegal.

Danny and Ty Ross were *nice*.

They worked the pick-and-roll. When they had a chance to get out and run on the fast break, Ty would get the ball off the boards and throw a blind pass nearly to half-court, knowing Danny would already be there.

Or: Ty would draw two of three defenders to him in the low blocks and then kick it out to Danny, who kept launching that funny shot of his — though he was getting it more out in front, like Richie had showed him — and scoring with ease from the outside.

Then Richie would wait to see a smile or a fist-pump from his kid, or any kind of change of expression.

Only Danny never would.

Like this was the way it was all supposed to be.

There was a taller guard with a skinhead haircut who Danny couldn't guard sometimes, at least when Danny would let the skinhead get to his spot in close to the basket. But *only* if he could get to his spot.

Danny's team won the first game of eleven baskets easy, Richie keeping score to himself, into it now, and they were about to do it again. It was 9–4 and here was Danny dribbling through a double-team — the skinhead and the freckled kid who was just a little taller than Danny — beating them at the top of the key and stopping at the foul line and no-looking Ty with a perfect bounce pass for a layup.

Richie felt himself give a little fist-pump.

As he did, he heard: "Rich."

The voice made him jump the way Ali had that night outside the house. Like he was wearing some kind of sign these days that said, Please sneak up on me.

Or maybe he was just so used to living deep inside his own head, blocking out everything: Noise. People. The world.

He turned around to see Jeff Ross.

"Hey," Richie said.

"Hey yourself."

Ross put his hand out. Richie shook it, studying him as he did: The little polo pony on the shirt, expensive sunglasses, what still looked to be a summer tan on him, hair a little grayer and a little thinner than Richie remembered from the last time he'd seen him a couple of years ago, but the hair still hanging in there.

You still look like money, Richie wanted to say, you always did. But you're no kid anymore.

Of course, how old do I look to him?

Ross nodded at the court. "Kind of fun watching the next generation have at it," he said.

Danny and Ty came up the court on a two-on-one break, passing the ball back and forth between them at warp speed, neither one of them taking a single dribble, Ty finally blowing past the long skinny black kid trying to defend them and Danny lofting a little pass that Ty caught and shot in one smooth motion.

The crowd around the court, adults and kids, cheered like it was a real game.

"Ball didn't touch the floor," Ross said. "Just like I teach them."

Richie turned so he was looking right at him. "Speaking of that, how did my kid not make your team, if you don't mind me asking?"

Getting right to it. Knowing he sounded like every father of every kid who hadn't made the team, and not giving a rat's ass.

"Well, first of all, it's not *my* team," Ross said. "And secondly, I didn't pick the team. My son was trying out, too, and I'm the president of Middletown Basketball as well. So I took myself out of the process."

Richie let it go, like a bad shot that wasn't even worth contesting. They both knew it was bull.

"Let me put it to you another way: What kind of process do you guys have going here if a kid that good doesn't make your team?"

Ross took off his sunglasses, folded them, stuck them in the front of his polo-pony shirt, like it was all part of a rich-guy pose, buying time. He even cleared his throat.

"My understanding with Danny — whom we all love, by the way — is that it just turned out to be close with him and a group of other guards and he unfortunately had a bad second night of tryouts."

"Who gives a sh . . ." Richie put his hands out in front of him, trying not to get hot. "Who cares?" he said. "Have you been watching what I've been watching here? Anybody who knows anything about basketball can see how good he is. And he was on travel the last two years. Now you guys take him off because he has a bad night? Because he's too small? No kidding, Jeff, what's up with *that?*"

It was clear that the only thing Jeff Ross had heard was the part about Danny being small. "Who said he didn't make the team because he was too small?"

"Didn't you tell those crackerjack, basketball-savvy talent scouts of yours that you wanted the team to get bigger this year?"

"No, Rich, I most certainly did not. Did Danny tell you that?"

Richie ignored him. "In sports, the best kids are supposed to make the team."

103

Peabody Public Library
Columbia City, IN

"The evaluators were as fair as they could be. . . ."

"Maybe they were fair," Richie said. "But if they don't know what they're watching, they shouldn't be picking the stinking team."

"I'm sorry you feel that way," Ross said. He put the sunglasses back on, like he was putting a mask back on. "But sports isn't always fair. I guess you know that better than anybody."

Now they were getting to it, and Richie knew they weren't just talking about the kids on the court.

Ross said, "Here's something else you know: Sometimes the little guys have to play a little bigger when it counts."

"You turned away the wrong little guy and you know it."

"For somebody who's not around very often," Ross said, "you've certainly taken a passionate interest in Danny's career all of a sudden."

"I'm taking an interest in my kid, who just happens to be a hell of a player. That okay with you?"

Ross said, "Not all the players in town get the chance to be you. Even when they're related to you."

They were both watching the court now.

As if on cue, Danny went behind his back with his own long arms — but those small hands — and dusted a fat kid who had just entered the game.

"There used to be a rule, back in our day, where you could add a kid after the tryouts," Richie said. "Put him on the team, Jeff."

"And what do I tell the other kids who didn't make it? No, he can try out next year. That's the system."

"Then the system stinks worse than the town dump."

Jeff Ross didn't say anything, so Richie kept going. "So that's the way it's gonna be? You're gonna get back at me through my kid?"

"This has nothing to do with you and me, Walker. But since you're such a concerned parent now, why not have your own damn system?"

Dropping all pretense that they were going to be any more polite to each other now than they had been twenty years ago.

"Maybe you should start your own team," Ross said, trying to be sarcastic. "The Richie Walker All-Stars."

Richie was silent. Staring at the court. Ross started walking toward the pond, away from the game, saying, "You were always a big movie guy, Rich. But life isn't always a movie. The little guy doesn't always win the day. I'll see you around."

"Yeah."

Ross left him standing there. Alone again, watching the kids playing ball.

Watching his kid.

Richie Walker's all-star.

He had to be leaving.

When his dad came over for dinner, when it was an official visit to the house, scheduled in advance and not a drop-by, it almost always meant he was leaving the next day.

At least he had stayed a whole week this time. Longer, if you counted that first night in the driveway.

"Hold on there, Mr. Gloom and Doom," Ali Walker said when Danny ran his theory past her. "He didn't say anything about his travel plans."

"He never does, until the last possible minute."

"He just asked if it would be all right if the three of us had dinner. Even offered to take us out, sport. I told him to save his money, I'd whip up my famous Wasp Girl Lasagna."

"At least he got to see me play at the fair," Danny said.

She was setting the table. Resetting it,

actually. That meant she was putting the forks on the outside of the napkins, knives on the inside, after Danny had once again managed to do it the other way around.

She looked up. "You didn't tell me you saw him at the fair."

"I don't even know if he saw me see him. He was in the distance, kind of, just watching the game."

"Anyway," his mom said, "if he is leaving, he'll tell you."

"You don't mind, by the way? Him coming over?"

She was back in the kitchen, opening the oven door, checking out the famous lasagna, which was better than you got at Fierro's in town. "He's your father. I have never tried to keep you two apart, you know that. I told him tonight that if you guys wanted to have a boys' night out, go for it. He said, no, I was included."

"He's never not leaving when it's one of these."

"Double negative," his mom, the English teacher, said.

"Just negative," Danny said.

His dad showed up at six-thirty sharp, wearing a blue buttoned-down shirt, khaki slacks, the kind of nubuck shoes kids wore with their school clothes, his hair slicked back and still wet from his shower. He was carrying a bottle of wine.

Danny had been up in his room playing last year's NBA game on PlayStation when he heard the doorbell. When he came down the stairs he noticed that his mom had found time to change out of her school clothes, into a green, silky-looking blouse with some kind of print on it you didn't notice at first, and khaki-colored pants of her own, her slacks looking a lot nicer than what his dad had on.

The kind of dress-up clothes she'd wear when she went out to dinner with a friend. Male or female. Though, Danny had to say, there weren't a lot of males in Middletown she would give the time of day to.

It was Danny's impression that his mom was about as interested in dating as she was in video games.

But she'd dressed up tonight for his dad, whatever that meant. Maybe he'd ask Tess online later how much he should read into something like that.

Danny Walker, even at twelve, was smart enough to know this about girls: They were smarter than boys already. They were smarter about all the important stuff in life that didn't include sports, and would stay smarter from now on, which meant that he and the rest of the boys would be playing catch-up, trying to come from behind, the rest of the way.

"You look nice," his dad said.

"You still clean up pretty well yourself," his mom said.

It was Will Stoddard's theory that adults, even cool adults, behaved like space aliens about half the time, and now here it was right in front of Danny's eyes: With all the rotten things his mom could say to his dad when they were alone, she still wanted to look her best when he came over.

The three of them sat in the living room before dinner, eating cheese and crackers. His mom drank some of the wine he'd brought. His dad drank beer out of a bottle. Danny got to have a Coke. On account of, he figured, this being a special occasion.

Whatever the occasion was.

His mom tried to find out how things were going for his dad in that casual way she had, asking questions you were supposed to believe had just popped into her head, all the time getting to the one she hoped would make you spill your guts.

He was still living in Oakland, he said, even though his lease was about to be up.

Said the Warriors had talked about him doing some work for them in community relations, but he hadn't decided yet. He had done some scouting for them in the past, but had quit that, saying he was tired of watching people he didn't know or care about play games he couldn't play.

He had thought assistant coaching might be different, taking a job at the University of San Francisco last season.

But he had quit that, too.

He had quit a lot of things since the accident, Danny knew.

"So it's back to the card shows," Ali Walker said. "Which you love so dearly."

The most money he'd made the past several years was from making appearances at card and memorabilia shows.

"It's not so bad if you limit the conversation."

"Your specialty." His mom smiling when she said it.

"Most people are all right. Step right up and see the guy who used to be Richie Walker."

He drank down about half his beer in one gulp, like he was incredibly thirsty all of a sudden.

"You're right," he said. "I hate it."

Now came one of those record-breaking, world-class silences that made you wonder if any member of the Walker family would say anything ever again.

Until Danny said: "When are you leaving?"

"It's actually what I wanted to talk to you both about."

She clapped her hands together. "Well, let's do it at the dinner table, before the lasagna turns into leftovers."

They passed the rolls and salad around. His dad remarked that her lasagna was as good as ever. She said, thank you, sir. She asked how things were at the place known in Middletown as the Inn. He said, hey, they even had cable there now.

Finally he put down his fork and said, "Listen, I'm thinking about hanging around for a while."

His mom had her wineglass nearly to her lips, stopped it right there. "In Middletown?"

"Yeah."

Danny thinking: *Yeah!*

His mom said, "What about the fabulous card-show appearances?"

"There's enough of them around here," he said. "Even though the money's not that great for somebody like me anywhere." He gave her a look and said, "As you know better than anybody else."

"We're all right, Rich."

Danny couldn't wait.

"What are you going to *do* here?" he said.

Richie Walker said, "I was thinking about coaching."

Danny's mom said, "You're going to coach a team in Middletown?"

"Yeah, an opportunity just presented itself in the past couple of days."

Danny and his mom waited. Sometimes you could try to wait his dad out on something and he'd be out the door and gone and you'd still be waiting. But this time was different, Danny'd had this feeling there was something he'd been waiting to tell them since he walked in the front door.

"To tell you the truth," he said, "it's an opportunity I sort of created for myself."

"Dad!" Danny didn't mean it to come out as loud as it did, but there it was. *"Who are you going to coach?"*

"You," he said.

"Me."

His mom said, "In the Y league?"

Richie Walker was smiling now.

Even with his eyes.

"You know what this town needs even

113

more than cable TV at the Inn?"

Danny grabbed his arm. *"What?"*

"Another seventh-grade travel team," his dad said.

9

Richie came back from the kitchen with a brand-new beer, drinking it out of the bottle this time. When he sat back down, Danny started asking questions immediately.

Like: "How are we going to get games?"

His dad said, "I'll call the Tri-Valley League and see if they've got room for one more team. If not, I'll get phone numbers for coaches and call them on my own. It's seventh-grade ball, after all. We're not trying to join the Big East."

They were all sitting around the coffee table, Danny and his dad on the floor, his mom on the couch, his dad showing them the to-do list he'd been scribbling on Runyon's napkins.

Ali said, "But won't they have their schedules set?"

"There's still a month to go before the season starts. I'm hoping they'll try to work something out, on account of . . ."

"On account of," she said, "you're Richie Walker."

"Yeah," he said. "What's left of him, anyway."

Danny said, "Even if we come up with enough players, where are we going to practice? Everybody was saying at the fair that because of what happened to the Springs gym, there's not enough practice time for anybody."

His mom said, "I can help at St. Pat's. But you may have to practice at some weird hours. Maybe after homework instead of before, as long as all the parents are willing."

Richie said, "What do they charge?"

"I don't honestly know. But I'll ask."

Danny said, "You think we can really get into the league?"

Richie said, "If we don't, we'll be one of those independent teams, like they have in minor-league baseball. You know, where all the bad boys go when they come out of drug rehab and nobody will give them a job."

His dad held up a couple of his napkins and said, "Hey, I don't have all the answers here, least not yet."

Danny said, "But if we don't get into the league, how do we get into the tournament?"

Richie said he might have one more

beer. Ali said, "Why don't I go make up a quick pot of coffee instead," not even asking if he wanted coffee.

She came back five minutes later with two mugs, handing Richie one, saying, "Milk, two sugars," as she did. They all sat down on the living-room floor, like they were unwrapping some kind of Christmas present.

On the kind of Christmas morning, Danny thought, they'd never had.

"Listen," his dad said, "all we are right now is the Middletown Cocktail Napkins and you're already worried about making the tournament?" Giving Danny a shove to let him know he was playing. "If we pull this thing off," Richie said, "maybe it'll be enough for us to win the championship of all the kids who got told they weren't good enough."

Danny said, "But all the good players are taken."

"No," Richie Walker said, "they're not."

Danny looked up at the standing grandfather clock that belonged to some grandparent and saw that it was past ten o'clock now. Past bedtime. His mom hadn't said anything about that, at least not yet.

Maybe because she was getting into it about the Middletown Cocktail Napkins the way the boys were.

It had turned into another night Danny didn't want to end.

Now she was the one who said, "I know there are still good players out there, present company certainly included. But Danny's right: Are there enough so it doesn't turn out to be Danny and the Bad News Bears?"

Danny started ticking off names on his fingers: "There's me. Bren. Will."

Richie: "Can Will play?"

Danny: "He can make an open shot. And he can defend almost as well as he can talk."

Richie: "Could he start with you in the backcourt?"

Danny: "Bren's better."

He saw his mother's head going back and forth like she was watching a tennis match. A grin on her face, even though it was basketball talk, which she said usually was about as riveting for her as interest rates at the bank.

Just not tonight.

Danny said, "The only really big guy left is Matt Fitzgerald. He's already wearing size thirteen kicks. But he needs to be coached."

His dad said, "You know what I say."

The three of them at once, as if they'd

118

rehearsed it, said, "You can't teach tall."

When they stopped laughing, Danny said, "That's only four guys."

"We don't need to come up with a whole list of possibles tonight," his dad said. "Over the next day or so, try to think of all those fabulous bubble guys Jeff Ross talked about. Or maybe some kids who didn't try out. All we need is ten, tops. And we could play with eight."

"I'll ask around," Danny said.

Ali said, "I don't want to throw cold water on this. But leagues cost money, Rich. Teams like this cost money, and not just for the gym."

He shrugged, held up a napkin. "I've got some thoughts on that. Hell, everybody's got a salary cap these days. Ours might just have to be a little lower than everybody else's."

He started to get up. And for a moment, it was as if he had forgotten how many busted parts he still had. He got halfway up before making a face, then started the whole process again, this time putting a hand on the coffee table to steady himself, then taking it much more slowly from there.

Danny wanted to help him, just wasn't sure how.

"Sweet dreams, kiddo," he said to Danny.

Danny thinking: You can say that again.

The two of them were still outside, standing next to his car.

Danny had snuck down the stairs once they were outside, gone out the back door, got behind where the garbage cans were, and eavesdropped on his parents like he was on a stakeout.

His mom was saying, "You can't start this and not follow through."

"You mean like my jobs."

"I mean with everything."

"I can do this."

"No," she said. "Now you *have* to do this."

"Okay," he said. "I can do this, I have to do this. I *will* do this."

"Because if you don't, you really will break this boy's heart this time."

Small silence.

"Hell, Ali, this is *about* his heart."

"You know you're not going to get any help from the Association. Thinking outside the box in this town can get you arrested."

"Screw 'em if they can't take a good joke."

"There's the old Rich."

"Listen," he said. "I know I'm not much of a parent. Not a parent at all, most times. But the more I listened to Jeff Ross, the more it occurred to me that my ass is just worn out having guys who can't find their own jockstraps running sports. At any freaking level."

"I'll help any way I can."

"Figured."

"You can pull this off?" she said. It came out a question.

"We're sure as hell gonna find out," his dad said.

"Well, okay," Will Stoddard said, looking around the basketball court at St. Pat's, eight o'clock the next Saturday morning. "We're looking to assemble the first all-guard basketball team in history."

"Plus Matt," Bren Darcy said, correcting him.

"Plus Matt," Danny said. "Just so's people won't get the idea we're a sixth-grade team."

"I've seen sixth-grade teams bigger than us," Will said.

Danny and Will had written up fliers and left them around both Springs and St. Pat's, announcing tryouts for a new seventh-grade travel team this Saturday. Will, who said he knew more about computers than Bill Gates, had even figured out a way to set up a temporary Web site, though the Web site basically had the same information as the fliers.

The largest type on the page announced that this was all at the invitation of Coach

Richie Walker, Middletown's most illustrious basketball alumnus.

Will had thrown in the last part.

They had left fliers at the Candy Kitchen and Jackson's stationery store and Fierro's and on the bulletin board they still kept in the lobby of the Middletown movie theater.

After all that, eight kids showed up.

Danny. Bren. Will. Matt Fitzgerald, who didn't just look tall, he was also as wide as one of those double-wide trailers at the trailer park outside of town when he stood next to the rest of them. Michael Harden, another decent St. Pat's kid. He was another fifty-five incher who'd given up on trying out for the real travel team the year before.

There was one Springs kid, Oliver Towne, a round black kid known to his classmates as the Round Mound of Towne, a play on words that came from Charles Barkley's old college nickname, the Round Mound of Rebound. Oliver was a little taller than Danny, but not by much.

Danny actually thought Oliver took up about the same space horizontally as he did vertically, as if every inch taller he got also became an inch wider.

Will used to call him Roker, because he was as fat as the weatherman on *The Today*

Show used to be, but that was before the *Today* guy did that deal where he had his stomach stapled shut.

Will always seemed to know stuff like that, believing that most useful information in his life came from *People* magazine.

Whatever Oliver Towne weighed, he was the closest thing to an actual forward in the gym.

Finally, there were the only twins at St. Patrick's School, Robert and Steven O'Brien, who announced to the other kids they were only there because their mom had made them.

"She told us that if we weren't going to play hockey this year because we were tired of getting up at five in the stupid morning, we were going to do *something*," Robert said.

Or it could have been Steven. Danny was never completely sure which was which. The only ones who seemed to be able to tell the O'Brien kids apart *were* the O'Brien twins.

The other twin said, "She said our winter sports schedule wasn't going to consist of us sitting on our skinny butts and playing video games."

Danny took a quick survey of his teammates and in his head heard one of those

NBA-arena announcers shouting, "Give a big Middletown welcome to *your* . . . *Middletown . . . Cocktail Napkins!*"

Now, if they could scare up a couple of more players, maybe they could even scrimmage.

Danny's dad hadn't made much of a speech when he realized the eight players in the gym were the only ones coming. He addressed the kids, and a few of the parents who'd hung around to listen. Michael Harden's dad, Jerry, had played with Richie Walker on the championship seventh-grade team, even if he looked a lot older now, having gone bald and put on a few since his playing days. He was a lawyer in Middletown, and after he gave Richie a hug, he asked if he needed any help.

"All I can get," Richie said.

"I can help coach, I can make calls, I can organize a phone list, you name it," he said.

"All of the above," Richie said.

Then he told the kids that if they were here today, it meant they had a passion for playing ball, and he'd always had a soft spot for guys like that.

And told them that maybe, if he managed not to screw them up, they could all have a basketball season that was a lot more than a consolation prize.

His dad said, "Danny knows I'm the last guy who ever wants to give a speech. But bottom line here? Maybe, just maybe, we can turn out to be the kind of team nobody wants to play."

One of the O'Briens raised a hand.

"Mr. Walker? How do we do that if we don't even have enough players to play each other?"

"What's your name, son?"

"Steven O'Brien."

He was in the red T-shirt. It meant Robert was in black.

He motioned the other twin over. "And your name, son?"

"Robert."

Richie looked hard at one face, then the other, stood back. To the red-shirted Steven he said, "I think you've got a few more freckles than your twin brother there, Steven, though that's not going to help me a whole lot when you're out on the court, so we're going to have to ask you to color code each other at every practice."

They both nodded. "We switch T-shirts sometimes when our mother leaves the room."

"Zany," Will said.

"Anyway," Richie said, "I'll tell Robert

126

and Steven and the rest of you that by the time we're ready to get serious here, hopefully we'll have found a couple of more players. If not, Mr. Harden and I will play when we want to go five-on-five."

Danny stared at his dad.

Because as far as he knew, the last time Richie Walker had played in any kind of basketball game was with the Golden State Warriors.

"One last thing before we start," his dad said. "There's only going to be three basic rules on this team, and I'm going to expect you all to follow them. One, if you're open, shoot. Two, if somebody has a better shot than you, pass the ball, let him shoot. Three? Have fun." He looked from face to face. "Did I go too fast for anybody?"

Will had to get the last word, of course.

"What if we're missing our shots?"

Richie said, "Keep shooting. That will be rule number four. Now get in two lines and let's see what we got here."

Nothing, Danny decided after the first hour.

They had nothing.

They were either hopeless or helpless, he could go either way.

He kept thinking that if the Vikings

could see them, they'd think they were trying to get on one of those *Funniest Home Video* television shows.

Even the guys who could play couldn't play dead today.

Danny knew that Will and Bren — Bren especially — knew how to run a three-man weave fast break drill the way they knew their own screen names; they'd all had to run the weave for any team they'd ever played for in their lives.

Just not today.

Not to save their lives.

And when they'd mess it up again, his dad would just look at them calmly, no problem, and say, "Same group, let's try it again."

One time Matt was the last guy to get the ball, which meant he was supposed to shoot the layup. Only the pass from Michael Harden was too low and Matt had about as much chance of reaching down and catching it, and then shooting it, as he did of getting a good grade in Spanish.

But he did manage to drop-kick the ball off the court and up onto the stage.

Will immediately imitated one of those Spanish soccer announcers you heard during the World Cup.

"Goooooooooaaaaaalllllll!"

Even Richie Walker, whom Danny knew wasn't exactly the life of the party in the best of times, laughed at that one.

To keep from crying, most likely.

When Richie said they were going to try four-on-four, full-court, push the ball every chance you got, Danny thought things might get better, even though nobody had the height to guard Matt.

Instead, they got worse.

Even I stink today, Danny thought.

He kept checking out the old clock above the stage, knowing his dad had said they would only go to ten o'clock today.

Danny praying that none of the play-practice kids would come early and see a team that he was now thinking of more as the Middletown Rugrats. One that had scrimmaged for more than half an hour and managed to produce exactly five baskets, three for his team, two for Bren's.

Danny had all the baskets for his team, Bren had the two for his. He might have been slightly off with his math, but there had also been about six thousand turnovers.

Richie Walker finally put two fingers to his mouth and gave a sharp whistle, told them all they were done for the day and to come to the middle of the court.

"We suck," Danny said under his breath to Will.

Will said, "You're being much too easy on us."

Danny told Will his Rugrats line and Will said, "If you remember the show, I'm pretty sure Phil and Lil are bigger."

Richie Walker knelt down in the middle of them. When he did, he had to put his right hand out to keep himself steady, or from falling over on his side.

Maybe those weren't sad eyes on his dad as much as they were hurt eyes.

Richie said, "Before anybody starts to get down on himself, remember: This was our first practice. Wasn't even a practice, really, as much as it was, like, orientation. So hang in there, okay?"

Then he said, "Hey, the team I played on? The one that won? Our coach threw us out of the gym three times the first month we were together."

Jerry Harden nodded. "Think it was four, actually."

One of the O'Brien twins raised a hand. "Are we going to practice this week? We need to know because we've got piano."

Will, whispering into Danny's ear, said, "Maybe they can *play* piano."

Richie Walker's response was a sigh.

Then he turned and looked at the clock.

They sat in front of 422 Earl for a few minutes after his dad drove him home from practice.

"You could come in," Danny said, "if you want."

"I've got some calls to make when I get back to the Inn. It's a big job — two jobs, actually — being both general manager *and* coach in travel basketball."

Danny could see his mom's blue Taurus in the driveway. Somehow he could feel her watching them from somewhere inside the house. Maybe even hearing what they were saying. He liked to tell her that she had the kind of mutant hearing that could have landed her a spot fighting crime with the X-Men.

There was just nothing much to hear right now in the front seat of the rental car.

Until: "Dad, why are you doing this?"

Richie turned in the front seat so he could face him, forgetting that the shoulder harness from his seat belt was still attached. He caught himself when he felt the pull of it, but even a sudden stop like that made him wince in pain.

"Why're you asking, bud?"

"Because you don't even *like* basketball anymore. And you *didn't* like coaching, even though you're trying to make this sound like something you couldn't live with yourself if you passed up. That's why."

Deep breath.

Keep going.

Danny said, "The only reason you play with me in the driveway when you show up is because it's a way for us to have some kind of common language that doesn't involve us talking."

He shot him a look to see how that one went over. His dad was actually smiling, like Danny had gotten off a good shot. Swish.

"You're pretty smart for twelve," his dad said. "Smarter than I was, that's for sure."

"Whatever."

Richie said, "Can I talk *now?*"

" 'Course you can."

"I don't hate basketball," Richie said. "Do I hate what happened to me? Yeah. Do I spend most of my life feeling sorry for myself? Yeah, I do, though I'm trying to cut down. I really hate what happened to me, that I never got the chance to find out how I stacked up against the big boys. And I did hate coaching the first time around.

132

College boys with their attitudes who I could have run circles around when I was their age." His dad was the one who took a deep breath now, letting it go.

"Dad, I didn't mean . . ."

Richie carefully turned himself back around, so he was facing forward, those big hands on the steering wheel. "I hate that I don't have the game in my hands anymore. Or ever again. But I don't hate the game, bud, and I never will."

His dad never talked about the car accident that nearly killed him. Never, never, never. This was as close as he ever got, what losing control of his car on the wet road had done to him, how it made him feel. The whole thing feeling as if it were right next door to them.

"But why do you want to coach us?" Danny said. "We're gonna stink."

"You don't know that. And I have to say, if you act like you're giving up after just one practice, the other guys are gonna do the exact same thing, and we're all wasting our time here."

"I'm not giving up."

"I watched you today, Dan. You're the only one who acted like he hated basketball, every time you or somebody else would screw up."

"Yeah," Danny said, knowing he sounded just like his father.

"Yeah," Richie said. "And you can't let it happen again, because I need you. Because I'm gonna put this team in *your* hands. Give you more responsibility than you've ever had in your life."

Out of the corner of his eye, Danny saw his mom standing on the front porch, waving at them.

"What if I'm not good enough?" he said.

Richie said, "No, it was the other guys who told you you're not good enough."

Danny sat there. "It was a bad day."

"Let me tell you something I learned the hard way," Richie said. "There's no such thing as a bad day if you're playing. On a team you weren't supposed to be on. In a season you weren't even supposed to have."

"*We* weren't supposed to have."

"There you go. Go take a shower and tell your mom I'll give her a call later and talk about the availability of the gym."

Danny was going to tell him he loved him, the words were right there, ready to spill all over the dashboard.

But he didn't.

Because he never did.

He just got out and ran for the front

door, trying to bluff his mom by looking happy.

It wouldn't occur to him until later that his dad still hadn't really explained why he was doing it.

11

They practiced twice more during the week, each one a little less awful than the first one.

But not by much.

It was the Saturday of Veterans Day weekend, most of the town at the parade. They had to practice in the morning today, insanely early in the morning, seven o'clock, because the theater had been taken over by the Science Fair and the Drama Club kids needed the gym at nine. Mr. Harden was playing on the skins team with Will and Bren and Matt. Danny's dad was moving stiffly around for Danny's team, the shirts, pretending he was playing center, just as a way of putting a bigger body on Matt in the scrimmage and making the sides look even.

Matt Fitzgerald moved about as fast as a traffic jam on the Long Island Expressway, so even though the best Richie Walker could do was limp-jog up and down the court himself, they could sort of keep up with each other.

They were about forty-five minutes into what was half game and half practice, Danny's dad stopping them every few minutes to give them one more variation on the offense he wanted them to use against a man-to-man.

It was then that Danny spotted Ty Ross standing just inside the double doors, at the opposite end from the stage. He was in his baggy white shorts, down to his knees, new McGrady blue-and-white sneakers you could spot from a mile away, a Middletown High T-shirt with the sleeves cut off, Ty apparently wanting to show off arms as skinny as his legs.

Danny gave him the chin-up nod, Ty did the same back.

When Richie Walker spotted Ty, he told everybody to take a water break and relax for a minute.

Danny and his dad walked over to Ty, Danny saying, "You must be in the wrong gym, dude."

"Hey, Ty," Richie said.

"Mr. Walker." Ty ducked his head. "My mom was on her way over to Springs, she has to help them set up for some auction or something tonight. I was supposed to help her, but then I remembered that you guys practice early on Saturday." He grinned. "She sort of gave me a reprieve."

They all stood there for a moment, nobody knowing what to say about that. Then Richie said, "You want to play some?"

"Would that be okay?" Ty said.

Richie said, "If it's okay with your mom."

"She's cool."

Danny said, "What about your dad?"

Ty looked down at the McGradys, the left one untied. He was wearing those socks that barely made it above the top of your high-tops.

"He's playing tennis right now."

Richie put a hand on his shoulder. "It's just basketball, son. But I don't want you to get into trouble with your father."

"My mom said that as long as it was okay with you, it was okay with her, we — the Vikings — don't practice again until next Tuesday."

"Well, then, thank you for coming, Ty, because you may have saved a broken-down old man's life. You play with Danny. And I am going to sit my worn-out butt down."

Then he changed the teams around a little, stacking the other guys, making it Will, Bren, Matt, Michael Harden and his dad. He put Oliver Towne and the O'Brien twins with Danny and Ty.

"Let's play some damn ball," Richie Walker said.

They started over, jumping it at center court, Ty against Matt. Ty back-tipped the ball to Danny and as soon as he did, Danny gave him the eye, Ty breaking toward their basket, Danny feeding him perfectly, Ty catching the long pass on one bounce and laying the ball in off the backboard.

As they ran back to set up on defense, Ty changed lanes so he could give Danny a quick low five. He was smiling over the play, as if they'd drawn it up beforehand.

Danny wasn't.

He's not the one in the wrong gym, Danny thought.

I am.

When practice was over, Ty used Will's ever-present cell to call his mother and ask if he could go with Will over to Danny's house.

Most of the other kids had beat it out of the gym when Richie had said they were done for the day. A bad sign, Danny knew, for a bunch of guys who were supposed to be there because of their burning love of the game.

Of course the only reason Danny'd had any fun was because he'd had Ty to pass to.

Ty said he was getting a busy signal on his mom's phone, but she was probably on her way, since her shift at Springs ended at nine, and there was a better chance of her robbing the King Kullen supermarket than there was of her being late for anything.

So they were all standing outside in front of the gym — Danny, his dad, Ty, Will — waiting for Mrs. Ross when Mr. Ross pulled up in his black Mercedes, left the car in the fire lane that was really just a drop-off spot in front of the gym, came up the stairs fast at them, taking the last steps two at a time.

"What's *he* doing here?"

He was talking to Richie about Ty, as if Ty weren't even there.

Richie said, "You should probably ask Ty that."

"I'm asking you," he said, pointing a finger at Richie, not quite touching him, but getting it up there near his face.

"Ty showed up and it was lucky he did, because we're short players. I asked if it was all right and he said that his mom said it was, she's the one who dropped him off."

"My *wife*," Mr. Ross said, "doesn't make our son's basketball decisions for him."

Danny wasn't as interested in Ty's dad as he was in his own, wanting to see how he was going to play this, Mr. Ross bossing him now the way he liked to boss everybody else in town.

"You're making a big deal out of nothing," Richie said, standing his ground, not backing up, keeping his voice calm. Putting his eyes on Mr. Ross and calmly keeping them there.

"He doesn't belong here."

"He's twelve," Richie said. "If he can find a game on a Saturday morning, he ought to be allowed to play in it, you ask me."

Mr. Ross said, "You think I can't see what you're doing here?"

"You mean other than getting up to ten kids so we could scrimmage."

"Dad," Ty said.

"Stay out of this."

Richie said, "C'mon, Jeff. He didn't do anything wrong. I didn't do anything wrong. I told him that if he doesn't have a conflict with your team, he can practice with our team anytime he wants to."

Then Richie said, "And backing up a second? What *do* you think I'm doing here?"

"You've made it abundantly clear by putting this team of yours together that you think some grave injustice was done to the kids who didn't make the cut. Well, I don't. And I don't want the other kids on the Vikings to even get the idea, from my son, that they have some sort of alternative if they don't like the way things are going."

Richie Walker barked out a laugh. "You think I'm, like, *recruiting* your kid?"

Danny stood there, not moving, barely breathing, curious to see when Mr. Ross, the most important guy in Middletown, was going to figure out what a jackass he was making of himself, in front of them, in front of his son.

"You just coach your little team and I'll coach mine," he said. He took Ty by the arm now and said, "Let's go."

Danny was afraid that Ty was the one about to cry over basketball.

But he didn't.

Richie said, "Why don't you go easy on the boy?"

Mr. Ross stopped, turned around, nodding, a phony smile on his face. "You know," he said, "there's nothing I like better than getting parenting advice from the experts."

He and Ty went down the stairs to the

car. When they got there, Mr. Ross stood on the passenger side and opened the door, waiting there until Ty was inside.

When the car was gone, Danny said to his dad, "He was pretty angry."

And his dad said, "Only for the last twenty years or so."

12

Danny imagined the scene at the Ross house afterward being something out of one of those *SmackDown!* wrestling shows, but Ty called the next morning and asked if Danny wanted to do something.

"I thought you'd be under house arrest until Thanksgiving or something," Danny said. "Now you get to do something with me?"

"It was a mom deal," he said.

Then they put both their moms on the phone and told them to work it out.

"Hey, Lily," Ali Walker said when Danny handed her the portable, then chatted with Lily Ross for a few minutes before she put her hand over the phone and said, "Do you want Ty to come here or do you want to go to his house?"

Danny waved his arms in front of him as if he'd been attacked by bees. "It's like going to the *big* house. No way, Mom. Here. Definitely."

Mrs. Ross, who seemed way too nice to

144

be married to who she was married to, brought Ty over after lunch. The two moms went into the kitchen for coffee and gossip, while Danny and Ty went upstairs and began putting together their own superteams on *NBA '05*, where the object was to have a final score of about 188–186.

Danny said, "How *did* you get to come over?"

He was on the bed with his controller, Ty slouched in a beanbag chair on the floor with his.

Ty said, "They had a big fight about it that lasted into the night. She said I could play with who I wanted to play with. He asked whose side was she on, his or your dad's. She said she wasn't aware there were different sides on everybody's children being happy. One of those."

"My parents fight like that sometimes," Danny said. "But that's because they're only together sometimes."

Ty said, "Your team has my dad pissed, that's for sure, dude."

Danny paused the game. "You've seen us. You think *your* team has anything to worry about?"

"He thinks your dad is trying to show him up."

"I don't think it's like that. I think my

dad, like, thinks this is something he had to do for me, even though he didn't."

Ty said, "You guys just need a couple more players, you'll be pretty good."

Danny said, "I know who the players are, too. Shaq and Duncan."

"Really. You just need one guy to catch and shoot, and one guy to rebound."

"Like I said. Shaq and Duncan."

Danny unpaused the game.

In a soft voice, one you could barely hear over the PlayStation crowd noises in the bedroom, Ty said, "Dude? I'd rather play on your team."

Danny didn't even look up from the game.

"I know."

Then they went back to fantasy basketball, which was almost always a lot simpler than real life.

The next practice was Tuesday night.

Danny and the rest of the Rugrats — he couldn't get the name out of his head now, like they were a rock group — were waiting to get on the floor while the seventh-grade girls' travel team finished their own practice.

Will and Bren were on the stage, quietly dogging the girls as a way of entertaining each other, Will doing most of the talking, of course. Danny was up there with them for a few minutes, but then left, knowing that if they actually started bothering the girls, or were overheard by the girls' coach, Ms. Perry, one of the phys ed teachers from the high school, he'd be going down with them.

He went and sat with the other guys on the floor.

Richie Walker sat in a folding chair on the other side from them, legs stretched out in front of him, watching the girls.

Danny walked over there when the girls went past eight o'clock. Ms. Perry had shouted over and asked if it was all right if they went a few extra minutes, and Richie Walker said, go ahead, he was in no rush.

Danny said, "Even they're better than us."

"Who is she?" Richie said.

Danny didn't have to ask who "she" meant. "That's Colby."

Colby Danes was out there doing what she always did in girls basketball, which meant scoring all the points, getting all the rebounds, passing like she was ready at twelve to go play for the women's team at UConn or Tennessee or one of those other colleges where the women's team was better and more famous than the men's. Danny had always thought of her as the girl player that Ty would have been, almost as tall as Ty, with her red hair in a ponytail, smiling her way through practice even when she'd occasionally do something wrong.

Another tall St. Pat's girl.

Richie said, "What do you think of her?"

"I think she's great," Danny said. "For a girl."

"She's great, period," Richie said. "Those two knotheads making fun of her up on the stage ought to be paying attention to the way she plays. On account of, they might learn something."

With that, Richie spun around suddenly and stared straight at Bren and Will, as if training a searchlight on them. They both froze, Will with his mouth still open.

Richie went back to staring at Colby Danes.

Really staring.

"Dad?"

"Huh?"

"You seem pretty interested in Colby."

"I just like watching people who know how to play. Girls or boys. That's all."

Ms. Perry announced next basket and they were done for the night.

"You think your friend Colby —"

"— I wouldn't really call her a friend —"

"— would like to practice with the boys sometime?"

On the court, Colby got the ball near the basket and turned and made a baby hook over the girl guarding her, a Chinese girl from Springs. Emily Ming.

"Dad?" Danny said. "What are you doing?"

"Doing what your mom said people should do more of in this town. Thinking outside the box."

"But she's a *girl*," Danny said.

"Yeah," Richie said, "a girl who knows what to do when you pass her the ball. A girl who can catch it and shoot it and go get it. And can run the court on her long legs almost as fast as you can, Dan the man."

On the court, Ms. Perry blew her whistle and told the girls to bring it in. Danny's dad pulled himself out of his chair, picked up the bag of balls that had been sitting next to him.

"You know what she is, if we're strictly talking basketball here?"

"What?" Danny said.

"The girl of your dreams."

Richie talked to Ms. Perry first. Ms.

Perry told him to ask Colby's dad, Dr. Danes, who was standing with the rest of the girls' parents at the other end of the gym. Then Richie was standing with Colby and Dr. Danes and everybody was doing a lot of smiling and nodding and before you knew it, Colby was in the layup line with Danny and the guys.

Will whispered to Danny, "I knew nothing good was gonna come out of Annika playing golf with the boys."

Behind them Bren said, "This is just for practice, right?"

Then Danny heard himself saying, "Let me ask you basketball geniuses a question: Could Colby make us any worse?"

"Okay," Will said, "Walker has officially turned into the coach's son."

In the first five minutes of the scrimmage, she set a great pick on Will, rolled off it perfectly, and took a smooth bounce pass from Danny for a layup. Like Stockton and Malone. The pick-and-roll.

Then she went down to the other end of the court, stole the ball from Michael Harden, passed it to Danny, who passed it right back to her, then watched as she beat everybody down the court for another easy layup.

Danny looked over at his dad, still standing with Dr. Danes.

Richie Walker, no expression on his face, shrugged.

It went like that for half an hour and then Dr. Danes yelled out to Colby that she had homework to do. Even that made Colby smile. "One more basket?" she said. "Please, Dad?"

"One more. But then that's it."

Danny brought the ball up. He passed it on the wing to Colby. As she came up, Bren came from the other side and set a back-pick on Oliver Towne, who was guarding her now. Colby left-hand dribbled into the open, near the foul line, and had a wide-open shot.

When she went up for the shot, with everybody watching her, Danny cut for the basket from the other wing. Colby never stopped her shooting motion or seemed to even alter it as she went into the air, passing the ball off to Danny instead.

He caught it and, in the same motion, showing off a little — for a girl? — made a little scoop shot from the left side.

He looked over to see what Colby thought but she was already walking over to her dad.

When practice was over, Danny said to his dad, "Colby coming back?"

"Thursday," he said.

"Who *is* going to pay for this great team of ours?" Danny said to his mom when he got home.

He'd asked his dad if he wanted to come in after practice, but he said he had to be somewhere. At ten o'clock, Danny just assumed the somewhere had to be Runyon's bar.

"Your father wrote a check to the school for the gym time," his mom said, "I know that. Beyond that, if this thing keeps going forward, I assume he'll pass a hat with the parents for team uniforms, warm-ups, referees and whatnot. I forget all the costs, it's been a couple of years since I was a travel basketball mom."

Ali Walker was sitting at the kitchen table, grading compositions. Danny had finished his homework and had been watching a show in the living room where the contestants tried to see how long they could keep live grasshoppers and crickets in their mouths.

"Don't worry about money," she said. "Parents do that. You worry about school and sports. In that order, I might add."

She looked up at him over her reading glasses, which always made her look more like Mrs. Walker the teacher than his mom.

"Is there something else on your mind?"

"I was just wondering if Dad's going to stay at the Inn the whole season, now that he's staying," Danny said.

"He mentioned the other night that he might look into getting a small apartment somewhere if it was cheaper than the Inn."

" 'Cause I was thinking, he could stay —"

"No," she said. "He could not stay here."

She put down her reading glasses as she said it, for emphasis, a judge banging her gavel, case closed.

"So he's okay for money right now?"

"He says he is, that he'd had a few good months doing those shows of his before he got here."

"You believe him?"

His mom said, "You don't?"

It was somewhere between a question and an observation.

"I just don't know what this whole deal is about sometimes," he said.

"Well, I thought it was about putting together a team for a bunch of boys —"

"— and girls. I think Dad's fixing to put Colby on the team."

That stopped her.

153

"*Your* father is going to put a *girl* on *his* basketball team?"

"He didn't come right out and say it. But he let Colby practice tonight and he says she's coming back on Thursday."

Ali Walker said, "Will wonders never cease."

"What's that mean?"

"It means your father, in his youth, was not exactly the biggest fan of girls' basketball."

"She's pretty good, you know."

"I know. For a girl."

Danny said, "You were about to tell me something before I told you about Colby."

"I was just going to say that I thought this was a team for a bunch of kids who'd been told by a bunch of adults they weren't good enough." She gave him a long look, then said, "Or big enough."

"He wants *us* to prove a point then?"

"Would you mind telling me what you're getting at here, Daniel Walker?"

"Sometimes I just think Dad's the one trying to prove some kind of point to somebody."

"Maybe it's to you," she said. "Ever think of that?"

Danny's thinking was more along these lines:

He wondered if the someone Richie Walker was trying to prove something to was himself.

CROSSOVER2: Hey, picture girl. You there?
CONTESSA44: We're here 24/7.
CROSSOVER2: Like those hotlines.
CONTESSA44: For troubled teens.
CROSSOVER2: I've only got b-ball troubles.
CONTESSA44: But I hear there's a new girl in your basketball life.

It was true, Danny thought.
News did travel faster than ever in the Internet age.

CROSSOVER2: Who told?
CONTESSA44: I cannot reveal my source . . . Yes, I can, it was Will.
CROSSOVER2: He's got a big mouth even on a Mac . . . And she's not in my life, she's on my dopey team.
CONTESSA44: Dopey? Uh-oh. Somebody's Grumpy tonight.

Tess Hewitt wasn't just a fast typist. She was fast, period.

CROSSOVER2: She won't change anything. We suck.
CONTESSA44: You haven't even played
a game yet.
CROSSOVER2: The only time I like
playing ball is when I play with Ty.

He waited longer than usual for her
reply. Which meant trouble, because the
longer she took usually, the longer the
reply.
But he was wrong.

CONTESSA44: Get over it.
CROSSOVER2: What?
CONTESSA44: Repeat: Get over it. As
in, all of it. Stop feeling so sorry
for yourself.
CROSSOVER2: Now you're my coach?
CONTESSA44: Just your IM cheerleader.
But on to more important stuff
. . . Do you think Colby's cute?

Danny felt himself smiling.
Just not about the tall girl on his basketball team.
He was smiling through all the magic of
computers, all the mojo, his screen to her
screen, all the way across Middletown, at
this girl.

CROSSOVER2: No.
CONTESSA44: You're cute.
CROSSOVER2: Gross.
CONTESSA44: Things will get better.

They were actually about to get worse.

13

First: the fight.

He and Will had gone to the new Jackie Chan movie at the Middletown Theater, the one with the old-fashioned marquee out front, somehow hanging in there against all the multiplexes in the area, including the new one outside Twin Forks, in the factory-outlet mall that was roughly the same size as Texas.

Danny's mom had brought him and Will, and Will's mom was supposed to pick them up at the Candy Kitchen afterward.

That's where they ran into Teddy Moran and Jack Harty and fat Eric Buford.

Will saw them come in, scoping out the room with his back to the wall in their back booth. He always sat facing the room, afraid he was going to miss something, even if it was only who'd just come through the door.

"Check it out," Will said. "Terrible Teddy actually found *two* people who wanted to go to the movies with him."

He said it in his boom-box voice, as if everybody in the Candy Kitchen had suddenly gone deaf.

"You better repeat that," Danny said, "I think a couple of guys in the kitchen might have missed it."

"C'mon," Will said, "you're the one who always says that calling Moran a snake is insulting to a lot of innocent water moccasins."

There may have been less popular twelve-year-olds in Middletown than Teddy Moran, whose father hosted his own show on the town's AM radio station. But if there were, Teddy was trying his hardest to take the crown.

Somehow Teddy thought his father's celebrity made him one, too. He went through life with even more mouth than Will, as if doing the play-by-play for himself and everybody else. He liked to think he had a lot of friends, but really didn't. In fact, if there was one enduring mystery in Middletown, at least among guys their age, it was this: Why Ty Ross had anything to do with him.

Danny just wrote it off to the fact that Ty would find good qualities in a guard dog.

He even managed to do it with a punk-face like Teddy, with those pig eyes, with a mouth set in a smirky way that made it look as if he were always on the verge of getting a flu shot. Teddy Moran: Who always got a lot braver when he had somebody as big as Jack Harty with him, even though Jack usually seemed to be embarrassed to be in the same area code.

Danny was hoping that if he and Will ignored them, they'd go away. No such luck. Will hadn't just talked too loudly, he'd made the fatal mistake of eye contact.

So the three of them came over and stood near the booth, Teddy in front of the other two. Danny thinking: Yeah, Moran, you're a born leader.

"Hey, Walker," Teddy said, "is it true you're playing with girls now?"

Looking over one shoulder, then the other, at Jack and fat Buford, like he'd gotten off a good one.

Will said, "It's easier for us with girls than it is for you, just because they don't run the other way when they see us coming. Or, in your case, smell us coming."

Teddy ignored him, saying to Danny, "What color are your uniforms going to be — pink?"

Will said, "Did somebody say punk?"

Danny leaned forward and sipped his root beer float, then looked up at Teddy. "Is there some point you're getting to, dude? Or are you planning to go from booth to booth busting chops, and just happened to start with us?"

Jack and fat Buford turned and went to the counter to order, somehow bored by the sparkling conversation.

Teddy stayed. "Hear you're spending a lot of time with Ross," he said.

"Jealous?" Will said.

Teddy shot him a sideways glance. "Nice hair," he said. "Come home with me later, you can scrub some of our dinner pots with your head."

"Holy crap, that's a good one," Will said. "I've got to get a pencil from one of the waitresses and write that one down."

To Danny, Teddy said, "One of these days, you and your pals have to get over not making the grade."

"You're absolutely right, Moran," Danny said, feeling himself starting to get hot now. "The other thing I've got to do is get my dad to sponsor the team next year, just to guarantee me a spot."

Garland Moran's station, WMID, *was* the Vikings' sponsor this season.

"Your dad?" Teddy said. "Sponsor a

161

team? With what, his bar tips?"

Will got up first. "Shut up," he said. *"Now."*

Teddy Moran started to turn away from them, on his way to the counter, but decided to say one more thing.

"Loser coach," he said, "for a loser team."

Danny, in a quiet voice, said, "Hey, Moran," to get his attention.

So he'd turn.

So Danny wasn't technically blindsiding him with what Will would describe later as a blinding first step, coming out of the booth and up into Teddy Moran, grabbing two fists' worth of Teddy's stupid F.U.B.U. sweatshirt as he did, Teddy thinking F.U.B.U. made him a cool-black white kid, driving him back into the swivel chairs at the counter.

Teddy was bigger and heavier than Danny the way everybody was bigger and heavier, but his lack of guts made it a fair fight.

The two of them went down in the opening at the counter where the waitresses brought out the food, Teddy hitting the floor hard as Danny heard people start to yell all around them, heard Teddy himself yelling, "Get *off* me."

Danny was on top of him now, had him by the front of the sweatshirt, had his face close enough to smell movie popcorn on Teddy's breath.

He could feel people trying to pull him off, but he wasn't ready to let go.

Still wasn't sure whether he was going to bust him in the face and knock the smirk off it.

"Take it back," he said.

He knew how lame it sounded as soon as he said it, but it was the best he could do, he could barely breathe, much less think clearly.

Even now, Teddy was still all mouth.

"About him being a drunk, or a loser?"

Now Danny pulled back his right hand, ready to pop him, see if that would finally shut his fat mouth. But Gus, the owner of the Candy Kitchen, the guy that kids considered the real mayor of Middletown, caught his hand like he was wearing a catcher's mitt and said, "How's about we don't make this worse than it already is?"

Will finished the job of pulling Danny off Teddy Moran.

Teddy was already on his feet, safely behind Jack and fat Buford, a complete phony to the end, trying to make it look as if he were trying to get around them and back at Danny, and they were holding him back.

"Truth hurts, huh, Walker?" he said.

Will was moving Danny slowly toward the door.

"You're the one who's going to get hurt," Danny said. "When it's just you and me, next time."

"You talk tough for a midget," Teddy said. "Everybody in town knows the *real* truth about your old man except you."

Danny tried to turn around, but Will had him in a bear hug, saying, "You're probably only grounded right now. Let's not shoot for life without parole."

They stood on the corner, Danny breathing like crazy now, gulping in air like he'd just run a hundred-yard dash, Will saying they ought to get out of there, he'd call his mom and tell her to pick them up at Fierro's.

"I should have kicked his ass," Danny said.

"Everybody in there thinks you already did."

They walked down the street. When they passed Runyon's, they saw Richie Walker at his usual corner stool, his face fixed on the television set. Danny didn't know what he was watching, but he recognized the look on his dad's face, the one where it looked as if he was staring hard at nothing, all the way into outer space.

Danny staring hard at him.

What had Teddy meant?

The real truth?

Danny was grounded for the next week, not even allowed to attend practices. He pleaded his case to his mom as soon as Mrs. Stoddard dropped him off at home that night, telling her what Teddy Moran had said, explaining that Teddy had lied when he told *his* mom that Danny had jumped him from behind.

He knew it wasn't going to help his case even a little bit, but he finished by telling her that if anybody in town deserved to catch a good beating, it was Teddy Moran.

"Are you finished now?" Ali Walker said.

"Pretty much. Yeah."

"You're right. He *is* a jerk. He happens to come from a long line of jerks, the biggest being his father. And having told you that? You're still busted, kiddo. You know my position on fighting."

He did, reciting it to her now the way he would have the Pledge of Allegiance. "The only thing fighting ever proves is who's the better fighter," he said. "And you usually know that before you start."

No phone privileges after dinner for a week. No after-homework television.

No computer of any kind unless it involved homework, which meant no instant-messaging.

"No IM!" Will said at school on Monday. Mock horror. "No tube? She's turned you into the Count of Monte Cristo."

What felt like one of the longest school weeks ever — no computer privileges always made him feel like he was stranded at night on some kind of desert island — finally came to an end. His dad stopped by Friday afternoon, telling him that he'd scheduled six games so far, the first one on the first weekend in December, the last of the six the Sunday before the Christmas holidays began. He also said that despite a lot of bitching and moaning — his dad's words — from Middletown Basketball, Colby Danes was leaving the seventh-grade girls' team and joining them.

He was at the front door when he turned and said, "Oh, by the way, one other thing? We're scrimmaging the Vikings tomorrow afternoon at St. Pat's."

"We'll get killed!" Danny said.

"I figure."

"You don't care?"

"Listen," he said. "I know *they'll* care, even though I'm not letting them use the scoreboard. They're not even supposed to keep score in a scorebook, though I figure they'll find a way. They're going to rub your faces in it. I just want to see what we've got, and who I should be scheduling, especially if it turns out we don't get into the league."

"The league hasn't told you yet?"

"They say they're still quote, considering my request, unquote."

"While they do, the Vikings get to use us as tackling dummies."

"It's just a scrimmage, not the Final Four."

Danny said, "More like a car wreck, if you ask me."

He felt like a jerk, talking about car accidents in front of his dad, as soon as the words were out of his mouth.

The stupid jerk of all jerks.

Inside his stupid head, he pictured himself using both hands trying to grab the words out of the air and stuff them back inside his mouth.

"What I meant . . ."

"Relax," Richie said. "I know you didn't mean anything. But it's not a car wreck, kiddo. It's just basketball. I used to think it was a matter of life and death, too. I found out the hard way that it wasn't."

It turned out to be a *train* wreck.

Mr. Ross hired a couple of refs Danny recognized from sixth-grade travel. Mr. Harden worked the clock. The Vikings wore black practice jerseys Danny didn't even know they had, with their own numbers on the backs and everything. Danny's team wore white T-shirts.

No spectators, not even parents. Just the players, the two coaches, the two refs.

In the huddle, Will said, "The refs want to know what our team is called."

They all looked at each other.

Will said, "I never really thought Rugrats was all that catchy, to tell you the truth."

Danny said, "How about the Warriors?" He looked up at his dad. "As in the Golden State Warriors."

For a moment, a blink of an eye, it was as if it were just the two of them, getting ready to play one-on-one in the driveway. His dad looked back at him, and winked. "Works for me," he said. "Warriors okay with the rest of you guys?"

"Why not?" Will said. "We'll be like the real Warriors. Just much, much smaller."

Richie had them put their hands in the middle, told them not to worry about who was winning or by how much, to play hard, have fun, work on their stuff.

When they broke the huddle and lined up to start, Danny looked around at the five starters for the Vikings, seeing how much bigger they were, knowing how much *better* they were. Then he leaned next to Will's ear and said, "Holy crap. Who *picked* these teams?"

The Vikings went with Ty, Jack Harty, Andy Mayne, Daryll Mullins, Teddy Moran.

Against: Danny, Bren, Matt, Oliver. And Colby Danes.

The only place where the Warriors had a height advantage of any kind was Matt against Jack, but that didn't mean squat, Jack Harty was a better player in just about every way.

Richie had Bren guard Teddy Moran. Danny took Andy Mayne, Colorado boy. As they all took their positions before the older ref, Tony, threw the ball up, Teddy walked close enough to Danny to say, "I was wrong. This team needs *more* girls."

Somehow Matt got the opening tip from Jack, back-tapping it to Danny, who immediately put one finger in the air and yelled "Syracuse."

It wasn't just the number one play in their offense, it was pretty much the only play, even if Richie had given them some options they could run, depending on how the defense reacted to it.

Danny passed to Bren, then cut away from the ball and set a pick for Colby on the right wing. She was supposed to cut toward the free throw line if the pick worked, and Bren was supposed to pass it to her if she was open. If she wasn't open, Danny was Bren's second option, cutting right behind Colby.

The Vikings switched on her, so Danny got the ball back. He was supposed to look for Matt underneath the way Colby would have. Because while they were doing their pick thing out top, Oliver Towne was supposed to be flashing across the baseline and picking Matt's man — Jack — and seeing if they could free Matt up for an easy layup.

It happened just that way, exactly the way Richie Walker had drawn it up for them, the way it happened when he had walked them through it the first time they'd practiced together.

Jack turned his head to see where Colby was after the first pick, even though Colby was covered. Oliver set a perfect screen, and Danny whipped the ball to Matt who, amazingly, did two things that qualified him for his own personal Book of World Records:

1. Caught the ball cleanly.
2. Made the layup.

One more time, Danny thought: Holy crap.

We're winning.

Even without a scoreboard, Danny had always been pretty good at keeping score in his head. Not just keeping score, but knowing how many points every player on the court had. He didn't know how he could do that, but he could, almost from the first time he started playing organized ball.

Just another part of having a head for the game.

But even he lost track now, as the Vikings scored either the next thirty, or thirty-two, points of the scrimmage.

That meant between Matt's basket and the two free throws Danny made with four seconds left in the first half.

Ty scored at least half of them, maybe more. The Vikings were doing fine just using their regular man-to-man, but then Mr. Ross had them put on their full-court press halfway through the first quarter, at which point they seemed to score ten baskets in the next twenty seconds.

The Vikings started double-teaming Danny in the backcourt as soon as he touched the ball. Instead of coming to help him out, the rest of the Warriors, with the exception of Colby, kept running away from the ball. When Danny would find somebody to pass it to, they hurried so much trying to get it right back to him, they usually threw it away, which usually meant another layup for the Vikings.

When by some miracle the Warriors did manage to get the ball over half-court, the Vikings would double-team Danny there, daring anybody else on his team to make a stinking basket.

While all this was going on, Teddy Moran was holding a non-stop, trash-talking festival, as if he were winning the game single-handedly. It was all Danny could do to keep his cool. But he did, knowing that you couldn't pick a fight when you were getting your doors blown off this way.

His dad tried calling a couple of time-outs.

They didn't help.

It was basically like trying to call a time-out right after somebody had yelled "Fire!" at a school assembly.

At halftime, Richie told them for what felt like the hundredth time to relax, telling them they knew how to play a lot better than this.

Will raised a hand and said, "You absolutely sure about that, Coach?"

"Mr. Harden talked to Mr. Ross," Richie said. "They're gonna take the press off for the whole second half. And that one's on me, we didn't work enough on breaking the press. For now, try to stay with your man, and do the best you can running the offense."

Danny said, "What offense?"

Richie gave him a look. "Hey." That's all it took, Danny felt like he'd gotten a good swat.

"Sorry."

"You knew these guys were better. And bigger. They've had a lot more practice time than we've had and most of them have been playing together a long time. Like I said: Don't worry about what they're doing, let's just work on our sh . . . stuff."

He almost used another s-word, didn't.

The real s-word happened with about five minutes left in the game, as it turned out.

There was 5:25 showing on the clock. Danny would remember the exact time when Mr. Ross called a time-out and put Ty and Teddy back into the game, after he'd sat the two of them for most of the second half. Danny had been out of the game since the middle of the third quarter, and had started to wonder if his dad was going to put him back in, or if he might be done for the day.

But now his dad poked him and said, "Why don't you go guard your buddy."

"Ty?"

"I was being sarcastic," Richie said. "Take the mouth."

"You heard what he's been saying the whole game?"

"I don't need to hear it, I can tell just by looking at his face," Richie said. "I've been playing against guys like that my whole life. The only way to shut them up is to shut them down. So go do that."

After the substitutions, the Vikings took the ball out. Danny picked up Teddy as soon as he got the ball in the backcourt.

Teddy put the ball on his hip and said, "Look, it's Stuart Little."

But as soon as he put the ball on the floor, Danny took it from him, picking him clean off the dribble, and taking it to the basket for a layup. Teddy didn't even try to catch him, whining to the second ref, DeWayne, the one who looked like a dead ringer for Snoop Dogg, that Danny had fouled him.

Teddy let Ty bring the ball up next time. Ty started the Viking offense on the left side, while Teddy ran to the right. He waited until Ty passed to Daryll Mullins in the left corner, figuring everybody was following the ball. Including Danny, who was between his man and the ball the way he'd been taught.

As soon as he turned his head, Teddy stepped up and hit him in the neck with an elbow.

It felt like Teddy had hit him with a bat.

He couldn't catch his breath for a second, dropping to his knees and holding both hands to his throat while everybody else ran up the court after Daryll Mullins made his jumper.

"Hey!" Richie yelled to Tony, the ref closest to the play. "What was *that?*"

Tony saw Danny on his knees then, but made a quick gesture with his hands over his eyes; it was his way of telling Richie he hadn't seen what had happened. Then he blew his whistle, stopping play.

Richie knelt down next to Danny.

"You okay?"

He swallowed hard, the inside of his throat feeling as if he were swallowing tacks. "I'm okay."

"I'm taking you out."

"No."

"You sure?"

"Yeah."

"Hey," Richie said, putting both hands on his shoulders, looking him straight in the eye. "Just play, okay? No payback, at least for now."

Danny nodded.

Two minutes to go. Vikings' ball. Everybody on their team except Ty was goofing around now, doing whatever they wanted on offense, shooting from wherever they wanted to, making showboat passes, even though Mr. Ross kept making a show out of being pissed and telling them to run *their* stuff.

Danny noticed Ty giving warning looks to Teddy a couple of times. Like he was saying, Cut the crap. But Teddy ignored him.

Jack Harty, who hardly ever took a long outside shot, decided to fire one up from twenty feet. Danny and Teddy ended up underneath, each trying to get position to get the rebound. Ty was there, too, already having the inside position on Will.

While everybody was looking up for the ball, Teddy gave Danny another elbow, this one in the side.

Enough, Danny decided.

More than enough.

The ball had hit the back of the rim and bounced straight up in the air, as high as the top of the backboard.

As it did, Danny got a leg in front of Teddy Moran, planted it good and solid, and, as he did, used perfect rebounding position, elbows out, to shove Teddy hard to the side, his left elbow like a roundhouse punch into Teddy's rib cage.

It knocked Teddy off balance, made him stumble to his left, just as Ty Ross, who had gone high up in the air when the ball had finally stopped bouncing around on the rim, was coming down with the rebound.

Danny saw it all happening like it was super slo-mo on television.

Or in a video game.

Only this wasn't fantasy ball.

This was Ty landing on Teddy instead of the basketball floor at St. Pat's.

This was Ty Ross, not just the best twelve-year-old player in town but the most graceful, the one who never made a false move on the court, rolling over Teddy's back, the ball flying out of his hands, nothing to break his fall as he landed hard on his right wrist — his shooting wrist — with a crack on the floor that sounded like a firecracker going off.

Then Ty was rolling on the floor at St. Pat's, cradling his right arm to his stomach, screaming in pain.

14

There was a secret place in his room, next to his closet, the wall hidden behind the poster of Jason Kidd.

It was where Danny had been measuring himself for a long time. Where he could check the progression he had made, say, between February 26 of fourth grade to October 16 of fifth grade.

He would use a pen, afraid pencil marks would fade over time or disappear, writing the date and the year, hoping there'd be one year where he'd see the growth spurt Dr. Korval kept promising him.

Only the growth spurt never came.

The lines just kept crawling their way up the wall.

Danny Walker was fast everywhere except here.

He would carefully untape the poster when it was time to make another entry, lay it flat on his bed, take his place next to the door frame, reach back, put the pen flat on his head and point it toward the wall, make another line. He never cheated. Not even on September 17 of this year, a couple of weeks after he started school, when he was desperate to break the fifty-five inch mark he'd hit back in July.

Except he didn't break the speed limit that day.

Or on October 2.

Or October 14.

His mom called him a streak of light and he even thought of himself as a streak of light sometimes when he was flying up the court, but he kept moving his way up the wall like an inchworm.

Now he took the Kidd poster down when he got back from the Vikings scrimmage, stared at all the lines and all the dates — the only progress he could see was that his penmanship was improving as he got older — and thought about measuring himself for the first time since October.

Instead he just sat in the beanbag chair Ty had been sitting in the other day.

Feeling smaller than ever.

Trying to squeeze his eyes shut so that he would stop seeing Ty lying there on the floor, rocking from side to side on his back, his injured hand not leaving his stomach.

Only closing his eyes didn't help. He

kept seeing Ty. And hearing the voice of Teddy Moran.

"You happy now?" Teddy had said in the gym after it happened.

This was after Mr. Ross had decided not to wait for an ambulance and to take Ty to Valley General Hospital, just outside of town on Route 37, himself. The two of them had walked slowly out of the gym, Mr. Ross with his arm around Ty's shoulder, Ty holding his right hand in front of him with his left, the left hand shaking so bad you wondered why he even bothered.

"You couldn't have a real season for yourself so you had to wreck ours?" Teddy yelled at Danny when the Rosses were gone.

In a voice the size of a penny Danny said, "It was an accident."

Not even sure why he was saying anything back to him.

"He shoved me into him," Teddy said, addressing the rest of the Vikings now, not dropping the sound of his own voice one bit. Most of the Vikings were still there, along with some of the parents who'd shown up a few minutes early for pickups. Teddy pointed right at Danny and said, "*He* did this to Ty."

"It was an accident, you moron," Will finally said.

"It was," Danny said again.

"You keep telling yourself that, little man," Teddy said to Danny. "You tried to get me and you got Ty instead. Does *that* make you feel big?"

"I didn't mean to," Danny said.

He was going to say something else then, something that would explain what had happened, to the Vikings, to their parents, to the Warriors.

Maybe to himself.

Except his throat closed up suddenly, the way it had when Teddy got him in the neck with his elbow, and he started to feel his eyes fill up, and no words would come out.

He felt his dad's hand on his elbow.

"I'll run you home," he said.

"Nice team," Teddy said now, to both of them.

"Shut up, kid," Richie said.

Teddy's father, Garland, was standing next to him. Garland Moran had the same pinched face as his son, same pig eyes, just an adult version. "Hey," he said, "you can't talk to my son like that."

"You ought to try it once in a while," Richie said. "It might teach him some manners."

Then father and son began walking out

of the gym, but not before Teddy hit Danny with one more sucker punch.

"He actually told me you were his *friend*, Walker."

Danny didn't turn around, kept walking toward the front doors. Wanting to run.

Now he felt as if Teddy's words had chased him all the way to his room. He got out of the beanbag chair, that move taking as much effort as his dad usually showed getting out of a chair, took a pen off his desk, put a mark about an inch above the floorboard, and the date.

You're as big as you think you are, his mom always told him.

You're as big as you feel.

He was in his room the next afternoon, lying there on his bed and listening to the Jets game on the radio instead of watching it downstairs, content to stay here by himself until it was time to go to high school.

"Hey there," his mom said, standing in the doorway. "It's my solitary man."

"Huh?"

"Another old song."

Danny turned down the volume on the radio when it was clear she was staying. That she was there for a Mom Talk.

"I just got off the phone with Lily Ross," she said.

He waited.

"It turns out he only broke one bone in the wrist," she said. "So that's pretty good news, right?"

"Wow," he said, "a broken arm. That's *great* news, Mom!"

"You know what I mean," she said. "Your father thought it could have been much worse just because of the way he landed and the pain you guys said he was in. The doctor told Lily that some Jets quarterback had a wrist injury in about the same spot a few years ago —"

"— not some quarterback. Chad Pennington —"

"— and broke four bones and had some ligament damage."

"They operated on him that time. Did they operate on Ty?"

Ali Walker nodded. "To put a pin in there. He'll be in a cast for a while."

Danny sat up on the bed. "How long?"

"They'd only be guessing."

"Okay, what was Mrs. Ross's best guess?"

"She didn't talk about how long he'd be in the cast, just that the whole healing process was going to take at least three months, probably closer to four."

November. December. January.

Back in February.

Maybe.

The official Tri-Valley League season, Danny knew, started the first week of January and lasted until the middle of February. The tournament was the last week of February.

So if Ty was lucky, he could get a game or two in before the tournament.

"So he'll be able to play again this season?" Danny said.

His mom said, "She didn't say that. The doctor reminded her that they just needed to keep their fingers crossed. And that if everything went well, he *might* be able to play again this season, as long as he is convinced — this is Dr. Marshall, the orthopedic surgeon, talking — that there is no chance of Ty reinjuring himself."

Danny let himself dead-fall back on his pillow, staring up at the Stockton poster.

"He *might* be able to play."

"If not, he'll be ready for baseball."

"Yippee."

"Might be able to play is better than won't be able to play."

Danny said, "You think I could maybe call him?"

Ali Walker didn't say anything.

Danny raised his head back up off the pillow, repeated himself as if she hadn't heard him the first time. "Mom? You think I could call Ty?"

"Maybe you ought to wait a couple of days. Lily said he doesn't want to talk to anybody right now. Including his own parents."

"You think it would be all right to e-mail him?"

There was another pause, not as long as the one before, and she said, "Why don't you just wait on that, too."

Danny said, "He blames me, doesn't he?"

"Honey, I think he's just hurting in general." She came over and sat on the end of the bed. "And you're hurting."

"I'm fine."

"You want to talk about this?"

"No," he said. "But I can see you do."

"I thought it might be better if you just talked it out a little instead of sitting up here and brooding about it."

"Actually, I've been partying."

"It was an accident," she said.

"How much did that help Dad?" Danny said.

"He learned the hard way," she said.

"Accidents happen in life. Sometimes they just happen, and nobody's to blame."

"Somebody was to blame this time," Danny said.

The week after Thanksgiving, Richie Walker stopped by the house, saying that the Port Madison Pacers had dropped out of the Tri-Valley at the last second. It turned out only seven kids showed up for their original try-outs, and then three of them decided they wanted to play hockey instead. When they had a second tryout, only two more seventh graders showed up, at which point the Port Madison Basketball Association surrendered.

Richie Walker said he'd just gotten a call from the league telling him that, and also telling him the Warriors could take Port Madison's place as the Tri-Valley's eighth team.

"I had the check ready, the paperwork, the insurance forms," he said, sounding pretty proud of himself. "I had already scheduled some games I hadn't told you about yet, against some other Tri-Valley teams. They said I could pick up the rest I needed from Port Madison, use as much of their league schedule as I wanted. And a few nonleague games before Christmas if I wanted them."

"Do we play the Vikings?" Danny said.

"No," his dad said. "We just needed twelve official league games. We can play the six teams besides them twice, and that's enough." He looked at Danny and said, "I didn't see any point."

"But we could see them in the play-offs, right? Doesn't everybody make the play-offs?"

"Eight teams, three rounds, like you're starting with the quarterfinals. Yeah, if it falls right, we could play 'em in the play-offs. Depending on what our record is. And theirs. They'll be pretty good even without Ty, I figure."

"I can figure what our record's gonna be."

Richie grabbed him by the arm, turning him slightly. The grip on his arm wasn't enough to hurt. Just enough to let Danny know his dad meant business.

He said, "I want you to stop feeling so sorry for yourself. I mean it. Grow up, for Chrissakes."

"I wasn't —"

"— Yeah, you were. You're feeling sorry for yourself today, you've been feeling sorry for yourself at practice, you've been feeling sorry for yourself since you got cut from the Vikings. And I want you to snap out of it. Or."

It was like he'd come to a stop sign.

"Or what?" Danny said, feeling some anger of his own now. "You're gonna quit? And leave?"

Richie looked down, and realized he still had Danny by the arm, let him go.

"I'm not quitting on you this time," his dad said. "All I'm asking is that you don't quit on me."

"I'm just being honest about the team," Danny said. "Aren't you the one who always says you are what your record says you are in sports?"

"It's an old Bill Parcells line," his dad said. "But we don't have a record yet."

"Right."

"You gotta trust me on something," Richie said. "We're gonna get better as we go. Swear to God."

"Oh, like you've got a master plan."

"I gave up on plans a long time ago," he said. The sad look came back then. "It's like your mom says. You want to make God laugh? Tell Him about your plans."

They both had calmed down now. Sat there talking their common language, basketball, Richie telling him he was going to press more, and feature Colby more, and that he'd even told Matt's dad that he was willing to work with him alone a couple of times a week.

"I was on a team once they said made magic around here," Richie Walker said. "It's time to make some again."

In the two weeks after the Warriors-Vikings scrimmage, Danny had left one message on the Rosses' answering machine, using Will's cell during recess one day even though it was against the rules at St. Pat's; he wanted to do it during school because he knew Mr. Ross would be at the bank and Mrs. Ross would probably be doing her volunteer work at the hospital.

Ty hadn't called back.

A couple of nights later, Danny tried e-mail.

And instant-messaging, when he saw that Ty was online.

He got zip in response.

On Thursday after school, he and Will had gone into town just to goof around. When they had gone past Runyon's, Danny had seen his dad at the end of the bar, a glass of beer in front of him, staring up at what must have been a rerun of a college basketball game played the night before, since it was only five-thirty in the afternoon.

Ty was back at school, Danny knew that. But he hadn't seen him at the Candy Kitchen on weekends. Hadn't run into him at the Middletown-Morrisville football game the weekend after Thanksgiving, even though he was hoping he would.

The next Friday, while waiting for his mom, Danny had even used his old hiding place on the stage while the Vikings practiced, just to see if Ty might be hanging around with them, fooling around with his left hand maybe.

He never showed up.

The next day at Twin Forks, they lost 47–22 and didn't score a point in the fourth quarter.

On Sunday, they lost 50–20 at Morrisville.

They never had a chance in either game, no matter how much switching Richie did with the defenses, no matter how many different lineups he tried, even though he had them pressing all over the court until the end.

At one point against Morrisville, Danny said to his dad coming out of a huddle,

"Uh, why are we still pressing?"

"Because it's the kind of team we have to be."

"Even though we're not even close to being that team yet?"

" 'Fraid so."

"Does that make *any* sense?"

"To me it does."

Then his dad gave him a push. Like: Just get out there and play. He played hard until the end, doing what he was always doing, which meant looking for Colby Danes every chance he got; the girl on the team being the only one he could pass it to and not be more scared than he was of spiders.

Danny and Will Stoddard were at the water fountain together when the Morrisville game was over. For once, Will talked in a voice only Danny could hear.

"Remember how your pop said we were going to be the team nobody wanted to play?" Will said.

Danny said, yeah, he remembered.

"Well, he was slightly off," Will said. "We're going to be the team *everybody* wants to play."

16

Their next practice wasn't until Tuesday night at nine.

Richie Walker, who was never late when basketball was involved, didn't show up until ten minutes after nine. Danny had gotten them into layup lines by then, using his own official NBA ball, his Spalding, last year's Christmas present — by mail — from his dad.

When they saw his dad come walking through the double doors, dragging his bag of balls, Will said, "Hey, Coach, we figured you finally deserted."

Richie said, "How about we have a new policy tonight? More playing and less talking."

Will, stung, said, "Hey, Coach, I was just saying . . ."

"Know something, Will? You're *always* just saying."

Danny, careful not to let his dad see him staring at him, watched him go to half-court and sit in the folding chair Ms.

Perry, from the girls' team, had left there.

Danny had seen him mad before, usually because of something that happened between him and Danny's mom. Danny'd get sent to his room and then the yelling would start. When he was younger, before he wanted to know exactly what was making them that mad, before he would eavesdrop at the top of the stairs, before he even had music to play or headphones to wear, he would just get on his bed and put pillows over his head until it stopped.

Until it was over.

It was part of it all. Being their son. Being the son of their divorce. The part he didn't like to dwell on very much.

Adults got mad sometimes, that was the deal. They yelled sometimes. And kids figured out pretty early that there wasn't one blinking thing they could do about it.

There was really no point in trying, the way there was no point in trying to figure it. The way there was no point in Danny trying to figure what had pissed off his dad before he got to the gym tonight.

A few minutes after Richie arrived, he yelled from the chair that they weren't going to start scrimmaging until they could make five straight layups with their off hands. It meant left hand for everybody on the team except Oliver Towne, who *was* left-handed. When they couldn't manage that after a couple of trips through the line he said, fine, they could run some suicides, maybe that would improve their layup shooting.

Suicides: Get on the baseline. Run and touch the floor at the free throw line extended. Back to the baseline. Then run and touch the half-court line. Come back. Then to the *other* free throw line. And back. Finally the whole length of the court and back.

Every kid who'd ever played basketball would rather sing in the chorus or go to the dentist than run suicides.

Matt and Oliver Towne finished last.

Richie made them run another one.

While they did, Will made the mistake of saying something to Bren and Bren made the even bigger mistake of laughing.

Richie made them run another suicide, since they thought suicides were so funny.

When they were finished, Richie got out of the chair, slowly and carefully, as always. Tin Man in *The Wizard of Oz*.

"You know why this team looked like a joke this weekend?" he said. "Because you guys treat it like a joke, that's why."

The Warriors were stretched out in a line

in front of him. Will and Bren still had their hands on their knees from running. Richie said, "Will and Bren, look at me when I'm talking to you!" Like he'd snapped them both with a towel.

They jerked their heads up.

"The worst crime in sports isn't losing," Richie said. "It's not competing. In my whole life I've never been associated with a team that didn't want to compete and I'm sure not going to start now. Now go out and let me see a real team."

Danny wanted to say, Make sure you tell us if you see it first.

There was only a half hour left for them to scrimmage, because they had to be out of the gym by ten.

Richie spent most of it yelling. Yelled, Danny thought, like every bad kid's coach he'd ever heard, in travel or rec leagues or at summer camp. Apparently yelled so much he had to keep going to the water fountain.

One time when he did, Will whispered to Danny, "Did he, like, forget we're twelve?"

Right before they finished, just a few minutes left, Matt Fitzgerald cut one way when Colby thought he was going to cut the other, and she threw a pass out of bounds.

"Come *on,* Colby!" Richie said. It was the first time he'd ever even come close to saying something in a mean voice to her. "Get your head out of . . . get your head in the game."

Colby took it better than he would have. Maybe better than any of the boys in the gym would have. She didn't look down, she didn't look away, she didn't try to make excuses. All she said was, "Sorry, Coach."

"No you're not," he said.

Everybody else on the court had stopped now, and was looking at Richie.

So was Ali Walker, standing with her arms crossed, just inside the double doors to the gym.

Richie saw her, too.

"That's it for tonight," he said. "Shoot around until your parents come."

Danny looked at his mom, still staring holes through his dad. She stayed where she was, nodding to the other parents who seemed to have showed up all at once for pickup, while Danny kept shooting free throws at one of the side baskets.

Richie made a big show of collecting the balls, as he tried to keep his distance from her. Finally, though, it was just the Walker family in the gym.

Richie said, "I didn't know you were picking him up tonight."

"I was on my way home from book club."

"Well, then, see you Thursday," he said to Danny, and slung the ball bag over his shoulder and started moving slowly, shuffling the way he did when he was tired, toward the door.

She still hadn't moved. "Rich?" she said. "I'd like a word with you. Danny? Go wait in the car. And I mean, *in the car*."

He walked out to the parking lot, carrying his ball, knowing his mom was watching him through the doors. When he got to the car, he turned around, waved, saw her close the door.

He waited two minutes and then snuck back. He carefully closed the front door, walked through the foyer, got on his toes, peeked through one of the windows in the double doors.

They were standing close to each other in front of the stage.

Danny cracked open one of the doors just slightly, praying that it wouldn't make some creaking noise that would be like a smoke alarm going off.

Now he could tell how pissed off his mom was.

Because she *wasn't* yelling.

Danny knew from experience it was the absolute worst kind of yelling there was.

Because she was speaking in such a low voice, he could only pick up bits and pieces of what she was saying.

". . . don't lie to me, Richard. Sally saw you last night."

His dad had his head down.

". . . can't be invisible, not in this town," she said.

His dad taking it all, the way they'd taken all his yelling in practice.

". . . not the children's fault that you're still hungover the next night."

He said something back now, but must have mumbled it, because Danny couldn't hear a single word he was saying.

Her voice came up a little. "Yes, you *can,*" she said. "We went over this already. You have to."

Danny could see him shaking his head, the head still down, acting as if he were the kid who'd done something wrong now, he were the one trying to act sorry.

Finally his mom said, "Quit drinking. Now. Or leave. No goodbyes, no travel team. No Danny. Just leave. It'll be better that way than letting your son be the last one to find out what a drunk you are."

She left him standing there, the ball bag still over his shoulder, and walked straight down the middle of the court.

While her streak of light streaked for the car.

Thinking as he ran about the magic they were supposed to make this season.

Wondering just when the magic was supposed to happen, exactly.

Everything his mom had said to his dad must have gotten through to him, because he was back to being the dad Danny always thought of as the Good Richie by the time they played their next game, against Hanesboro.

It's what you were always looking for from your parents, Danny had decided a long time ago, that they would show up with their good selves most of the time, in a good mood, not tired or pissed off about something at work. Or hungover. Just happy with you and the whole world.

The rest of the time, when their evil twin showed up, you just had to ride it out.

His mom drove him to Hanesboro, which was about an hour away, as far as they had to go in the Tri-Valley League. Danny couldn't tell whether it was because she wanted to see a whole Warriors game from start to finish, or because she thought she still had to police his dad.

"You didn't have to come," Danny said.

"I love sports," she said, and he couldn't tell whether she was the one being sarcastic, or not.

When they got to Hanesboro Middle School, his dad was on the court, moving around in his Tin Man way, shooting around with the O'Brien twins, and Oliver Towne, and Will.

He was even joking around with Will again.

"You been in the weight room?" Richie said to him. As he did he nodded at Danny, and winked.

"You want to touch these guns, Coach?" Will said, flexing his biceps in a bodybuilder pose.

Will was just making fun of his own skinny self, he knew everybody was in on it, that his arms, from wrist to shoulder, were about as thick as the lead in pencils.

Richie said, "They look more like cap pistols to me."

Will tried to look fierce as he kept staring at his right bicep. "You do *not* want any of this," he said. "Trust me."

When Colby showed up with Dr. Danes, Richie made a point of working with her in the corner, defending her with his arms up in the air, showing her how to get her shot against taller players.

Even Colby Danes, tall girl, was being asked to guard players taller than her, every single game. It was funny, Danny thought. Just not laugh-out-loud funny. Not funny the way Will Stoddard was. Because Colby had always been tall to Danny, from first grade on, the way Tess was taller. She was tall even when you put her up against most of the boys, she was tall when they'd have fool-around games in basketball or dodgeball or capture the flag at recess.

She still looked tall to him when the Warriors scrimmaged against each other.

Then they'd show up for a travel game and she'd go match up with the forward she was supposed to guard, or who was guarding her, and Danny would watch her shrink in front of his eyes.

Against Hanesboro, they didn't even have a size advantage at center, their guy was even bigger than Matt Fitzgerald.

It didn't matter over the first three quarters.

This time they were actually in the game.

It looked like another blowout when they got behind by ten points in the first quarter. But Richie told them they were "going small" in the second quarter, which meant starting Danny, Bren, Will, and Steven O'Brien, the better of the two twins.

And Colby at center.

He said they were going to play kamikaze ball, and they did, pressing after every Hanesboro basket, even pressing after a Warrior miss and a Hanesboro rebound, if they could match up quickly enough. Colby was smaller than their center, by a lot, but she was a lot quicker, and started beating him to rebounds; a girl doing that made the kid look as if he wanted to take up another sport. Every time Colby would get a rebound, the Warriors would run, and keep running, and Danny was dishing on the break, and by halftime the game was tied.

Richie stayed with the same group to start the third quarter, even though he got Oliver and Matt in there for a few minutes later.

It was still tied going into the fourth quarter.

Middletown 28, Hanesboro 28.

When the third quarter ended, the Warriors raced to the sideline, slapping each other five, pounding each other on the back. Feeling like a real team, maybe for the first time.

Danny, playing his best game, having assisted on just about every single basket they'd scored, was breathing hard in the huddle, like he'd just run a race, and gulped the red Gatorade that Richie handed him. As he took the bottle, the two of them locked eyes.

His dad made a small fist.

"Settle down now," Richie said. "It's not enough to just be in it. We're here to win it."

He looked around, talking to them in his quiet voice again. The one that had gotten their attention from the start.

Who knows, maybe he was the latest grown-up to crack the code on that.

"Don't change anything you're doing 'cause it's the fourth quarter," he said. "Get back as fast as you can, push it up as fast as you can. Okay?"

They all nodded.

"Same group that ended the quarter," he said. "Now bring it in."

He put his big hand out and then all these small hands were on top of it, and each other.

"One, two, three . . . *defense*," he said.

The Warriors yelled that out now, they were the ones doing the yelling, and came firing out of the huddle.

Danny scored the first basket of the fourth quarter, on a two-on-one break with Will. He was on the left with the ball, Will to his right. All game long, Danny had given the ball up on plays like this. The Hanesboro kid between him and Will expected Danny to do that again, especially coming at the basket on the left side.

The Hanesboro kid, a forward, all arms and legs — Danny was only worried about the arms right now — backed off at the last second, going with Will.

Danny slowed up just slightly, as if getting ready to make his pass.

Then he put it into another gear about ten feet from the basket, imagining himself exploding to the basket the way big guys did when they were going to throw down a dunk.

Pictured himself doing that, and flying.

Laid the ball up with his left hand.

Definitely not his strong suit.

But he put it in the exact right spot on the backboard, in the middle of the square behind the rim, got what one of the ESPN announcers always called the Kiss.

The ball dropped through and the Warriors were ahead for the first time in the game.

Hot dog.

Danny turned around as soon as the ball was through, looking over to his dad, pointed out of bounds, his face asking the question: Keep pressing?

Richie waved his arm hard, like a traffic cop. His face saying: Damn right.

The Warriors stayed right in their faces. Hanesboro hung in there. With two minutes to go, Danny dusted the blond kid guarding him, the one with the long mullet haircut, crossed over on him at half-court — the single crossover, not the double — and fed Will for an open fifteen-footer. Which he drained.

They were ahead by two again, 38–36.

Mullet Head got loose when Bren didn't switch and threw in a long one from his butt. They were tied again. Colby missed from the corner, Mullet Head missed, Will missed. Still tied. With thirty seconds left, their big guy got away with shoving Colby on a rebound, got the ball, had a wide-open layup until Colby grabbed him from behind.

Two shots.

He made the first, missed the second.

Hanesboro 39, Middletown 38.

Richie called time.

"You do not have to rush," he said. "Thirty seconds in basketball is longer

208

than church. Forget trying to run the play. Will, Bren, and Matt — you guys go over and stand on the left wing. We're gonna give the ball to Danny and let him and Colby run a little two-man . . ." He grinned, then said, "Two-*person* game over there on the right. Colby, do whatever you can do to get open. Step back from your guy like you want to shoot, and if he bites, and takes even one step toward you, bust it to the hoop. Okay?"

Still talking to them in the quiet voice.

But as excited as Danny had ever seen him.

"Dan? Just read the play. If she's open, get it to her. If the kid guarding you — the one with the Barbie hair? — turns his head, *you* blow by *him*. Will, after Danny and Colby make their moves, you be a bail-out guy in the left corner. Bren? You come behind Danny after he does whatever he's gonna do."

"What about me?" Matt said.

"As soon as somebody shoots, you crash for the rebound. Just don't foul anybody."

As they broke the huddle, Richie put a hand on Danny's shoulder. "You can do this," he said.

"Is this the fun?" Danny said.

"I'm pretty sure."

The guy guarding Colby didn't bite when she stepped out on him. When she ran for the basket, he ran right with her, step for step. Nothing there.

But she called for the ball the way she was supposed to, and Mullet Head turned his head for one second and, as he did, Danny crossed over to his left hand and broke by him and into the clear in the lane.

At first he thought he was going to have a clear path to the basket. But Will had run to the corner too soon, and not deep enough into the corner, which brought his guy, a Hawaiian-looking guy, into the play. The Hawaiian-looking guy left Will and came over on Danny.

Danny could hear Mullet Head yelling "Switch! Switch!" even though Will's guy had already done that.

Eight seconds left.

Seven.

Six.

Danny wanted to dish one more time, to Colby, who *was* wide open now in the left corner, just because his first instinct was always to give it up.

But he was worried that there might not be enough time.

He was going to have to shoot it before the Hawaiian guy was in front of him and before Mullet Head got back in the play: The passer having to put it up.

He was two steps inside the free throw line when he released the ball over the Hawaiian guy's long left arm, which suddenly seemed be made of elastic; which seemed to keep growing like he was a comic-book guy.

Danny released the ball in front of him, the way his dad had been teaching him, not off the shoulder, and felt like he'd put perfect rotation on the ball.

Saw the last of the time disappear from the clock behind the basket as the ball came floating down toward that basket.

Saw the ball catch a piece of the front rim, but softly, bouncing just slightly as it settled on the back of the rim, hanging there for what only felt like three or four hours, as if making up its mind about how this one was supposed to come out.

Then it fell off like it had rolled off the end of the kitchen table.

Hanesboro 39, Middletown 38.

Final.

His mom kept trying to cheer him up on the ride back to Middletown, he had to give her that.

Somehow he felt like he was with some

smiley-faced nurse trying to make him feel better about being at the doctor's.

"C'mon, it was a great game," she said, "even if it didn't come out the way you wanted."

"Ya think?"

She had let him sit in the front seat. Technically, they both knew he didn't weigh enough, wasn't big enough, to get out of the backseat yet, even though he was twelve and just about everybody his age was sitting in the front seat with their parents. But she had said, ride with me today, I want the company. As if she knew making him sit by himself in the back today would make him feel worse than he did already.

"You guys looked really good in the second half," she said.

Danny, sitting there with his ball in his lap, said, "Great."

"I would think," she said, "that a game like this would have you excited about the rest of the season."

"That might be the only chance we have all season to win a game," he said.

"Get 'em next time. Right?"

Danny turned to face her. "Mom?"

"You want me to stop trying to cheer you up now."

"I'll clear the dinner dishes for a week

and load the dishwasher if you'll stop trying to cheer me up."

"And take out the trash?"

"Mom."

"Okay, okay, I'll stop."

He went straight up to his room when they got home. Noticed when he got there that he'd left his computer on. Again.

The IM box was up there and waiting for him, along with a message from Tess.

CONTESSA44: Hey? You there? I heard about the game.

Danny thought: God Bless America. It was one of his mom's expressions when she wanted to swear. God Bless America, the air traffic control guys couldn't track airplanes the way kids his age tracked travel basketball in Middletown.

He heard the doodlely-doo now.

A new message.

Maybe she had radar tracking him, knowing he was back in his room.

CONTESSA44: C'mon, you must be back by now from HanesUnderwearBoro.

He walked over and shut off his computer and cranked up PlayStation2, then proceeded to stack one of his teams on *NBA '05* with all the best guys: Duncan, Iverson, Shaq, McGrady, Kidd, LeBron.

The guys on the other team were all scrubs.

He was going to get a sure thing somewhere today.

God Bless America, why hadn't that stupid shot fallen?

He had let everybody on his team down. And he knew it was his team more than anybody else's, there wouldn't even be a stupid team, his dad wouldn't even have invented the Warriors, if he hadn't gotten cut from real travel.

Real travel, he thought.

As Will liked to say, Ain't that the truth?

I need you, his dad kept saying. Don't you quit on me, his dad had said. Then, when he had a chance to make one stupid shot to win one stupid game, he couldn't measure up.

He got up suddenly, shut off his game, cranked up his computer, ignored another IM from Tess — he'd explain to her tomorrow why he hadn't felt like talking — and Googled up the place where he could watch his dad dribble out the clock against L.A. in that championship game.

Watched again as young Richie Walker

was in complete control of everything: The clock, the game, himself, his team, the other team. The moment. Like he was the one alone in a driveway.

He didn't choke.

Maybe you only got one nonchoking point guard per family, maybe that was it.

Then he shut down the computer for the night, hearing one more IM jingle before he did. Tess, for sure. But he didn't want her trying to cheer him up any more than he did his mom.

It was definitely a girl deal, wanting to put a Band-Aid on the whole thing.

He didn't want to feel better tonight. He *wanted* to feel like crap. He *wanted* to remember what this felt like so that maybe — maybe, maybe, maybe — he wouldn't let everybody down the next time.

Danny remembered listening to his mom on the phone once, talking to one of her friends, saying that the best thing about youth sports was that an hour after the game ended, most kids couldn't even remember the final score.

Not this kid.

Not this score.

Hanesboro 39, Middletown 38.

Final.

God Bless America.

$$18$$

His mom was meeting Will's mom for a girls' brunch after church on Sunday. She asked if Danny wanted to be dropped at the Stoddards' so he could hang with Will while she and Molly Stoddard went into town. He said, no, he wanted to meet up with Tess at McFeeley Park.

He changed after church into jeans and sneaks and last year's shooting shirt from sixth-grade travel, then grabbed his ball, knowing he'd get time to shoot around because Tess was always late.

"Why don't you show up a few minutes late, then you don't have to wait for her?"

Danny said, "Me waiting for her, that's part of our whole deal."

"Oh," his mom said. "Sometimes I forget I was a twelve-year-old girl once."

"Duh."

"But if you and Tess go into town, you'll have to carry your ball with you."

"So?"

"You don't mind?"

"I like carrying my ball with me."

She sighed. "And I know *nothing* of significance about twelve-year-old boys," she said.

When they drove through the high arch that was the entrance to McFeeley, she said, "You seem to be feeling better today."

"Only 'cause I couldn't feel any worse."

"I know we've gone over this before," she said, "but basketball isn't a matter of life and death."

He smiled, to let her know he was playing, and said, "No, it's much more serious than that."

She said she'd pick him up in front of the Candy Kitchen at four. Then she called out the window that she loved him. He waved good-bye as if he hadn't heard.

You never knew who might catch you telling your mom you loved her back.

He heard the bounce of a single basketball as he came up the hill toward the big court at McFeeley. He couldn't see who was up there right away — he was too short, the hill was way too steep — but as he got near the top he gave a little jump and saw that it was Ty Ross.

Danny had told Tess he'd meet her by the tennis courts. He turned one last time and saw she wasn't there yet, kept going toward the basketball court. Ty didn't look up until he heard Danny bouncing the ball at the other end of the court.

Having just come from church, he wasn't sure whether he should be praying for stuff like this, but he was praying hard now that Ty Ross didn't really hate his guts.

Maybe there was a way they could talk basketball with each other the way he talked basketball with his dad when neither one of them knew what else to say.

Danny thought: What would guys do if they couldn't speak sports?

"Hey," Ty said.

"Hey."

Danny could see his fingers sticking out of the top of what looked to be a pretty light cast, one that had more writing and graffiti-looking squiggles on it than some of the subway cars he'd see going past Shea Stadium when he'd go to a ball game there.

It was pretty cold out, down to the high forties, his mom had said, but Ty was wearing a Knicks' orange sweatshirt with the sleeves cut up to his shoulders, black sweats, and brand-new sneaks that Danny would have been able to spot a mile away.

The new LeBrons from Nike.

Ty turned away from Danny and pushed a simple layup toward the basket with his left hand, making it look like shooting with that hand was the most natural thing in the world.

Holy crap, Danny thought, he looks better shooting with his weak hand than I do with my good one.

Danny stood at half-court, holding his favorite ball, as Ty stepped back with his—
— same model, an Infusion — and made the same shot Danny had gagged on against Hanesboro.

He's better than me at basketball with a broken wrist.

"Yo," Danny said.

Changing the conversation up a little.

Ty turned.

Then Danny just came out with it, knowing he'd better do it now before he lost his nerve.

"I'm sorry," Danny said. "I am *so* sorry about what happened, I've been trying to tell you —"

Ty raised his right hand, his way of telling him to stop, forgetting that it was the hand with the cast on it.

"I know," he said.

Danny kept going anyway.

"Teddy had cheap-shotted me right before with an elbow, then he did it again under the basket, and I just reacted and gave him one back. But I never meant —"

"I know all that," Ty said.

You had to drag things out of him the way you did with Richie Walker sometimes; Danny had been reminded of that just hanging around with Ty in his room that day.

Ty Ross was really good at a lot of things — *excellent* at a lot of things — but conversation wasn't one of them.

"How do you know?" Danny said. "Teddy's been telling everybody I did it on purpose."

Ty said, "His name should really be Teddy Moron."

"Thought you guys were buds."

"Not anymore."

"Because?" Danny dragged the word out the way Tess did sometimes.

"Because once I stopped feeling sorry for myself I knew you weren't the guy he wanted me to think you were." Ty smiled. *"He's* the guy he wanted me to think you were."

Danny bounced his ball in front of him, left hand to right hand to left hand. Feeling better for the first time since he'd missed the shot against Hanesboro.

Maybe it was seeing Ty with the cast on his wrist, and realizing things weren't so bad, after all, that missing a game-ender wasn't an epic tragedy.

Danny said, "Who told you about what happened before you fell?"

"Tess," Ty said.

"You guys talk?"

Ty laughed. "Now we do. My mom thought I should try something new while my wrist was getting better. Something *not* sports. We decided on that photography course at the Y. On Wednesdays?"

Danny nodded. "The one Tess is in."

"The first one was last Wednesday. She grabbed me as soon as it was over, said I was gonna listen to something she had to say." Ty made a whoosh sound. "Man, she's got this way of getting you to do what she wants you to do."

"Ya think?"

"Anyway, she told me what happened. And that I couldn't blame you, because she wasn't gonna allow it."

"She's the best-looking girl our age in this whole town," Danny said. "But she's already got some mom in her."

Ty said, "Ya think?" He flipped another left-handed shot toward the basket, missed. The ball bounced away from him.

"I got it," Danny said, passing Ty his ball while he retrieved the other.

"I'm supposed to be meeting her here," Danny said.

"I know."

Danny smiled. Imagining a cartoon lightbulb going on over his head. "She told you to be here."

Ty shrugged. "She said you'd expect her to be late."

Tess Hewitt. Secret Agent Girl.

"She said she told you twelve, but wouldn't be here until twelve-thirty," Ty said. "You want to play H-O-R-S-E?"

"I can't shoot well enough left-handed," Danny said. " 'Course after yesterday, I'm not even positive I'm *right-handed* anymore."

He told Ty all about Hanesboro 39, Middletown 38.

"You'll make the next one," Ty said. "That's the way I always look at it." He nodded at the basket. "I'll shoot lefty, you shoot righty."

Danny said that if he lost, he was definitely quitting basketball. Ty said, fine, they could both take up photography.

They played H-O-R-S-E and talked. Ty said he didn't really know how fast his wrist would heal. Said he hoped he'd be able to get in a couple of games before the play-offs. In the Tri-Valley, he said, you didn't have to set your official roster until the week the play-offs began. So even if he hadn't played at all, his dad could still have him on the roster.

When they were both at H-O-R-S, Danny said, "Your dad know you're here, by the way?"

"He's out of town on bank business. My mom brought me."

"What would he do if he knew?"

"Yell."

Ty twirled the ball on the tip of his left index finger as effortlessly as Richie Walker did.

"He's not so bad, really, my dad. He just tries too hard."

"With sports?"

"With everything."

Danny said, "He doesn't seem to like me very much."

"I don't think it's you," he said. "It's the whole thing. You. The Warriors. Your dad. My dad likes to be the biggest guy in town. Like he waited his whole life to be the biggest guy in town. Now there's this bunch of little guys . . ."

His voice trailed off.

Danny shot and missed. Ty shot and

missed. Down the hill, Danny could see Tess getting out of her mom's Volvo station wagon.

Danny dribbled to the spot where he'd missed against Hanesboro. Not that he was still fixed on that or anything. Then he shot the ball a little higher than usual, higher than he had yesterday, and hit nothing but net.

Sure.

Today he hits nothing but net.

Ty missed, then missed the extra shot you get at the end of the game.

"Good game," Ty said.

"That," Danny said, knowing he was getting off the kind of pun Tess usually did, "is a left-handed compliment."

Ty gave him a low five with his left hand as they heard Tess say, "Fancy meeting you boys here."

Tess: In a ponytail today. With some kind of long red sweater, one that went nearly to her knees, with the sleeves pushed up to her elbows. Tess in jeans and Timberland boots, the Timbys looking as new as Ty's LeBrons.

Carrying her camera.

She snapped one of Ty and Danny standing there next to each other.

"You two look like a team to me," she said.

"I wish," Danny said.

The three of them went down the hill, destination Candy Kitchen. Danny didn't even mind walking between them, looking like their little brother.

They decided to spend Christmas together, like a real family.

Or, Danny figured, as close to a real family as they were likely to get.

His dad said he probably wouldn't get up early enough for the opening of presents, telling Danny that the only part of him that was still a ballplayer — that still *worked* — was his body clock. But he said he would be there for Christmas dinner, the roast beef dinner with all the trimmings that Ali Walker had promised them, followed by strawberry shortcake for dessert, Danny's favorite.

According to his mom, dinner would be served at what she called a "soft two o'clock."

"What does 'soft' mean?" Danny asked.

"It means that showing up on time, for anything other than basketball, has always been real hard for your father."

Christmas was still Christmas when his dad wasn't around, when it was just him and his mom. But after all the waiting for it, all the anticipation, it sometimes seemed to be over for the two of them before Christmas Day was even over. They'd go over to have Christmas dinner with friends sometimes, families like Will's and Bren's that had four kids each in them, and there would be presents everywhere, under the tree and all over the house.

It was smaller with him and his mom.

Always came back to that.

Danny didn't know how much teachers made at St. Pat's, or anywhere else, for that matter. Even if his mom told him what her salary was, he wasn't sure he'd understand where it fit into the whole grand scheme of things. The one time it had come up, a couple of years ago, his mom had said, "I make more than a year's allowance for you, and somewhat less than Michael Jordan used to make." Then she laughed. She always went for a laugh when the subject was money, but Danny usually thought it was like the fake laughter you heard on television shows even when nothing funny was happening.

Her heart never seemed to be in that, the same way it never seemed to be in dating the guys who would come to the house to pick her up sometimes.

There were some subjects Danny tried to avoid at all costs, and one of them was this: Whether his mom would ever get married again.

"What?" she said when they talked about that one from time to time. "And give up our life on Easy Street?"

Then she would fake-laugh again.

Danny could never figure out, on Christmas Day or any other day of the year, why they *weren't* on Easy Street. His dad had made it to the NBA, even if his career hadn't lasted very long. *Those* salaries he did know something about, even if he didn't know squat about what teachers made. And he knew that if you were a first-round pick, even back when his dad was a first-round pick, you got a three-year contract, guaranteed.

So there had to have been some money in the family once, right after he was born, when his mom and dad were married and they were a real family more than one day a year.

Where had it all gone?

That was one he never asked either of his parents about, how it worked out that his dad didn't seem to have any money left and why he and his mom were living in the Flats, at 422 Easy Street. . . .

Tess had helped him shop for his mom. She had asked him exactly how much money he'd saved up from allowance and birthdays, and he told her.

Tess said, "I just need to establish our price range."

"I'll give you the money and you get her something," Danny said. "I hate to shop. You know I hate to shop."

"You'll love it," she said. "Shopping with me is like playing a round of golf with Tiger."

She took him to Wright's, the only jewelry store in Middletown, and helped him pick out a silver charm bracelet. Done, Danny said when they'd agreed on the one they both liked, thinking how quick and painless the process had been, jewelry shopping with a girl four days before Christmas.

Tess said they weren't quite done, and then somehow talked the woman behind the counter into throwing in a single silver charm — a basketball — for an extra five dollars.

The bracelet, with the tiny ball hanging from it, made his mom cry after he insisted she open her present first, really cry, as he helped her fasten it on her wrist, his mom telling him it was the most beautiful piece of jewelry anybody had ever given her, ever.

Then she hugged him and started crying all over again.

He was never going to understand girls of any age as long as he lived, he was sure of that. But he was going to run upstairs the first chance he got and IM Tess and tell her that they'd hit the stinking jackpot with the charm bracelet.

It was his turn to open then.

Real jackpot.

His mom had bought him a new laptop, the first brand-new laptop he'd ever had in his life, a Sony VAIO.

And even a dope about money knew it was way out of their price range.

Way, *way* out of their price range.

"Mom," he said, when he was able to get some words out, imagining how buggy his eyes must have looked to her as he stared at the inside of the box, afraid to even lift the unit out of there. "You can't . . . we can't . . ."

"Can," she said. "Did. Done deal. Merry Christmas."

"But —"

"But nothing," she said, helping him get the white Styrofoam out of the box so they could gently remove the computer. "Been

230

doing a little extra tutoring on the side."

"You ask me, it must have been a whole *lot* of extra tutoring —"

"What*ever*," she said in her dippy mall-girl voice, as a way of ending the conversation.

Then, in her real voice, about as soft, Danny thought, as the snow starting to hit the ground outside the living-room window, the Christmas snow she seemed to have ordered, his mom said, "I knew that if I made enough money on the side I could buy myself the kind of Christmas-morning face I'm looking at right now."

She hugged him again and then had him open another box, the one that had the new LeBron James Nikes in it, the ones like Ty's he had described to her after he got home from McFeeley that day.

The sneaks were so cool, coming right on top of the laptop, that he managed to act excited while he opened the remaining boxes, the ones with the shirts and sweaters and new school khakis in them. Then the two of them went upstairs to his room and unplugged and unhooked the old computer, somehow managed to follow the directions — the two of them giggling their way through the whole thing — until they had the Sony up and running with

Microsoft Word and e-mail and IM and passwords and codes and all the rest of it.

When they were done with that, they attached his old speakers to it.

His mom kept telling him, Do *not* lose anything.

He said he was being careful.

She asked where he was going to put the box and the directions and the warranty. His closet, he said. "Oh no!" she said in *Freddy vs. Jason* fright. "Anywhere but there!"

She left him alone then, knowing he was twitchy to IM Tess and Will and the rest of the Danny Walker Network, telling them about his stuff and asking about theirs.

Then he could hear the Christmas music coming from downstairs as she went to work in the kitchen; nobody liked Christmas music more than his mom, she started playing it in the house and in the car the day after Thanksgiving. Always telling him that if Christmas shopping had started, it was time for Elvis to start singing "Blue Christmas."

Even when the presents weren't as jackpot big as they were today, even when Christmas wasn't as big as it felt like today, his mom loved Christmas as much as he did.

New laptop on the desk. New LeBrons on his feet. Snow coming down. His dad coming over for Christmas dinner at a soft two in the afternoon.

The Warriors might still suck.

Today didn't.

His dad showed up early, saying the roads were getting bad as the snow came down harder, and he didn't want to take any chances.

"You were the one who always wanted a white Christmas," his dad said to his mom when he was inside, brushing the snow out of his hair. "This white enough for you?"

"There can never be enough snow on Christmas to suit me," she said, taking the old Syracuse letter jacket he was wearing, navy with orange trim, and leather sleeves.

"Enough to you always meant snowed in."

"I'll take that deal," she said.

He was carrying a big paper bag, set it down near the tree and just left it there. He didn't say anything about it, so neither did Danny.

His mom had a fire going in their small fireplace. She made popcorn for everybody, and said she'd whip up some eggnog while Danny took his dad up to show him his new computer. That didn't take long, his dad not being a computer guy, so Danny challenged him to a game of *NBA '05* instead. His dad said he was almost as bad at video games as he was with computers, where he was the absolute world's worst, but he'd give it a shot.

"I haven't even whipped your butt yet and you're already making excuses," Danny said.

He showed him how to work the controllers. They each got into a beanbag chair, even though Richie said that once he settled in it might take a forklift to get him out.

Richie Walker wasn't the world's worst at video ball, as it turned out.

"Ringer," Danny said.

"Is that what you kids call a guy trying to get the most out of his ability?"

"Ringer," Danny said.

He was either a ringer or the fastest learner Danny had ever met, because it was 112–112 with ten seconds to go.

Both of them clicking away like madmen.

"Don't let me win," Danny said.

"Wasn't planning to," Richie said.

McGrady, who was on Danny's team, made one over Vince Carter at the buzzer and Danny's team won, 114–112.

"Yes!" He jumped up and made one of those dance motions with his arms like he was stirring some huge pot.

"You cheated," his dad said, still clicking away even though the screen was frozen. "There was one second left!"

"Was not."

"Was so."

A much calmer voice from the doorway said, "Dinner, children."

They turned their heads at the same time and saw Ali Walker in her Santa apron, smiling at them, hands on hips.

"What's so funny?" Danny said.

"Oh, nothing."

Richie said, "There was one second left."

"Was not," Danny said.

The three of them went down to have Christmas dinner.

As soon as Danny picked up the bag, he knew it was another ball.

"You didn't need to get me a new ball," he said. "You got me a cool ball last Christmas."

"Not this ball. Open it."

The Spurs were playing the Nets on television. The fire was still going strong. The snow was coming down even harder, making it hard to see across Earl Avenue.

Richie had just announced that he better be going soon.

It was an official Spalding NBA game ball.

Danny twirled it slowly in his hands, then ran his right hand over the surface of it.

"Leather," he said.

"Full grain," Richie said.

From the couch, Ali Walker said, "You say that like it's pure gold."

Danny looked at his dad and they both shook their heads sadly, that one person could be this ignorant about something as important as an official leather ball.

"Sorry," she said, and went back to reading *Vanity Fair*.

Richie said, "I think you ought to check it out a little more closely," and pointed to where "NBA" was.

There were autographs on either side, so neat and legible you could have thought the ball came with them.

Jason Kidd.

John Stockton.

"Your two poster guys," Richie said.

"The two you say were the best."

Richie corrected him. "The best *lately*."

"How did you get them both to sign it?"

"I just told them it was for a point guard

they ought to be rooting for the way people always rooted for them."

Danny went over and hugged his dad. No man hug here. The real thing.

Richie hugged him back. "Merry Christmas, kiddo," he said.

They were both on the floor. When Danny pulled back, Richie pulled himself up on his second try.

"I sound like a pocketful of loose change," he said.

To Ali he said, "I didn't know what to get you."

"You got me all you needed to get, Rich."

To Danny he said, "First game back, we're going to use this ball as our gamer. I have a feeling it's going to change our luck. Then if it works, we'll save it for the next time we need our stinking luck changed."

Danny put out a closed fist. His dad touched it lightly with one of his own.

Richie said, "On account of, our luck is due to change."

They all stood near the front door while he put on his Syracuse jacket. Ali said that he should drive carefully. He smiled at her. "I always do," he said.

"Now, anyway," he said, with that shy duck of the head he gave you sometimes.

He opened the door, turned around.

"This was a good Christmas," he said to both of them. "Been a long time since I had a good Christmas."

"Drive carefully," Ali Walker said again.

"See you at practice," Richie said to Danny, and then walked slowly on the slippery walk toward his car, looking more like an old man than ever.

Danny and his mom went and stood on the porch in the snow, watched the car pull away from in front of the house, watched it until it made the turn on Cleveland Avenue and disappeared.

He had the basketball under his arm.

When they got back inside, she took it from him.

"Go ahead," she said.

"Huh?"

She grinned at him and dribbled the ball twice on the floor in the foyer. Not really dribbling it so much as slapping at it, as though trying to squash some bug sitting on top of it.

"Go ahead," she said, handing the ball back to him.

Danny tricky-dribbled around her and then past her down the hall and through the kitchen and into the dining room.

Dribbling through the house like he was a young Richie Walker.

Having the names of Stockton and Kidd on the ball didn't help.

"Stockton and Kidd *handling* the ball, now that would help," Bren Darcy was saying.

"We need *that* Kidd, not the kids we've got," Will Stoddard said.

"No *kidding*," Danny said. "Get it?"

Will said, "Okay, we have to stop now."

They tried the new ball in the first game back, against Kirkland, and lost by six points. Tried it again the next day, played well for three quarters against Piping Rock, the best team in the Tri-Valley with a record of 8–0 coming in, but ended up losing by ten.

Colby missed a couple of shots in the last two minutes, and after the second one, Bren made a face. Danny called a time-out, and when they got to the huddle, Will told Bren that he could make faces when people missed as long as *he* never missed, and Bren said that Will should be worrying more about winning the game than sticking up for Colby. Before Danny knew it, they were nose-to-nose and Danny had to get between them.

"You guys have been buds as long as I've been buds *with* you guys," he said. "So cut it out."

Will said, "Tell him to stop making faces."

Bren said, "Tell *him* to mind his own freaking business."

"Hey!" Danny said. "Both of you. Zip it now. We're getting better, let's not blow it now."

They *were* getting better.

Matt Fitzgerald, in particular, was starting to look like a real center, the private work he'd been doing with Richie finally starting to pay off. Colby got better every game. Will was taking basketball seriously — or as seriously as Will could take anything — for the first time in his life.

No team, no matter how big, wanted Danny and Bren Darcy harassing them in the backcourt.

"It's like being chased by freaking *bees*," one of the Kirkland guards had said the day before.

They just couldn't win a freaking game to save their lives.

It was the middle weekend in January

now, about a month from the start of the play-offs, and their record was 0–9. They were kidding about Jason Kidd in the layup line, getting ready to play Seekonk at St. Pat's.

Colby showed up a little late, and the minute she walked through the door, everybody spotted her new kicks:

Old-school Converse high-tops, white, yellow toward the heel, some purple in there, too; even guys their age knew these were the ones Magic Johnson used to wear for the Lakers.

Danny had known from the start how cool Colby Danes was, not that he would have admitted that to his buddies. Now it was official.

A girl in Magic's Cons.

"Girlfriend is *stylin'*," Will Stoddard said.

Bren slapped him five on that, their fight at the end of the Piping Rock game already ancient history.

Oliver Towne, their only black kid, said, "Stoddard, you are, like, *pathetically* white."

"Oh," Will said, trying to act hurt, "like you have to rub my pasty face in it."

Colby, who was now one of the guys on the Warriors, because she was cool *and* could play, said, "You are all sooooooo jealous that a girl has cooler sneaks than you."

Will couldn't let her have the last word. Will would sooner leave town before he'd let somebody have the last word.

"Maybe I can borrow them someday," he said. "If I ever grow into them, of course. Like, when I'm in college."

But this time, Colby got him.

"You're right," she said. "This is, like, totally messed-up. Isn't it the boys who're supposed to have big feet and the girls who are supposed to have big hair?"

The rest of the guys whooped as she took her place in line, casually high-fiving Danny as she passed.

Danny looked around and thought: We act like a team, we have fun like a team.

When do we play all four quarters like a team?

It turned out to be against Seekonk.

The Seekonk Sailors — they were the next town up from Port Madison, on the Sound — were even smaller than the Warriors. And not nearly as well coached. They didn't have anybody who could get in front of either Danny or Bren, anybody who could stay with Colby, anybody who could keep Matt Fitzgerald off the boards.

When they tried going with a two-one-two zone, Will made five outside shots in a row, an all-time personal best.

The 0–9 Middletown Warriors were ahead 18–4 after the first quarter.

They were ahead 26–10 at halftime.

They were ahead twenty points by the fourth quarter, and Richie had them making ten passes before they were even allowed to look at the basket. By then, he had the O'Brien twins in the backcourt, Michael Harden playing center, Will and Oliver Towne at forward.

Richie had taken Danny out halfway through the third quarter.

"I think your work here is done," Richie said.

Danny took a seat next to him. "Somebody said these guys have won two games," he said. "I don't know how they did that, but they're not going to win another one the rest of the season."

"Don't worry about them," his dad said. "You were worried we weren't going to win a game the rest of the season."

"Excellent point."

"And when it's over? You make sure the rest of the guys — and girls — act like they've won before."

"Even though we haven't?"

"Especially because we haven't."

It ended up Middletown 42, Seekonk 22. Final.

Richie Walker said for the players and parents to meet at Fierro's about five o'clock, the pizza was on him.

"Is your mom here?" Richie said to Danny.

Danny nodded to the row of folding chairs up on the stage. "She came late with Tess."

"See you all at Fierro's," his dad said.

They tapped clenched fists.

"We're on the board," his dad said.

They were on the board.

His dad still wasn't there at five-thirty.

"See?" his mom said. "The game's over. He thought it was a soft five."

The Warriors and their parents had taken up most of the front room at Fierro's, pushing four tables together. They finally decided to order, a bunch of plain pizzas and a couple of pepperonis, huge greasy paper plates covered with mountains of French fries, pitchers of Coke and Sprite. They were playing oldies on the old-fashioned Fierro's jukebox as usual, but nobody could hear them over the mega-amped-up noise of the place, and laughter, and excitement, as the kids on the team replayed just about every basket of the game.

In honor of the Warriors' first win, Al Fierro announced that the ice cream sundaes were on him today.

The waitresses, all of them from Middletown High, were starting to clear away the plates and pizza platters when the pay phone on the wall next to the front door rang.

Al Fierro answered it, called out "Ali," and motioned for her to come up there.

Danny watched his mom take the receiver.

Watched the smile leave her face.

Saw her free hand come to her mouth.

"Not again," he heard her say.

She nodded hard a couple of times, placed the receiver back in its cradle, walked over to where Danny was sitting between Will and Tess.

"It's your father," she said. "There's been an accident."

21

She convinced him in the car that his dad wasn't going to die.

"But he's broken up pretty badly," his mom said, her hands gripping the steering wheel like she was holding on for dear life.

Maybe she was.

"But they can put him back together, right?" Danny said.

"They did it before, they can do it again. It's his hip again, his shoulder. One of his lungs collapsed, but they said they fixed that when he got to the hospital. However they fix things like that."

"He must have stopped somewhere after the game," she said. "They say he lost control of his car, right before that big curve where 37 intersects with 118. You know where that is, right? Near the Burger King and the Home Depot?"

Danny said he knew it, but he didn't remember a big curve.

"At least he was wearing a seat belt this

time," Ali Walker said, turning her head slightly to talk to him.

They were doing it by the book today, Danny sitting in the back where he belonged.

"Coming home from a game, just like last time," his mom said, not really talking to him now, more like she was talking to herself.

"You okay?" she said.

"I'm okay."

He wasn't going to cry, that was for sure. Somehow crying to him meant that the whole thing was worse than he wanted it to be.

We're on the board, his dad had said.

Danny sat in the waiting room looking at the pictures in the front of *Sports Illustrated*, just so he had something to do while his mom talked to the doctors.

When they finally got into his dad's room, all he could see were tubes, coming out of Richie Walker's arm and stuck in his nose. There was a thick bandage covering his forehead.

"Did I miss a good party?" Richie said when he saw them at the end of his bed.

"We're not staying long," Ali said. "The doctors say you need your rest."

"Before they do their body and fender work on me in the morning."

"Well," Ali said, "it's not like the hip and shoulder they gave you last time around were top-of-the-line, anyway."

Richie said, "I asked them to try something besides used parts this time."

"Good one, Dad," Danny said.

He realized when he took his jacket off that he was still wearing his Warriors Number 3, the jersey hanging all the way down to the knees of the gray sweats he'd put on after the game.

His mom stood on one side of the bed now, he stood on the other. Richie reached out with his left hand, the one not in the sling, and took Danny's left hand.

Danny squeezed it hard.

"I wasn't drunk," Richie said, holding on to Danny but looking at Ali.

She said, "Rich, you don't have to —"

He said, "I know I don't. But I want to. I'm not going to lie to you, I thought about breaking the pledge, stopping for a cold one, just to toast our great victory. But I knew better this time."

"Don't talk," she said.

"Hey," Richie said to her. "Did you ever think you'd be telling me not to talk?"

She said, "This is like being in class.

What part of 'don't talk' aren't you getting here, mister?" She tried to smile at the end of it, but then she got that lower lip going and made Danny afraid she was the one who was going to lose it.

But she didn't.

Danny had always known she was the toughest one of all of them.

"The doctors said they're going to fix up Dad as good as new, didn't they, Mom?" Danny said.

"Only if they're grading me against the curve, right, teach?"

"Close your eyes now," Ali Walker said.

He did, and a few minutes later, was sleeping.

They were scheduled to operate on his right hip and his right shoulder at nine the next morning. Danny didn't want to go to school, but his mom made him, saying he wasn't going to do his father or anybody else any good hanging around the hospital and staring at the clock.

"You'd rather have me sitting in class and staring at the clock?" he said.

"You're going to school," she said. "I'll wait it out at the hospital. The second he's out, I'll call."

Mrs. Stoddard picked him up. Right before first period, the principal at St. Pat's, Mr. Dawes, an old guy who was retiring at what Will said was the age of dirt at the end of the school year, came over the intercom and said all students should keep Danny Walker's dad in their thoughts today, even though he was sure Mr. Walker was going to come through surgery that morning with flying colors.

They were in their English classroom by then.

Will leaned over and said, "Hem and Haw Dawes makes the operation sound like a pop quiz your dad is trying to pass."

Danny had already decided that he wasn't going anywhere today without either Will or Tess — or both — with him.

Danny said to Will, "You're my official spokesman today."

"Finally," Will Stoddard said. "Finally, my brother, you have seen the light."

They still hadn't heard anything at lunch, but Tess said that wasn't unusual for a hip operation.

"How do you know that?" Will said.

She stuck her nose up in the air. "I know things," she said.

"You, like, researched Mr. Walker's surgery?" Will said.

"Last night," she said. "Some people actually use Google to look up things besides somebody's lifetime batting average."

"Mom said the same thing," Danny said. "She said that if they were done by lunch, that would be fast."

Will and Danny had already finished eating the hamburgers they usually got in the cafeteria on Mondays. Tess cut off a small corner of hers, and chewed it carefully. As usual, she was working on her food as though it were some kind of tricky math problem.

"Can I ask a completely selfish question?" Will said.

Tess said, "We'd expect nothing more of you."

"Or less," Danny said.

"Who's gonna coach the team if your dad is laid up a while?" Will said.

"I knew it was going to be something incredibly messed-up lame," Tess said. "He's not even out of *surgery* yet."

"It's okay," Danny said, putting a hand on her arm. "I've been thinking about it, too. Just to have something to think about *besides* the surgery."

"You guys never cease to amaze," she said. "All guys never cease to amaze."

"No, really, Will's right," Danny said. "Mr. Harden's going to be out of town on a case for the next month, Michael was talking about that at the party. Oliver's only got his mom. Bren's dad is all jammed up coaching his brothers in hockey. Mr. O'Brien's got that Wall Street job that has him in London, England, half the time. Colby said that the only time Dr. Danes ever coached her was in soccer, that he gave up coaching anything after that because he's on call so much on the weekends."

So who *would* coach them, Danny wondered.

Fifteen minutes into Spanish, Mr. Dawes — who reminded Danny of Alfred, the butler from the Batman cartoons — appeared in the doorway, and motioned for Danny to come out in the hall.

For the first time since they'd all been at St. Pat's, Mr. Dawes was smiling.

"Your mother just called from the hospital," he said. "Your father made it through the surgery just fine. He's a little worse for wear, but there were no surprises, she said to tell you, and no complications. She wanted me to tell you that she'll pick you up here after school and drive you over there."

Danny thanked him, even shook his long, thin bony hand.

When he came back into class, he gave a thumbs-up to Will and Tess, sat down at his desk, and thought: His dad had been a little worse for wear for as long as Danny could remember things.

Ali Walker called off Warriors practice on Tuesday night. But after dinner that night, the whole team went to visit Richie at the hospital.

Colby brought the present they had all chipped in to buy him, ten bucks a kid:

An official Spalding NBA ball they'd all signed in Magic Marker.

"Now you've got a gamer of your own," Danny said to his dad.

Richie still had the IV-tube attached to his right arm. With his left, he placed the ball next to him on the bed.

"Just because I'm a little stiff," he said, "I'm going to let you knuckleheads off without making you learn a couple of new plays I've got cooked up against the man-to-man."

There were only two chairs in the room; the O'Brien twins grabbed those. The rest of them stood at the foot of the bed so Richie could see them without turning his head. Any time he tried to move at all, Danny saw, there was a look on his father's face like somebody had punched him. In addition to everything else that had happened at the intersection of 37 and 118, he'd broken two ribs.

He let the kids do most of the talking. Will made everybody laugh — Richie included — by asking him if he'd mind just sliding over on the bed a little and handing Will the remote for the television set that came down out of the ceiling.

Richie said, "The surgery didn't kill me. But you making me laugh with busted ribs might make me do myself in."

"It's a burden I have to bear, Coach," Will Stoddard said. "Some people are just too funny."

Richie promised them all he'd be back before they knew it. The room then filled with the sound of *Cool* and *That's right* and *Now you're talking, Coach.* Even though they all knew he was lying, just by the looks of him, by what their own eyes were telling them.

Finally the kids ran out of small talk and nobody knew what to say and it was at that moment, as if on cue, that the nurse stuck her head inside the door and said it was time for them to go, her patient needed his sleep.

Danny was the last one to say good-bye.

And now, after three days of holding everything in, even when he was alone in his room at night, thinking alone-in-his-room thoughts, he started to cry.

And, as he did, he blurted out something he'd been holding inside along with the tears:

"Why does this crap keep happening to you?"

In a voice that was about one level above a whisper, Richie said, "You mean why do I have to be the victim of the world?"

"Yeah, basically."

"I'm not a victim," his dad said. "Even though I've been playing one for a hell of a long time."

He told Danny to tell his mom he was going to be a few extra minutes, then to come back and pull up one of those chairs, it was time for him to set the record straight, once and for all.

22

"You have more than just the best head for basketball I've ever seen — and that includes me," his dad said. "You've got a great head, period. So I'm going to talk to you like you're older."

Danny didn't know what to say to that, so he didn't say anything. Just sat there thinking again how quiet hospitals were, especially at night, the only loud sound he could hear being the soft ding of the elevator down the hall.

"I didn't just come back for you," his dad said. "I came back for me."

"I didn't care why you came back," Danny said. "You were back, that's all that mattered to me."

"But I can't have you feeling sorry for me anymore," Richie said, trying to sit up a little, squeezing his eyes shut for a minute as he did. "I've been letting people feel sorry for me, you included, for as long as you've been alive."

He made a motion toward the glass of

ice water on the table next to him, and the pain pill the nurse had left for him. Danny got up and handed both to him, waited while his dad swallowed the pill, then took the glass back. "Your mom's right about something. Something she's been telling me for a long time. That's no way to live, just a slow way to die."

Danny nodded, as if he understood.

His father smiled.

"I don't expect you to get all of this. But it's important that you get this: The accident that wrecked everything, for all of us, it was my fault."

"The roads were bad that night," Danny said. "I've read all about it a bunch of times. You lost control of the car."

"I lost control of the car because I was drunk."

Now the only sound in the room was the ticking of the clock above the bed.

"I never liked to let the sportswriters see me drinking after the game. Didn't want to screw up my image. But I'd always liked a few after the game, even at Syracuse. I had this equipment room down the hall where I'd go before I went out after the game. Even had a little cooler back there. That was one of the nights I drank a whole six-pack before I got in my Jeep."

"Why are you telling me this now?" Danny said. "Why do I have to know this now? I know you drink, okay? I heard you and Mom that night at the gym. I heard her call you a drunk. Okay? I don't need to know any more bad stuff right now."

He was shouting.

His dad didn't shout back, came at him with a voice so soft Danny imagined the words barely making it off the bed.

"It's time you knew," Richie said.

Danny heard the ding of another elevator, wishing it were the bell telling him it was time to go to the next class.

"The cop who found me in the ditch took me to the hospital, as busted up as I was. He told them afterward that he was afraid to even call an ambulance, he thought I was dying. They asked him why he wasn't afraid to move me, and the guy — Drew Nagelson was his name — said he was afraid not to. He could smell the beer on me. He had to know I was loaded. But I remember him telling me in the car that he was a big Warriors fan." Richie Walker smiled. "They always want to tell you that. Anyway, he asked me if I could chew some gum. I said, 'What?' He said, 'We've got to get the beer stink out of you.' He threw my shirt away, put a blanket on me, took me to the hospital. The doctors worked on your old dad all night. By morning, it was too late for them to take a blood alcohol test."

"Huh?"

"It's a test they have to see how much alcohol you have in your blood system."

"Oh," Danny said.

"Sergeant Nagelson came by the next day, and I thanked him for saving my life. He said, 'And your rep.' I said, 'Yeah, and my rep.' " Richie reached out and ran his hand over his new basketball. "And from that night on, everybody has felt just awful about America's lovable little point guard getting a bad break like that. Having his career end that way. And I let them, kiddo. I let them."

"Does Mom — ?"

"Yesterday," he said. "When I finished telling her, I told her it was the drugs talking. But it wasn't. It was the truth, the whole truth, nothing but. There was, like, a million times when I started to tell her. But I never did. And you want to know why? Because as mad as I knew she was at me for leaving the two of you, I wanted her to feel sorry for me, too." He looked at Danny with those sad eyes as he worked his mouth into a crooked-looking smile. "The rest of the time, when she was yelling at me how drinking had ruined my life and hers more than the accident had, I just didn't have the guts."

"No," Danny said, not wanting to believe it.

"Yes."

"All these years, you just let Mom think — ?"

"That I was still the toughest guy going."

"But what you did," Danny said, "that was, like, the opposite of tough."

"But it kept up the myth of little Richie Walker," his dad said.

Richie said he was too tired to tell him all of it tonight, all about his drinking life. Another time, he said, when they had more time. When he had the strength to get it right.

"It's funny how things work out, though," his dad said. "The thing that started everything — drinking — is the thing I kept turning to after I felt like my life had turned to crap."

Danny told him about Teddy Moran saying one time that people knew the "real truth" about him, and Richie shook his head, no, saying that people suspected he was drunk that night, just because he drank as much as he did after the accident. But the only people who knew the "real truth," at least until now, were Richie Walker himself, and Sergeant Drew Nagelson, big Warriors fan.

"Why did you come back?" Danny said. "This time, I mean?"

"I didn't have a specific plan," his dad said. "I just knew you were my best part, and that I had to do something about that before you got too big."

Now Danny smiled. "Me? Too big? Not a problem."

"The only time I got drunk after coming back was that one night at Runyon's, when I started to think that starting this team was a big dumb mistake, that you guys getting your brains beat out every game was worse than if you didn't have any games at all."

"The yelling day."

"The yelling day," Richie said. "I let myself get messed-up 'cause of drinking one last time. Haven't touched a drop since, if you want to know."

"I don't, Dad," Danny said. "I don't care."

"I know," he said. "But I do."

The door opened. The nurse's head appeared again and she said in her perky nurse voice that it was getting late, and we needed our rest, didn't we, Mr. Walker?

"One minute," Richie said to her.

To Danny he said, "I wanted us to have this season."

"We still can."

"*You* still can," Richie said. "I was full of it with the other kids before. I'm going to be on the disabled list for a while."

Might as well ask him.

"Who's gonna coach us?" Danny said.

"Don't worry," Richie said. "I got a guy in mind who'd be perfect."

Kelvin Norris — the great Coach Kel from last year's travel team, cool-guy hero to all his players and all their parents — was waiting for them in the gym when they showed up for Thursday's practice. With the exception of Danny, who knew Coach Kel was coming, the rest of the players were expecting Mr. Harden to run his last practice with the Warriors before leaving town the next day.

Except they walked into St. Pat's at six-thirty and there was Coach Kel, in baggy sweats almost as dank as his skin and a bright yellow T-shirt that read "B. Silly." The sight of him got an immediate whoop out of Bren and Will, the guys he'd coached before. And even from Matt Fitzgerald, who remembered him as being cool just from having tried out for the sixth-grade team.

"You couldn't tell me he was coming?" Will said to Danny. "Not even a stinking hint?"

Danny shrugged. "I wanted to surprise you."

Will said, "Once trust is gone in a relationship, what is there?"

From across the court, in a boom-box voice, Coach Kel said, "Stoddard, why don't you go run some laps instead of runnin' your mouth."

Will's mouth opened and closed and, for once, nothing came out.

Coach Kel grinned. "I'm just playin'," he said. "You know."

Bren said, "I can't believe you're here."

"When Richie Walker calls from his damn hospital bed and asks for a favor, you don't say no, I'm not in the mood, Richie Walker. On, no, I'm too busy, Richie Walker."

Coach Kel went around and introduced himself to the other Warriors.

"Say hello to your substitute teacher," he said. "You ever hear of a movie called *To Sir With Love*? Starring the great Sidney Poitier?"

He got blank looks from everybody, as if he'd started speaking Russian to them.

"In that case," he said, "go get in two lines and shoot some damn layups."

He told them Danny was going to be his assistant coach tonight, just so they could make things feel like normal, run practice the way they usually did when Coach Walker was there.

"Just want to see your basic stuff," he said.

You always got the feeling with Coach Kel that he wanted to use another s-word instead of *stuff*, but kept it inside him like he was a bottle with the cap still on it.

Once they got going, got into their stuff, Danny realized this was exactly like the picture of the court, the other players, he'd take sometimes when they were starting their offense; when he didn't even have to look at the left side of the court when he was over on the right side because he knew where everybody was. He knew what drills they were supposed to run, in what order, what plays his dad had them working on at their last practice, the new way he had them set up when they went to a zone press.

Coach Kel leaned over at one point and said, "Even when you were just eleven, I used to tell people I was just waitin' on that little body of yours to grow into that big basketball *brain*."

"You sound just like my dad," Danny said.

"Gonna take that there as a compliment," Coach Kel said.

He had shaved his head completely bald, and as soon as he started getting on the court and showing them how he thought they should be doing something, you could see the little raindrops of sweat start to form on top of his head. He was also wearing retro Air Jordans, the red-and-black ones.

Will once said that guys would notice what sneakers you were wearing before they noticed whether or not you were carrying a paint gun.

They scrimmaged hard for the last half hour, really hard, Coach Kel saying he was going to push them, that he really wanted them to show him what they all had. And they did. Maybe it was because of what had happened to Danny's dad, but it was serious ball with the Warriors tonight, even less messing around than when Coach Walker was in the gym and blowing the whistle and calling the shots.

Somehow — and not just because Coach Kel was a high-energy guy who always kept you fired up, about basketball and life — they all seemed to know what they were supposed to be doing tonight without being told.

Go figure.

When they were done, right before parents started showing up, Will said, "See you Saturday, Coach K."

Coach Kel looked at him. "Say what?"

"I said, we'll see you Saturday," Will said. "For the Kirkland game."

Coach Kel said, "Won't be here Saturday, big hair. I guess I should have told y'all from the jump. I'm coaching the JV at Christ the King this season. I just came tonight to get you *through* tonight. Like I was sayin', as a favor to Coach Richie."

"Then who's going to coach us against Kirkland?" Bren Darcy said.

"Don't know," Coach Kel said. "Danny's dad just said that him and the other parents were gonna come up with a Plan B by then."

Will said, "Excuse me, but we thought you were Plan B."

"Only for tonight."

On their way out of the gym, Will said to Danny, "You got any bright ideas, Mr. Point Guard?"

"I thought you were the idea man," Danny said to him.

"Not this time."

Danny said, "Then we better do what we always do when we have a crisis."

He looked at Will and at the same time they both said, "Call Tess."

267

★ ★ ★

It had been arranged with Ali Walker before practice that Coach Kel would drive him home.

"Keep your eye on the prize, little man," Coach Kel said when he got out of the car.

"I'm trying, Coach K," Danny said. "I'm trying."

When he got inside, his mom was walking around with the portable phone. She put her hand over the mouth part and said, "I'm talking to Mrs. Stoddard, we're trying to come up with a plan for Saturday's game, and the other games before the play-offs."

He went upstairs to work on some English homework he hadn't been able to finish in study hall, just because his mind kept going back to his dad's crazy plan. When he was done with homework, he opened his door a crack and gave a listen. His mom must have finished with Molly Stoddard, because right then he heard the chirp of the phone.

He had a feeling he knew who it was, and what was coming next.

Knew there was probably going to be some yelling in the house.

The first thing he heard: "No. Absolutely not. Out of the question."

Danny didn't cover his head with a pillow this time. He pulled on his new hooded Gap sweatshirt, part of his Christmas clothes, grabbed the Infusion ball out of the closet, went quietly down the stairs, slipped out the back door, put on the driveway floodlight and the light over the basket, went out on the part of the driveway near the basket he had shoveled himself, having managed to keep that area — his area — bone dry despite all the snow they'd been having lately.

He had forgotten to shut the back door. When he went over, he heard his mom say, ". . . a head injury the doctors must have missed. Because you can't do this, Richard. I won't let you."

"Richard" was never good, that had been Danny's experience.

He closed the door firmly this time, shot around for a couple of minutes, then stepped away from the basket and went right to the double crossover.

He went back and forth with the ball. Then again. Then again. Three times without missing, then four, never looking down at the ball once. His fingers felt like icicles in the night, but even that didn't matter, because for this night Danny felt as if he had the ball on a string.

269

As if he could do anything he wanted with it.

His mom was still on the phone when he came back inside. But now she had closed the door to the small study off the dining room that served as her office.

At least she wasn't yelling anymore.

He snuck over, put his ear to the door, heard: "I understand you can't quit now. That they can't quit now. It's why we're having the parents' meeting here tomorrow night. . . . No, *you* can explain it to them, Rich."

They had at least moved off "Richard."

Danny went to the kitchen, microwaved himself up some hot chocolate, took the mug up to his room.

Time to get Tess into the loop.

CROSSOVER2: Hey. Tall Girl. You there?

When in doubt, *always* talk to the tall girl.

CONTESSA44: On 24-hour call. Even when doing our dopey outline on *The Pearl.*
CROSSOVER2: You mean Earl the Pearl?
CONTESSA44: Don't tell me. Another legend of the hardwood.

CROSSOVER2: Hardwood?
CONTESSA44: You forget. My dad talks like he goes through life doing the six o'clock sports report.

Danny went to his door, poked his head out. No yelling from downstairs. No talking, period. Unless she'd worked herself all the way down to whispering.
Maybe she was actually listening.
He went back to his new Sony.

CONTESSA44: What's on your mind, cutie?
CROSSOVER2: ShutUP.

It was like they were waiting each other out. Or she knew he had something on his mind.
As if she could read his mind, too.

CROSSOVER2: We have to get a new coach. Or we're toast.
CONTESSA44: I heard.
CROSSOVER2: Coach Kel did tonight.
CONTESSA44: Will told me. But just tonight, he said.
CROSSOVER2: Yeah.
CONTESSA44: So we need a plan.

Downstairs, he thought he might have heard a laugh.

CROSSOVER2: My dad actually came up with a plan.

He could hear his mom coming up the stairs.

CONTESSA44: Who does he want to coach?

It didn't take long to type out his answer.

He could keep up with her when he kept it this simple.

When he'd replay the scene in his head later, another scene he thought would have to be in the movie, he remembered getting the answer he wanted from the two women in his life pretty much at the exact same moment.

His mom was in the doorway when he turned around, hands on her hips the way she had been on Christmas Day when she had watched him and his dad finish up their video game.

Basically smiling the same smile.

"Hey, Coach," she said.

He turned back to the screen when he heard the old doodlely-doo.

CONTESSA44: Cool.

When he didn't respond right away, she did.

CONTESSA44: Very VERY cool.

Before he got himself calmed down enough to think about going to sleep, he took the Kidd poster off the wall, carefully laid it out on the bed, made sure to smooth out any wrinkly places, took off his LeBrons, went over to the wall, placed the pen on top of his head.
Made his mark.
Turned around.
The new line was an inch higher than the line he'd made in October the last time he'd measured himself.
Fifty-six inches.
He took out the tape measure just to make sure.
Fifty-six on the button.
He'd grown an inch!

24

"What finally convinced you?" Danny said at the kitchen table.

It was way past his bedtime, but his mom wanted to talk. And Danny knew by now that when she wanted to talk, the Walker house turned into the place where time stood still.

She had made them some real hot chocolate from scratch, boiling the milk in a pan on the stove, slowly stirring in the Hershey's chocolate from the can.

After she poured it into their mugs, she even threw a couple of marshmallows on top.

His mom thought microwaved hot chocolate was for sissies.

"What convinced me?" she said, pushing her marshmallows slowly around with a spoon. "I guess you'd have to say it was when your father hit me with, 'We're one-and-nine with me coaching, how could the kid do any worse?' I have to admit, that one got a good laugh out of me."

Danny said, "Not a lot of laughs around here lately."

"No," she said, "there haven't been."

She saw that his cup was almost empty, got up without asking him if he wanted more, poured the last of the hot chocolate from the pan. Usually she guarded against any kind of chocolate intake around bedtime. Like she was the Chocolate Police.

Not tonight.

Danny took a look at her as she made sure not to spill any. A good look. His friends liked to needle him sometimes by telling him his mom was hot, knowing that would get a rise out of him. But he didn't need them to tell him that, he knew she was pretty, movie pretty, that was a given. You could count on that with her, the way you could count on her always wearing nice clothes, never really looking like a slob, even when it was just the two of them hanging around the house on what his mom would sometimes call slob weekends. And when he compared her to some of the other moms, it was no contest. Some of the other moms, it was like they'd packed it in, they didn't care how they looked anymore.

Ali Walker always cared.

But tonight he saw how tired she looked,

noticed the bags under her eyes, what he thought of as worry bags.

She said, "I had been telling him — yelling at him — for most of the conversation about what a ridiculous idea this was."

"I heard."

"Figured," she said. "But I didn't care, I meant it. I told him it was way too much pressure on a twelve-year-old boy, even one with supernatural basketball powers, and that on top of that, I wasn't sure the other parents would go for it."

"What did Dad say to that?"

Ali Walker, elbow on the table, nested her cheek in her hand, as if keeping her head propped up. He could see it was going to be a fight to the finish now, her need to talk against her need to go to bed. "He did what he always used to do when I was yelling at him," she said. "Waited me out."

"Yeah, but when he finally said something, it must've been pretty good." He reached over and plucked the marshmallow out of her cup and swallowed it.

"Hey," she said.

"I could tell you didn't really want it."

"What would I do without you?" she said.

Danny said, "Dad always says that it was

harder turning you around on stuff than it used to be playing UConn on the road."

"I know," she said, and sighed. "Anyway," she said, "he told me that this had been your team from the start, not his. That you knew it better than he did. That for all the normal screwing around the other kids did, they all took their lead from you, even through all the losing. That no matter how much they hung their heads, they didn't quit because you didn't quit."

"He said that?"

"He did. Then he hit me with this: Kids always make the best game."

"Wait a second," Danny said, "that's my line."

"He told me it was. And you know what? I knew he was right. Then he finished up by telling me that you might learn more about basketball doing this, even for a few games, than you've ever learned in your life. And then he said one last ultimate thing that sealed the deal for old Mom."

"What?"

"He said that even he never had the guts to coach one of his own teams."

She reached across the table now with both of her hands, with those long, pretty fingers, and made a motion with them for him to get his hands out there. He did.

His mom's hands were always warm.

"Truth or dare," she said.

Danny said, "Truth."

"You can do this?"

Danny made sure to look her in the eyes. "I can do this."

"You're sure?"

"If it's okay with the guys —"

"— and Miss Colby —"

"— and Colby. If it's okay with them and the parents say they're good with it, yeah, so am I."

"We're going to have a team meeting here, tomorrow night, seven-thirty," Ali Walker said. "We'll run the whole thing up the flagpole, bud, and see who salutes."

"You have some very weird expressions, Mom, have I ever mentioned that to you?"

She came around the table, pulled him up out of his chair, put her arms around him, leaned over as she did and put her face on top of his head.

"I grew an inch," he said.

"I thought there was something different about you," she said. "I just assumed it was the stature that comes with your new job."

"Funny."

"Go to bed," she said. "And no more IM."

Danny said, "Haven't you heard about

278

how little sleep dedicated coaches get?"

"Not when they're in the seventh grade," she said.

Tess was waiting on the sidewalk in front of the school when Danny and his mom came around from the teachers' parking lot. As soon as Ali Walker was gone, Tess said, "We're good to go."

"Where?"

"Everybody on the team is completely fired up about you coaching," she said. "With the possible exception of the wimp-face O'Brien twins."

"What's their problem?"

"Not a problem, exactly. They just said what they say about practically everything."

"What?"

"You're close," Tess said. "Actually, it was what*ever.*"

"You already conducted a poll this morning?"

"Last night, right after you IM'd me."

Danny said, "Well aren't you a busy little bee?"

"*Queen* bee," she said, giving her hair a little shake.

The Warriors all sat together at lunch, at the big table by the window facing the soccer fields. Before they got around to talking about their team, Will and Bren informed the group that Colorado boy — Andy Mayne — had suffered a severe high ankle sprain, worst kind, the day before, playing touch football in the parking lot after school.

"Black ice," Will said. "Never saw it."

"Heard he was lucky he didn't break his ankle instead of just twisting it like a pretzel," Bren said.

"They've got him in some kind of soft-cast deal for now, so he doesn't make it any worse," Will said.

"Might be back for the play-offs, might not," Bren said.

"That means they'll only beat us by twenty points in the playoffs," Will said.

" 'Stead of forty," Bren said.

"I don't want to talk about them," Tess said. "I want to talk about us."

Danny knew he probably had the goofy look on his face that he felt come over it when Tess Hewitt said or did something that really got to him, but he didn't care.

"Us?" he said.

"Yes," she said. *"Us."* She looked at him and said, "What, you thought I was going to sit the big adventure out?"

Then she wanted to know if everybody

had followed her online instructions, and kept their big fat stupid mouths shut around their parents about Danny coaching the team.

"Explain to me again why it has to be a surprise for all the mummies and mummified daddies," Will said.

"It's just better if Mrs. Walker tells, is all. So nothing gets lost in translation." She hit Will with her raised eyebrow and said, "Mrs. Walker," she said, "is, like, *good* with words."

"Go ahead," Will said, trying to act wounded. "Lash out at the ones you care the most about even on this happy day."

Bren said, "I'm asking the new coach for shorter practices."

"And no suicides, ever," Colby Danes said from across the table.

The Warriors applauded.

The O'Brien twins were dressed exactly the same today, so nobody had any idea which was which.

"Are we going to have to play more minutes?" one of them said.

The other one said, "This season feels too long already."

"Hey, Mary-Kate and Ashley," Will said to them. "Zip it."

Colby said she had a question.

"What if the league says you can't coach, that we need a grown-up?"

Danny said, "My mom thought about that already, she says she's got a backup plan."

"Oh, good," Will said. "Now we go from Plan B to Plan C."

Tess smiled now.

"No, Plan D," she said. "For Danny."

She held his hand under the table.

And he let her.

The Walkers' doorbell rang at six-thirty, even though the parents' meeting wasn't scheduled to begin for another hour.

Ali Walker yelled down for Danny to get it, she was still getting dressed, and if it was somebody selling something, tell them it was too late to be coming around.

When he opened the front door, Mr. Ross was standing there.

"Hello, Danny," he said.

"Mr. Ross."

"Is your mom home? I saw the car."

Danny jerked a thumb over his shoulder. "She's upstairs."

"Would you mind if I come in? I've got something I want to say to both of you."

Danny called up to his mom and told her Mr. Ross was here. Then, trying to think what she'd want him to do, he asked if he could take Mr. Ross's black overcoat, which felt as soft as a baby blanket as Danny started to hang it on the coat rack.

"Would you mind using that little hook up by the collar?" Mr. Ross said.

They went into the living room to wait for his mom. Mr. Ross sat down on the couch.

"I hear your dad is feeling much better," he said.

Danny felt like saying, compared to *what?*

"I've been meaning to stop by the hospital and see him," Mr. Ross said.

Danny said, "I'm sure he'd appreciate that," only because he couldn't say what he really wanted to say, which was that his dad would appreciate that about as much as having his bones broken all over again.

Ali Walker came breezing into the room then, saying, "Well, isn't this a surprise."

Mr. Ross got up and looked like he was leaning over to kiss her on the cheek when his mom stopped him by putting her hand out for him to shake, stopping him the way a crossing guard would have.

"I was going to call first," Mr. Ross said. "But I had an errand to run and I was passing the house, and I just decided to drop by."

Even Danny knew that was bull.

"So," Ali said, "to what do we owe the honor?"

Danny was in one of the chairs on the

other side of the coffee table from the couch, one of the two that they'd just had done over with new flowered covers that looked exactly like the old flowered covers to Danny. Ali Walker sat down in the other.

They both waited patiently for him to get to it.

"Well," he said, "I came with an apology, and what I think is a pretty neat idea."

Danny looked over at his mom, in her dark blue dress, hands folded in her lap. She smiled at Mr. Ross. Still waiting. Danny folded his hands in his lap and did the same.

Mr. Ross said, "First, I want to apologize to you, Danny. I don't know what my evaluators were thinking, but you should have been on the Vikings this season."

His mom still didn't say anything, and neither did he.

"Sometimes," he said, "adults don't know when to get out of the way when it comes to youth sports. And sometimes they don't know when to get *in* the way."

Danny was staring, fascinated, at Mr. Ross's white shirt, whose collar looked as stiff as a board.

"What I'm saying," Mr. Ross said, "is that I should have done something. And

285

we all should have seen the greatness in you."

Now Ali Walker spoke. "Tough to miss," she said.

"I realize that now, Ali. I was so hell-bent on maintaining the integrity of the process —"

"— right, the *process*," she said, nodding, as if trying to be helpful.

"— that I let a talented boy like the one sitting across from me not make a team he should have made."

He cleared his throat.

"Anyway," Mr. Ross said, "Richie said something to me that was absolutely correct, but I didn't want to hear. He said the best kids are supposed to make the team. And we all should have realized that Danny's always been one of the best kids in this town, despite —"

"— his size?" Ali Walker said.

Who was more helpful than her?

"— his size. Yes. But it seems this time his size worked against him for whatever reason —"

Holy *schnikeys*, Danny thought. A made-up Will word. *Whatever reason?* The reason, Mr. Rossface, was that you told them to make the team bigger.

"— and that's wrong."

There was another silence. Danny had been watching *SportsCenter* on the kitchen set when Mr. Ross arrived, and he could still hear somebody in there screaming about something.

Danny had sat in on his mom's class a few times, she said she wanted him to see her work, to have a better understanding about what she did, why she loved it so much, why she had gone back to college to give herself a chance to do it for a living. And every time he saw her teach, he saw how she'd go out of her way to help out any kid struggling to find the right word or the right answer. Sort of like she was throwing the kid a life preserver.

Now she seemed perfectly willing to let Mr. Ross go under before she'd make this any easier for him.

"Which brings me to the second reason for my visit," he said, "now that I understand there may be a problem with Danny's team."

"The Warriors," he said.

"Quite right, the Warriors. By problem, I mean insofar as your dad is going to be laid up for a while, and Ty says there may be a problem finding another parent willing to make the time commitment necessary to fill in for the rest of the season."

Danny looked over at his mom. He wasn't sure if Mr. Ross saw her give one shake to her head — basically telling him to shut up — or not.

Danny got her meaning, though.

"So I thought Danny could come play for the Vikings," Mr. Ross said. "Where he would have had the ball all along, if we hadn't dropped the ball."

He looked at his watch, as if he needed something to do with his hands after his big announcement.

"Even with the loss of Ty and young Mr. Mayne —"

"Andy Mayne was their point guard, Mom." Danny knew he was interrupting, which he was never supposed to do with grownups. But he wanted her to know. "He wrecked up his ankle yesterday. Might be out for the season."

"That must have hurt," Ali Walker said. "Both him and the Vikings, I mean."

"Knowing we'd be getting Ty back for the play-offs," Mr. Ross said, "I thought we had enough talent to make it out of the state and go all the way back to the nationals. And even without Andy, I think we still can, especially if I can convince Danny here to come aboard."

His mom leaned forward. "What about

the rest of Danny's team?" she said, in a pleasant-sounding voice.

"Well," he said, "if they can find another coach, of course, they can go ahead and finish the season." He shrugged and made this gesture with his palms turned up. Like: Who cares? "And if they don't, well, they'd only be missing a handful of meaningless games. I'm sure that even Danny would admit that they haven't exactly been tearing up the league."

Ali Walker answered that one by turning to face Danny.

"My husband always said that it's not the team you start with that matters, it's the one you end up with," she said. "Isn't that right, sweetheart?"

He'd almost missed the question, all he heard after "my husband" — which she never ever said anymore — was blah blah blah.

"Dad says he wants to see who's out there and what they're doing the last two minutes of the game, not the first two."

"I didn't mean any disrespect by what I said about the other Warriors," Mr. Ross said. "Really, no offense, to either one of you."

"None taken," Ali Walker said.

"Danny's different from the others," Mr. Ross said.

"He was in October, too," she said, and

stood up. "I've got some people coming over. I'll leave you and Danny alone, this is his decision, then I'll come back and see you out, Jeff."

She left them there.

"I finally figured out what you and Ty have known all along," Mr. Ross said. Giving him a weird grin that made him look like a jack-o'-lantern, as if the two of them were buds all of a sudden. "You two knotheads should be playing together."

Danny couldn't help it then.

He laughed.

"Did I say something funny, Danny?"

"Not really," he said. "It just kind of occurred to me that you're the biggest guy in our town, Mr. Ross. Seriously."

"Oh, I don't know about that."

"And here you are talking to me like *I'm* the biggest guy in town all of a sudden."

"I'm offering you a chance to play for a winning team."

"I'll take my chances with my team," Danny said. "Even *against* your team."

He stood up, came around the table, stuck his hand out, made eye contact the way his mom had taught him.

"But, sir?"

"Yes, Danny?"

"Thank you *so* much for stopping by."

★ ★ ★

Most of the kids on the team sat on the living-room floor. The parents sat on the couch, the two extra flowered chairs Ali Walker had brought in from the front hall, the four wooden chairs she brought in from the kitchen; the rest just stood around drinking coffee or wine or soft drinks. The Warriors were all drinking Gatorades out of plastic bottles. Tess Hewitt was with them, having come with Molly Stoddard and Will.

Danny's mom said she appreciated everybody taking time out to do this on a school night, and would do everything in her power to keep the proceedings brief.

Will Stoddard raised a hand. "Take as much time as you need, Mrs. Walker. I haven't done Spanish yet."

His mother smiled down at him like he was the most precious, wonderful boy in the whole world, then pinched his upper arm hard enough to make him yelp.

Danny leaned over and whispered to Tess, "You do not *ever* want to get the arm pinch from Mrs. Stoddard."

When Ali was convinced everybody had arrived, she laid out Richie's plan for them. She said that she knew that there were enough parents on the team with enough

291

free time that they could probably find a way to share the responsibilities of coaching the Warriors. But that Richie frankly didn't think that was good enough, that the kids were starting to come together, turning into the team he'd hoped they could be all along, and that the coach had to be someone who not only knew them, strengths and weaknesses, but also knew basketball.

And that in his opinion the one who fit the bill best was Danny.

Will said, "Please hold your applause until the end."

Molly only faked the pinch, but Will spazzed away from her anyway.

Mrs. O'Brien, the twins' mom, who'd always reminded Danny of a hummingbird with short black hair, said, "A *child?* Coaching the other children? I just don't know how that would *look,* frankly."

One of the twins, Danny thought it was Steven, he did the most whining of the two, said, "But Mom, you said you didn't care if one of the lunch ladies coached the team as long as you got us out of the house on weekends."

Danny bit down on the knuckles of his right hand, but then all of the adults in the room were laughing, so he did, too.

Mrs. O'Brien gave Steven a death look

and said, "Mommy was *joking*, honey. But we'll *discuss* all that in the *car* later."

It turned out that Mr. Harden was there, having flown back for the night from his case in Florida. He said, "I've been around this team more than anybody, with the exception of the players, of course. And from the start, Richie called Danny his coach on the floor. So I don't see his job description really changing all that much."

Molly Stoddard said, "I called over to the league office today. I didn't tell them why I was calling, just said that we might have some problems with logistics before the season was over, and was there an actual league rule about having an adult on the bench. And they said that there had to be at least one."

Ali Walker said, "That would be me."

Jerry Harden said, "*You're* going to be the bench coach?"

"Just filling in until you get back from West Palm," she said. "And if you don't make it back, I'll do it the rest of the way." She smiled. "I've learned from the best, after all," she said. "The former coach and his potential replacement."

Way to go, Mom.

She said, "I don't really care whether the other team thinks I'm coaching our team or not. If they think I've taken over, fine. But Danny will handle all the basketball stuff."

"There's no heavy lifting, I can testify to that," Jerry Harden said. "All you have to do, other than being a good cheerleader, is keep track of time-outs and fouls."

"I'm not even going to do that," Ali said.

"Who is?" Danny said.

Ali said, "Tess."

In a voice that seemed a little louder than she intended, Colby Danes said, "*Yes.* More girls."

Another laugh from the room. Mostly from the moms.

When it subsided, Molly Stoddard said to Danny in a serious voice, "You know we consider you a member of our family. But are you absolutely certain you want to do this?"

"My dad wants me to," he said.

He looked over at his mom. She winked.

"I appreciate that you want to do this for your dad," Molly said. "What I want to know — what I think we all want to know — is if you want to do this for yourself?"

Danny stood up, as if he had the floor now. As soon as he did, he could feel his hands shaking, the way they did when he'd have to get up and say something, or read something, in front of the class.

So he stuffed them into his pockets.

"I told my mom before everybody got here that if the guys on the team . . . and the girls," he said, giving a quick nod to Colby, "want me to do it, then I'm doing it."

Danny said, "I mean, they all said they were cool with it at school. But if anybody's changed their mind since we all talked about it at lunch, well, I'm cool with *that*, too. No harm, no foul."

He looked over at Will, who was sitting on the floor next to Tess now. Then at Bren. And Matt Fitzgerald.

For once, they were all looking *up* at him.

"My dad said that this started out as my team," Danny said, "and maybe it did. But now, like, it's all our team."

"Why don't we do it this way?" Ali Walker asked. "Why don't we ask the Warriors, and their new assistant coach, Tess, to vote."

Tess stood right up.

First in everything.

"I vote for Danny," she said.

Will got up. "Danny."

Bren walked over from Danny's right. "Dan the man," he said.

295

Then the rest of them got up, all of them looking a little self-conscious, knowing all the adults were watching them.

"Danny," they said, one by one.

Then Will Stoddard, clearly thinking everything was getting way too dramatic, turned the whole thing into a chant.

"DAN-ny! DAN-ny! DAN-ny!"

Even the parents joined in.

Danny put his hand about halfway into the air, the way you do when you think you may have the answer a teacher was looking for, but aren't really sure.

"Hey, guys," he said, "listen up. Okay?"

They had warmed up in two layup lines, the way they always did. Now it was time to actually start practice. His mom and Molly Stoddard were sitting up on the stage, not even paying attention to them, both of them with their yellow legal pads, making plans for the Valentine's Ball the parents had at St. Pat's every February.

So Danny was in charge.

Except he really wasn't, since no one was listening to him.

The O'Brien twins were doing what they always did when they thought there was a break in the action, which was sitting on the floor. Colby had walked away from the group and was shooting free throws at one of the side baskets. Will was trying to make outside shots over Matt Fitzgerald from the deep corner.

It reminded Danny of recess.

"Guys," he said, a little louder this time.

Nothing.

Tess was sitting in a folding chair at midcourt, watching him. She'd come with the Stoddards, explaining to Danny when she showed up, "If I'm going to be team manager, I want to see how things work."

"I thought your title was assistant coach?" Danny had said.

"I'm more of a management type."

Now Danny put his hands out to her, the way you did when you were pleading with somebody for help. Tess gave him a slow nod, as if she got the picture. But then, she always seemed to get the picture. Danny watched as she slowly got up out of her chair, cleared her throat as if she were about to sing some kind of solo at the spring chorale, then put two fingers into her mouth and issued one of the most ear-shattering whistles Danny had ever heard in his life, one that would have done a big-whistle NBA coach like Pat Riley proud.

The whistle got their attention.

"Thank you," Danny mouthed at her.

"My pleasure," Tess mouthed back, gave

298

him a quick little curtsy, sat down, as if nothing had happened.

Danny motioned for the Warriors to get around him at mid-court.

"I know this must be a little weird for you guys, because it's a *lot* weird for me," he said. "But we need to get to work. We've only got the gym for an hour tonight, we're playing Kirkland tomorrow afternoon, and we gotta get after it."

"Coach?" Will said. "Would you mind slowing down, you're going a little too fast for me."

Colby said, "Shut*upppppppp*," in a sing-songy voice.

Danny said, "We tried to go man-to-man against them last time, but nobody could handle their big guy."

"Bud Sheedy," Bren said.

"We couldn't handle him, we couldn't handle their press," Danny said. "So I figure we might as well go with a zone tomorrow. You guys okay with that?"

They nodded.

"But maybe not our normal zone," he said. "I thought we might try a one-three-one. Let me show you."

He went over to where he'd left his backpack, next to Tess's chair, reached into the side pocket, brought out the coach's board his mom had bought him, and the erasable laundry marker that came with it.

"Oooh," Will said, "he brought *toys*."

From her chair, Tess said, "Will Stoddard, if you don't zip it, I'm going to tell the whole team who you like."

Danny knew it was Colby. And he knew Tess knew. He couldn't believe she'd rat him out now in front of the team — in front of Colby herself — but sometimes he couldn't tell when Tess Hewitt was bluffing.

"What, now that he's the coach, this has turned into, like, a mirth-free zone?" Will said.

"Tonight it is," Tess said. "Are we clear?"

"As Clearasil," Will said, rather gloomily.

Danny drew up the zone he wanted them to play, then did some quick *X*-and-*O* work with their inbounds offense against the Kirkland press.

"See, Oliver, you're going to take it out instead of Matt," Danny said, trying to draw as fast as he was talking. "Matt, you're going to *get* the first pass instead of throw it. You flash to the near free throw line, with your arms up in the air, like you're a tight end getting ready to catch a pass."

He gave a quick look up. They were all really watching.

And all really listening.

Hot *dog.*

"Oliver, you make sure you give him the ball where he can handle it. Matt, as soon as you get it, you turn. Now you're a quarterback. Bren will be flying down the left side, like he's going for a bomb. I'll be at half-court, over on the right. But I'm just a decoy."

Colby Danes said, "I don't like this."

Danny ignored her. "If Bren's ahead of everybody, throw it to him. But *only* if he's wide open. If he's not, give it to Colby, who'll be a few feet away, on your left or your night, depending on where she is after the first pass. They won't be expecting her to bring it up. But she's going to."

"You and Bren are the ball-bringer-uppers," Colby said. "Don't make me bring it up." She brightened. "I'll pay you."

Danny said, "You can do this. You can handle the ball better than you think. Remember that dorky guy they had covering you in the first game? The one with the thingies in his hair?"

"Highlights," Colby said.

"Him," Danny said. "He couldn't cover you in the half-court, he's too slow. He's not gonna have a chance covering you full-court. When he sees you coming at him with the ball, and a head of steam, he'll start backing up like he just saw something in that *Blair Witch* movie we watched the other day in audio-visual."

"How do you know that?" Colby said, still sounding pretty skeptical.

"Can I say one thing?" Will said, looking over at Tess. "Without being threatened?"

"Okay, but just one," team manager Tess said.

Tess understood the situation, because everybody who knew and loved Will did:

He totally zipped it about as often as he saw Mars.

"He knows things," Will said. "I'm talking about basketball things. Don't ask him to fix a flat on his bike. Or burn a song."

"Don't even think about asking him to diagram a sentence," Tess called out.

"But if he tells you something is going to happen in basketball, it's probably going to happen," Will said. "Annoying, but true."

"This'll work great," Danny said to Colby. "Trust me."

"You want me to bring the ball up the *whole* game?" Colby said.

Just against the press, Danny assured

her, and then said, c'mon, they could all walk through it.

They did. The only person playing defense was Michael Harden, guarding Colby after she got the ball from Matt. Danny had told him to back off a few feet, the way he was sure the highlighted dork from Kirkland would, not try to steal it from her. But after they'd half run, half walked through it a few times, Danny motioned for Michael to get up on her.

And when he did, the Warriors' girl, looking as if she was about to have the ball stolen from her, put the ball behind her back — a move none of them had even seen from her — and just absolutely dusted Michael Harden.

Colby Danes did that to war whoops from the rest of them, with the exception of Michael, who was on the ground trying to get them to believe he'd twisted an ankle.

Danny went over to Colby, jumped up, gave her a high five.

"See," he said, "sometimes you can do stuff you didn't know you could do."

It was a short practice, but a good one, everybody rallying around Danny the way they had that night with Coach Kel.

303

At least until Danny yelled.

At Will.

They had all just decided — group decision — that next basket won in the scrimmage. They were going four-on-four by then: Danny, Bren, Oliver, and Colby against Steven O'Brien, Michael, Matt, Will.

Danny passed it to Colby, who missed. Michael got the rebound, fed Will, who was flying up the court. Matt had taken off down the court early, as soon as he saw nobody was going to contest Michael for the rebound. So it was Will and Matt in a two-on-one against Oliver Towne, the Round Mound of Towne, who was sucking wind big-time, the way he usually did by the end of practice.

Will on Oliver's left, Matt on his right.

Oliver was so tired, Will could not only have walked past him, but rubbed the top of his head for luck on the way by. Instead, maybe to show off for Colby, show that he could go behind his back, too, he threw this behind-the-back pass that Matt wasn't expecting, one that hit him on the side of the head, before bouncing harmlessly out of bounds.

"Hey, Will, cut the crap, okay?" Danny yelled, and just the way he did let everybody know he meant it.

His voice as loud in the gym as the air-raid siren they still used when they practiced evacuating school in case of an emergency.

Will looked at Danny as if he were the one who'd just gotten hit in the head by the ball, hurt and surprised at the same time.

Danny didn't know why he was as hot as he was. But he was. "What's the deal, it was too big a job for you to throw one simple pass so we could get our butts out of here?" he said. "Is that, like, some kind of *problem?*"

He looked around and saw the whole gym now the way he could see the court when he was coming up with the ball. Tess in her chair. His mom and Will's mom watching from the stage. The other players on the Warriors frozen in place as if somebody had hit the Pause button.

Will said, "You sound like a dad."

And, just like that, Danny knew his best friend was right.

He did sound like a dad. Like *his* dad had sounded that night when he was in a bad mood and his mom yelled at him about his drinking afterward.

At least Dad'd had an excuse, Danny thought now.

What's mine?

Sometimes he was a little slow out of the chutes figuring stuff out. Not now. Now he was the one who got the picture, just like that. He'd sounded like a schmuck and gotten busted for it. He looked bad in front of his friends, and knew he had to get out of it right now, even if it meant backing off and looking like some kind of wimp.

"I'm going to tell you something you already know," Danny said to Will. "Sometimes, I've got a pretty big mouth for a little guy."

He saw his mom watching from the stage, standing next to Will's mom. Ali Walker had always told him that there was no great skill to being right about something, anybody could carry that off. The trick, she said, was knowing how to be wrong.

Danny walked over to Will and put his hand out. No high five, no low five, no clenched fist, no secret handshake. He was just looking for a normal handshake. Strictly regulation.

"Sorry, dude," he said.

Will grinned. "You're the first coach ever to apologize for being too stinking loud."

"Nah, I was just another coach who forgot whose team it really is," Danny said.

Then he said, "We've been telling you to

shut up all night. Anything you want to say to the team before we call it a night."

"Yes," Will said. "Kirkland sucks."

Words to live by.

He and his mom stopped off at the hospital before they went over to St. Pat's for the Kirkland game. When they got there, his mom said he ought to have a few minutes alone with his dad, she'd be upstairs in the cafeteria having a cup of coffee and actually being able to read the morning papers for a change.

"The nurse said he had kind of a rough night," Ali Walker said. "He had a pretty high fever, which sometimes happens after extensive surgery like he had, but they finally got it under control a few hours ago."

Danny said, "He's going to be all right, though. Right? I mean, like, *really* all right?"

"He is," she said. "Just not as fast as he wants. Or you want."

"I don't get this," Danny said. "Everybody said all the operation stuff they needed to do went the way it was supposed to."

They were standing near the nurses' station. She walked him a few feet away, put her hands on his shoulders, scrunched

307

down a little so they were eye to eye. "Now pay attention," she said.

"What did I do?" Danny said.

"Nothing," his mom said. "You just have to understand something for today, and for however long it takes your dad to get better. Yes, the surgery went fine. Yes, he's *starting* to get better and *is* going to get better. Eventually, okay? But when he had the first accident, he was in the best shape of his life. Now it's ten years later, honey. And it's the second time the sky fell on him. And this time, he doesn't have any, well, *wellness* to fall back on the way he did when he was younger. So when I tell you it's going to take time, it's going to take time."

"But he's going to be able to walk okay."

"Yes."

"You promise?"

"Cross my heart."

"Do it," Danny said.

She stepped back, wrote a big *T* on the front of her sweater. "Now you go let your father get you all ready for the big game," she said.

Richie Walker's eyes were closed, and for a minute Danny thought he might be sleeping, even though the nurse had said he was awake, he'd just had an early lunch.

But when the door closed, Richie opened his eyes, saw who it was, and smiled, though pretty weakly.

Somehow, Danny thought, the cast on his dad's leg, going all the way to his hip, seemed even bigger than it had the last time he had visited him. And there seemed to be even more tubes than before. Even the bed seemed to have grown in the last couple of days.

All of it seeming to swallow up his dad.

Richie said, "Hey, Coach."

"Hey, Coach," Danny said.

"C'mon over closer, let me see you. Sometimes these pain pills give me such a jolt I feel like I've got the sun in my eyes all of a sudden."

Danny was wearing an old orange Syracuse sweatshirt his dad had given him a couple of years ago; Danny didn't like to wear it that often, mostly because he still hadn't grown into it.

But he figured he'd go with something from Syracuse today, the last place his dad still felt like the king of the world in basketball.

"Where's your mom?"

"She said she was going to have coffee. She's probably got one of the doctors against a wall, trying to get stuff out of him."

Richie said, "If I don't get out of here soon, they're going to make her chief of staff."

"She's pretty good at bossing people in that quiet way she has."

"Tell me about it," Richie said.

"We're on our way to the game," Danny said.

"You ready?"

Danny laughed, he couldn't help himself. "Heck no."

"You'll be fine."

"Easy for you to say," Danny said.

Richie moved his head from side to side on the pillow. "Nothing's easy for me to say these days. Not even, good morning."

Danny said, "I'm just worried that if I worry too much about coaching, I won't be worrying enough about playing. Which makes me worry that I won't be able to handle either job too well."

"That's way too much worrying over one travel basketball game," his dad said. "Just play. The rest of it will take care of itself."

"But what if I have the wrong guys out there? Or forget to get everybody enough time? You want another one? What if —"

"Daniel Walker?"

"What?" Danny had nearly what-if'd himself out of breath.

"Shut your piehole."

"I'm just saying —"

"Shut your piehole *now.*"

He did.

Thinking: At least now you sound like my dad.

"Let me ask you something, bud: Who would you rather be today — you or me?"

Danny looked down and studied the toe of his left LeBron. "Me," he said, without looking up.

"Maybe I told you this before, maybe not, I can't remember anything anymore. But listen up now: There isn't an adult who'll be in the gym today who wouldn't change places with you in a freaking heartbeat. You, or Big Matt, or Miss Colby. Or Will. You got that?"

He studied his right toe now. "Got it."

"Do you really get it?"

"Yes," Danny said.

"Good. Because if you put all this dumb pressure on yourself, then it means your mom was right the first night, her precious little boy can't handle this, boo freaking hoo."

Really sounding like his old dad now, the one who could cut you in half with a single word.

"The other players? They *want* to follow

you today. They'll be watching *you*. If you look like the whole thing makes you want to wet your pants, they're gonna want to do the same."

For some reason, Danny turned around, as if he could feel someone watching them. And there, in the window that faced out to the hall, the drapes just open enough for him to see her, was his mom. Not wanting to interrupt by walking in on them. But pointing at her watch, like they had to get going soon.

"It's your ball today," Richie said. "Your game. So don't worry about the rest of that . . . stuff."

Danny said, "You can say the s-word in front of me, Dad. Or any of the other biggies. It's not like I haven't heard them before. Or used them myself."

Then Richie smiled and used a whole bunch of biggies in one sentence, telling him what he should do with all his worries and what he wanted the Warriors to do to Kirkland.

Then he motioned for Danny to come close, like he wanted to whisper something, and kissed him on the cheek.

"Don't do it for anybody except yourself," he said. "Make yourself proud today."

Danny said, "I love you, Dad."

With his good hand, Richie gave him a little shove. "Beat it now," he said.

As Danny opened the door, he heard him say, "I love you, too, bud."

Danny turned back around then, smiling, trying to remember the last time he'd heard his dad say that.

"Remember the team rules," Richie said. "Play hard. Have fun. Shoot if you're open."

"If you're not," Danny said, "pass it to somebody who *is* open."

"And I want to add one more, just for today."

Danny waited.

"Beat Kirkland's ass," his dad said.

The Warriors were the ones getting their butts handed to them.

Total nightmare from the start.

Richie Walker had told Danny one time about what he said was the old coaches' nightmare. He said he'd heard it from a little guy who used to coach St. John's, one Richie called Coach Looie, at a dinner one time right before the Big East tournament.

"It's like a school nightmare you'll get someday, even when you're not in school anymore," Richie said. "It's one where you have to take a test, only you're scared out of your pants because you haven't been to class all semester. This is the basketball version. The coach wakes up with the heebie-jeebies in the middle of the night because his team is playing this game and, no matter what he tries, they can't make a single basket."

Danny was the twelve-year-old coach having the old coaches' nightmare now against Kirkland.

Only problem was, it was real.

The Warriors couldn't score a single basket.

The whole first quarter.

Kirkland 10, Warriors 0.

"I'm going to be the first coach to ever get shut out for a whole game," Danny said to Will with five seconds left in the quarter, while Kirkland's best player, Bud Sheedy, was making the first of two free throws.

Sheedy was a tall sandy-haired kid, taller than everybody else on his team, who was a lot like Ty, which meant he wasn't really a guard, or forward, or center.

He was another cool basketball kid whose real position was just basketball player.

"Well," Will said, "I *have* been telling people all week that you were going to make history."

Danny was playing tight; they *all* were. Will had missed at least three wide-open shots he would normally knock down. Colby fumbled the ball so much trying to bring it up against the press she reminded Danny of someone trying to play basketball wearing the kind of floppy oven mitts his mom would wear in the kitchen sometimes.

Every time there was a chance for the Warriors to get a rebound, Bud Sheedy was making Matt Fitzgerald look like he was the one who was fifty-six inches tall. Same with Michael Harden. Same with Oliver Towne.

Danny called his first time-out when it was 6–0, after they'd played just over four minutes.

"Everybody relax," he said in the huddle. "And when I say everybody, I'm talking to myself, too. Okay?"

"Roger that," Will said. "The way things are going, we figured it was only a matter of time before you started talking to yourself."

Danny heard some stifled laughs, as if they didn't know whether that was allowed or not.

"See, Will's starting to relax already," Danny said. "And listen, no lie, there's a long way to go."

Colby Danes said, "That's what I'm afraid of."

"We are gonna come back in this stupid game," Danny said. "For now, let's try to change the zone a little, make it more of the two-on-two my dad usually has us play. Maybe that will slow down these scumweasels."

On their way back out on the court, Will said, "Scum*weasels?*"

Danny said, "I didn't want to say scumwads in front of Colby."

The only thing keeping the Warriors in the game was that except for Bud Sheedy, no one was doing much scoring for Kirkland, either. But even after the time-out, the Warriors still couldn't make anything. When Matt picked up his third foul a couple of minutes into the second quarter, just to make matters worse than they were already, Kirkland had stretched out its lead to 14–0.

Danny called another time-out after Matt got his third, just to get him the heck out of there, afraid that if he left him in for even another minute, he might foul out by halftime.

They all gathered around him in the huddle — players, his mom with her clipboard, Tess with her scorebook — and waited for him to say something brilliant, or maybe inspirational.

Nothing came out of his mouth.

For one quick second, he felt so helpless — the way you do when some bigger kid gets you down on the playground and you can't move or even breathe — he thought he might cry.

He didn't, just because there was a part of him that knew it would go on his Permanent Record forever, worse than any black mark any teacher could put in there: How Danny Walker tried to coach the team and started crying.

The best he could do, finally, was: "Okay, listen up."

All he had.

He looked around at some of the faces, staring at him, waiting for the boy coach to start coaching. Only he still didn't have the words. Like he was the one with the whole game sitting on his chest.

Then, from behind him, he heard: "You guys are doing this all wrong."

Danny was on his knees in the middle of the huddle. He craned his neck around and saw Ty Ross standing there behind Oliver Towne and Michael Harden.

Ty said, "I played against Buddy Sheedy all summer in this camp league we have out at the beach."

They all turned to look at Ty now. Danny didn't even wonder about what he was doing here; he was just thrilled that someone seemed to know what he was talking about.

Ty said to Danny, "You've got to box-and-one him. That's what teams always do against me." He grinned. "It even works against me sometimes."

Danny had two thoughts, one right on top of another. One was that Ty was right about the box-and-one. The second was: How come *I* didn't think of that?

Box-and-one. One guy playing man-to-man against Bud Sheedy. Everybody else in a packed-in zone.

Ty said, "Put Will on him. Buddy's got the height. But Will can dog him all over the place." He gave Will a playful shove. "Maybe even talk to him a little bit."

Will said, "I think I can handle that."

The ref, Tony, their regular guy, poked his head past Ty and said to Ali Walker, "Fifteen seconds, ma'am."

Danny said, "Okay. Matt, I changed my mind, I'm keeping you in. Oliver, you play down low in the zone with Matt. Will, you've got Buddy, follow him to the bathroom if you have to. Colby, you sit for a minute. Bren, you're bringing it up with me."

They all put their hands in the middle and yelled "DEE-fense!"

As they broke the huddle Danny said to Ty, "You busy?"

Ty shook his head.

Colby was sitting on the folding chair

next to Tess and Ali Walker. Danny motioned for her to move over one.

"Have a seat," Danny said. "I'm deputizing you."

Will didn't care where the ball was when Bud Sheedy didn't have it. He just went wherever Sheedy went, like he had blinders on. And whenever the two of them were anywhere near Danny, he could hear Will talking to Bud, as if they were sitting together on the bus.

After one play when the refs couldn't decide who'd knocked the ball out of bounds, Danny went over and stood next to the Warriors' bench area.

"Will's gotta be careful he doesn't go too far," Ty said, "trash-talking really isn't allowed in the Tri-Valley League."

"He's not really talking smack," Danny said. "He's just talking."

Ty said, "About what? I'm too far away to hear."

"When they went by me a minute ago, I heard him saying something about the Knicks' playoff chances," Danny said.

It was 14–8 by then. Will had finally shut up long enough to make two open shots. Danny had put Colby back in for Oliver. Colby scored. Danny had assisted on all three baskets. Then he broke away for a layup when his guy thought he was going to pass to Colby again.

When Kirkland called time-out, Danny said to Ty, "The defense is working."

"So far."

Ali Walker said, "Is it really called the boxcar-and-one?"

At the same time, Danny and Ty said, "*Box*-and-one."

"Well," Ali Walker said, "I think boxcar is more vivid."

"Mom," Danny said, "we're trying to work here."

Ty said, "If Will starts to get tired, go to the triangle-and-two, and you help out."

Bud Sheedy started to get frustrated now, even complaining to the ref one time about Will's relentless chatter. He finally threw up a long hook shot, more in frustration than anything else. He seemed as surprised as anybody in the gym when it went in. Now it was 16–8, Kirkland. But Danny took the inbounds pass and beat everybody down the court and fed Colby for the layup that made it 16–10. Then Matt Fitzgerald shocked everybody by making two straight free throws for the first time all year. 16–12.

Right before the horn sounded to end

the half, the Warriors had a three-on-two break: Danny with the ball in the middle, Will on his left, Colby on his right. He passed to Will, who seemed to have a step on his guy. But the guy got in front of him. Will passed it back to Danny.

It was as if the ball barely touched Danny's hands.

He half passed it, half slapped it to Colby, who made another layup.

Kirkland 16, Warriors 14.

Whole half to go.

Game on.

Danny took them all out into the hallway at halftime. After his mom passed out the Gatorade bottles and the oranges she'd cut into perfect wedges, he said, "Anybody got anything to say?"

"I've got to save my voice for Buddy Boy," Will said. He ran a hand through his thick hair. Danny was surprised, as usual, that the hand could make it all the way through in one shot. "He still won't tell me whether he thinks Hilary Duff is hotter than Britney, by the way."

Ali Walker said, "Will honey? You could make prisoners of war talk."

Danny said, "Will, you just keep doing that mad thing you're doing to him. On account of, it's working. Matt, remember: No fouls. If you don't have a clean path to the rebound, forget it. None of that reaching-over crap." He gave a quick sideways look at his mom. "Sorry, Mom," he said.

"That's Coach Mom," she said. "I can take it."

Then he told Bren that the guy guarding him was backing off, and that Bren might get more shots in the second half than he'd gotten all season.

"Cool," Bren Darcy said.

Then Danny looked over at Ty. "You got anything?"

Ty said, "Just remember: The only other guy on the team besides Buddy who can hurt you is the kid up front who's almost as big as Buddy. I forget his name. He doesn't get to shoot much, but he can make an open shot. So Matt, you've got to keep an eye out for him down low."

Matt said, "He smells."

"But that doesn't mean he can't make an open shot," Danny said.

Matt said, "No, I mean he really *smells*."

Tess said, "Well, on *that* manly-man note."

They were all standing around Danny then. "I'm gonna tell you all the last thing my dad told me today when I went to see him," Danny said. "Beat Kirkland's —"

"Daniel," his mom said.

"— butts," Danny said.

Matt picked up his fourth foul halfway through the third quarter, doing exactly what Danny had told him *not* to do, going over the top trying to take a rebound away from the smelly kid.

Danny took him out and put Oliver Towne in the middle of the triangle, between Colby and Bren. Will was handling Bud Sheedy most of the time, Danny coming over to help out when he could, which meant any time he wasn't afraid that he was leaving about three guys wide open.

Six minutes into the third quarter, the game was tied at 24.

All of a sudden Colby Danes — the one Richie Walker had called the basketball girl of Danny's dreams — couldn't miss. She made the first three shots she tried in the second half, two from the outside, one of them *way* outside, the other one over Bud Sheedy after she took a rebound away from him and got an easy put-back.

Every time she made a basket, she'd jump a little higher in the air and her smile would get a little bigger, and then she'd go bounding down the court like a colt, pony-tail bobbing behind her.

It didn't take great powers of observation to notice that Bud Sheedy and the rest of the Kirkland Comets liked having a girl show them up — for the time being, anyway — about as much as they would have liked wearing her clothes.

Then, just like that, as if somebody had accidentally switched off the power, both teams seemed to stop scoring. It went on over the rest of the third quarter and into the fourth. It was either really good defense causing it, or really bad offense. Or maybe a combination of the two. By the time there were five minutes to go, the game was still tied, 28–28, and as excited as Danny was, as they *all* were, about having a chance to win, he was worried that Will was getting tired. So he replaced him on Bud Sheedy with Michael Harden.

But Michael couldn't stay with him. Sometimes Michael *and* Danny together couldn't stay with him. Bud got loose and made two straight shots for the first time since the start of the game. Danny knew he couldn't let him get hot, not coming down the stretch, when he could run them right out of the gym.

During a break in play, while the refs

tried to untangle one of the nets, Danny said to Tess, "How many time-outs do I have left?"

"Three," she said.

"Are you sure?"

Tess gave him the raised eyebrow. "I'm going to forget I heard that," she said.

Danny called time, walked down to where Will was sitting with a towel on his head that he'd fashioned into some kind of turban.

"Uh, Mohammed?" he said.

Will said, "I was actually going for that do-rag look defensive backs go with when they take their helmets off."

"You actually remind me of one of my dad's nurses," Danny said. "I need you to go back in and stay in the rest of the way on Bud."

"I may have to talk a little less," Will said, taking the towel off his head and spiking it as he stood up.

Danny said, "I can live with that."

They walked down to where the rest of the team was waiting in the huddle. As soon as Danny got in there, a laugh jumped out of his throat like one of those magician's bunnies jumping out of a hat.

"How much fun is *this?*" he said.

It came down to the wire — Kirkland

32, Warriors 30, with twenty-five seconds left.

Danny called for the same clean-out play he'd tried at the end of the Hanesboro game, him and Colby over on the right.

Kirkland played it about the same way Hanesboro had.

Danny ended up with pretty much the same shot, just inside the free throw line.

This time it was Bud Sheedy running at him from his left.

One step too late.

Danny got his shot up in the air. Telling himself to shoot it higher this time. Give it a chance to come down softer.

Drained the sucker.

It was 32–all. Fifteen seconds left. Before Kirkland could inbound the ball, Danny called his last time-out.

Ty said, "They won't expect you to put the press back on."

Danny had taken the press off when he put Will back in the game, just as a way of saving Will's legs, which were wobbly even after Danny had given him his short rest.

"No," Danny said to Ty. "Yes, you're right, they won't be expecting it. But no, I don't want to take the chance that somebody gets beat, especially without Matt back there to play safety."

He had put Matt back into the game with four fouls at the same time he put Will back in, but the big guy — who'd been coughing and wheezing with a cold all day and seemed almost relieved to be able to sit down for good — had fouled out a minute later.

Danny said, "They're going to try to isolate Bud. Because whatever they might want us to think they're doing, nobody else besides Bud will have the stones to take the shot."

He looked up at his mom. She just made a motion with her hand, like, just keep doing whatever it is you're doing.

Danny said, "He'll get the ball behind that double screen they've been running. Then everybody'll get out of the way, and they'll let him try to dribble through all of us."

Danny looked at Ty, who nodded.

To the Warriors, Danny said, "Everybody just play the D straight up, the way we have been. Once they see the press is off, they'll probably have the point guard bring it up. Will? As soon as he crosses half-court, you leave Bud and run right at him."

"Ex*cuse* me?" Will said. "We're going to leave Buddy Boy without anybody on him?"

"Trust me," Danny said.

"And what will you be doing?"

"Trying to win us a ball game," Danny said.

They put their hands together, came out, set up their triangle-and-two one last time. The point guard brought it up quickly, the way Danny had figured he would. Will was over on the right, where the smelly kid and one of the Kirkland forwards were coming out to set their screen.

Will was still with Bud.

As soon as the point guard crossed half-court, about twelve seconds showing on the clock, Danny could see him looking for Bud Sheedy.

Will ran at the kid with the ball like a maniac.

As soon as he did, the kid got bug eyes, and you could see he couldn't wait to give the ball up to Bud Sheedy. Who popped out, away from his screen, the way he was supposed to, even took a couple of steps toward the ball, not away from it, the way they were taught all the way back in Biddy Basketball.

Bud just didn't move toward the ball as quickly as a streak of light named Danny Walker.

Who had been playing possum behind

the double screen, arms at his side, like Bud Sheedy was somebody else's responsibility now.

The pass was in the air before the point guard, on Bud Sheedy, saw Danny making his move, cutting between them and grabbing the ball out of the air as if the pass had been intended for him all along.

He caught the ball and had the presence of mind to give one fast look at the clock over the basket at the other end — the *Warriors'* basket — as he did.

Four seconds left.

Will Stoddard had always said something about Danny that people used to say about his dad:

He was faster with the ball than everybody else was without it.

Will would tell him afterward that Bud Sheedy, no slouch himself when it came to running the court, was coming so hard he was sure he was going to catch Danny from behind.

"I knew nobody was going to catch Coach Walker," Bren said.

Everybody agreed on this: There was one second showing on the clock when Danny released his layup maybe one foot further away from the basket than he would have preferred.

He didn't know anything about where Bud Sheedy was, or how close he came to catching him, or the clock behind the basket. He was going by the clock inside his head, keeping his eyes on the prize:

That little square right above the basket.

He pushed off on his left leg, going up hard but laying the ball up there soft. He saw the ball hit the square as if there were a bull's-eye painted on it. The last thing he saw before he went flying toward the stage was the ball go through the net, right before the horn sounded.

He was sitting on the floor with his back against the stage when the Warriors came running for him.

Warriors 34, Kirkland 32.

Final.

When Danny managed to break loose from the Warriors, he saw Bud Sheedy and the rest of the Kirkland Comets still on the court, lined up and waiting to shake hands.

Danny said to his teammates, "Hey, we had enough practice losing. Now we gotta act like we know how to win."

Still coaching, to the end.

He was last in line. Bud Sheedy was last in their line. When it was just the two of them, Bud said to Danny, "We heard something about you coaching, but nobody really believed it."

"We sort of did it together," Danny said, and meant it. "Ty probably did more coaching today than I did."

"Nah, you did it to us and we know you did," Bud said. "You knew exactly what you were doing on defense with that last play." Bud smiled and shook his head. "That was, like, *sick*, dude."

The word always made Danny smile.

Somehow it had worked out that *sick* was

right up there with the highest possible praise one guy could give another.

"Thanks," Danny said.

Some of the Warriors were sitting on the folding chairs that served as their bench, some were on the floor, and all of them were eating the Krispy Kremes that Tess had brought in the green-and-white boxes that made your mouth water just thinking about what was inside. Tess waved at him, telling him to come over and eat.

But Danny was looking for Ty, who he thought was the real hero of the day.

He knew the Vikings had a game here in about an hour, against Hanesboro, and had just assumed that Ty would hang around for that. Only Danny didn't see him anywhere in the gym, and when he checked the back hallway where they'd had their team meeting at halftime, he wasn't out there, either. Or in the boys' locker room, where the Kirkland kids were getting into their coats. Danny asked Bud Sheedy if he'd seen Ty once the game ended. Bud said, "His dad showed up to watch the last few minutes. Stood over there in the corner by himself. Then as soon as you made your shot, I saw him come get Ty and take him by the arm." Bud hooked a thumb in the general direction of the front door of St. Pat's. "They went thataway."

Danny went back through the gym, made a motion to Tess like, one sec, pushed through the double doors that took him into the foyer, where all the glass doors were like a giant window facing out toward the front steps, and the parking lot.

Danny ducked over by the machine that dispensed bottled water, so they wouldn't see him.

They meaning Ty and Mr. Ross.

The two of them were on the top step in the cold, Mr. Ross doing all the talking. You could see his breath in the air between him and Ty, coming out of him in bursts, like machine-gun fire.

His face looked like the kind of clenched fist you made when you were looking to throw a punch, not tap somebody five.

Danny could see that as clear as day. He also noticed for the first time — he'd been too wrapped up in the game before to look past the game — that Ty didn't have his cast on his wrist anymore, just had it wrapped in an Ace bandage the color of his skin.

Good hand and bad hand, both at his sides, Ty stood there helpless while his father talked to him. Talked *at* him. Danny couldn't hear what he was saying through the thick doors, but could feel Mr. Ross's voice even in here, the way you could sometimes feel the beat of loud rap music from the car next to you.

Occasionally Mr. Ross would poke Ty in the chest.

Finally Ty couldn't take any more of what Mr. Ross was dishing out and started to cry.

Danny wanted to look away, this was the last thing he wanted to see. But he couldn't.

For a moment, Mr. Ross didn't say anything. Danny could just see his chest rising and falling, as if he had tired himself out.

It was then that Danny saw Mrs. Ross standing at the bottom of the steps. Maybe she said something to them, because Ty turned and saw her, too.

When he tried to leave, took just one step in his mom's direction, Mr. Ross grabbed his arm, turned him back around.

Then a pretty amazing thing happened:

Ty Ross shook him off, like his dad was just another defender who couldn't guard him, and walked down the steps to where his mom was waiting for him.

She touched him on the shoulder, still glaring up at her husband, and then she turned away and walked with Ty across the lot to where her red station wagon was parked.

The beginning of the end, that's the way Danny would think of the scene later.

Tess, who loved to play with words, said it was actually the end of the beginning.

Her description, they both decided, was more accurate.

They won again the next day against Seekonk, the team they'd beaten for their first win, in a game that now seemed to have been played when they were all in the fifth grade.

They were ahead by so much at halftime that Danny went with both O'Brien twins — at the same time, a first — for the entire second half, even though both of them were complaining by the middle of the fourth quarter that they were more tired than they usually got after sleepovers.

Three wins now for the Warriors, who'd started out thinking they weren't going to beat anybody.

One game to go, a rematch with Hanesboro, before the playoffs.

Maybe, Danny had started to think, they had finally turned into what they were supposed to be, what Richie Walker had talked about the very first time they were all together, the team nobody wanted to play.

Then Matt Fitzgerald's bad cold somehow turned into full-blown pneumonia and he ended up in the hospital.

Will called with the news, saying he didn't want Danny to read all about it in an IM box.

"Who do we call about ordering up some size?" Will said.

Danny told him he'd been asking himself that question his whole life.

Danny had three IM boxes going on his screen as he talked to Will: Will's, Tess's, Colby's.

"I would like to make one other observation," Will said.

"What?"

"Turns out it's a small world after all," Will said.

"You can't help yourself, can you?" Danny said.

"Other people say I *need* help," Will said, and then said he was getting off, if any other brilliant thoughts popped into his head, he'd send them along by e-mail. But not before adding, "Don't worry, you'll think of something."

Danny took down Will's box and Colby's.

Just him and Tess now.

Just the way he liked it.

CROSSOVER2: Matt's got pneumonia
and I'm the one who feels sick.

Her response didn't take long.

What did they used to say in the *Superman*
cartoons? Tess Hewitt was faster than a
speeding bullet.

CONTESSA44: You'll come up with a
plan.
CROSSOVER2: You sound like Will.
CONTESSA44: That is a cruel and heart-
less thing to say.

He looked out the window and saw a wet
snow starting to fall, the worst kind; if he
didn't shovel it right away around the
basket, it would be slippier than a hockey
rink out there before he knew it.

CROSSOVER2: I need a secret weapon.
When was the last time you
played center?
CONTESSA44: We're not that desperate
yet.
CROSSOVER 2: Getting there.
CONTESSA44: You don't need me.

Sometimes you had to let your guard
down, put yourself out there, not try to

be so much of a guy.

Which meant telling somebody the truth.

CROSSOVER2: I always need you.
CONTESSA44: I know. And back at you,
    by the way.

Before he could think of something
clever that would lighten up the mood, not
let things stay too serious, she was back at
him.

CONTESSA44: YOU'RE our secret
    weapon. 'Nite.

He left the computer on while he washed
his face and brushed his teeth, then went
down to say good night to his mom, who
had propped up a bunch of pillows and
had a blanket over her and was reading in
her favorite spot in front of the fire.

When he came back up to his room, he
heard the old doodlely-doo from the computer.

Incoming. Tess?

He walked over and stared at the message on the screen.

What?

He sat down in his swivel chair, closed
his eyes, opened them, stared at the screen

again, just to make sure it wasn't some kind of weird figment of his imagination.

It wasn't.

Then Danny Walker, knowing his mom would think he was a crazy person if she walked in on him, sat there and laughed his head off.

Will Stoddard *was* insane.

But he sure wasn't alone.

The Warriors beat Hanesboro the next morning, even without Matt Fitzgerald, mostly because Colby Danes had the game of her life, scoring twenty points and, according to ace statistician Tess Hewitt, grabbing fourteen rebounds.

Tess also pointed out after the game that Danny'd had twelve assists.

"You don't know how to keep assists," he said.

"I'm going to forget I heard *that*," she said. "First you act like I can't keep track of time-outs, something my cat could do. Now this ugly charge."

"You really know what an assist is?"

"When it all gets too complicated for me," she said, "I find a big hunky boy and ask him to explain whether that was a pass I just saw, or some kind of unidentified flying object."

Danny said, "I should drop this now, right?"

"I would."

Danny and Tess stayed at St. Pat's doing homework after the Hanesboro game, eating the lunches their moms had packed for them. When they were done with lunch they walked back to the gym to watch the Vikings play Piping Rock in the game that would determine which one of them finished first in the league.

He also wanted to see the new kid on the Vikings Ty had told him about. David Rodriguez, his name was, a five-eight kid from the Bronx who had been born in San Juan and whose family had moved to Middletown three days before. According to Ty, the dad was a policeman and had gotten tired of working for the New York police, and had up and taken a job on the small Middletown force.

"I only watched him at the end of one practice, when I went over to try shooting around a little bit," Ty had said. "I think the Knicks could use this guy."

David Rodriguez was even taller than Matt Fitzgerald and, without Ty in the lineup, the fastest kid on the Vikings as soon as he took his warm-ups off. Mr. Ross didn't put him into the game until the start of the second quarter, but Danny only had to watch him for two minutes to know he was the best center in town now, better than Jack Harty, better than Matt.

Great, Danny thought, just what the Vikings needed:

More size.

They hadn't just added a player, they had added a *New York City* player.

"Why couldn't he go to St. Pat's?" Danny said. "Then I could have recruited him."

"He is pretty good," Tess said.

"Only if you like a tall guy who plays like a little guy," Danny said. "I hear they call him Da-Rod. As in A-Rod."

"Who's A-Rod?" Tess said.

"Only the best baseball player in the world."

"One sport at a time, pal," Tess said, "one sport at a time."

They were sitting at the very top of the bleachers the janitors rolled out when there was enough of a crowd; the old-fashioned wood bleachers stretched from foul line to foul line. And as good as the game between the Vikings and Piping Rock turned out to be, Danny found himself watching Mr. Ross as much as he did the players. Figuring that if he studied him he could finally come up with an answer about why twelve-year-old travel basketball — *winning* at twelve-year-old travel basketball — seemed to mean so much to him.

And the more Danny watched him, and watched the dad coaching Piping Rock, the more he kept coming back to the same question:

Why were they even doing this?

It wasn't that either one of them was a screamer once the game had started; neither one of them was shouting at the players very much, or the refs. Danny didn't see either one of them really lose his temper one single time, even though they made plenty of faces every time somebody on the court did something wrong.

It was just that neither one of them seemed to be having any fun.

They looked like they were *working*.

Without even getting near each other, or really looking at each other, Danny still got the idea that they were competing against each other. It was like watching a college game on ESPN sometimes, at least until he couldn't take it anymore and had to turn the sound off. Even if it was a game he really, really wanted to see. Because the more he listened to the announcers, the more he started to get the idea that it was

344

Coach Kryzyzewski of Duke competing against Coach Williams of North Carolina instead of the Blue Devils going against the Tar Heels.

He always came back to what his dad constantly drummed into his head:

It was a players' game.

It just didn't come across that way on television, at least not often enough.

It sure wasn't that way here.

The two dads were coaching so fiercely, they were *missing* a great game.

And it *was* great, back and forth the whole second half, guys on both teams making plays, some of the plays so good Danny couldn't believe his eyes sometimes. He couldn't remember a single time in the game when either team was ahead by more than four points. The game was so great Danny understood now what Ty had been going through all season, sitting there watching while everybody else got to play.

Even though Danny had been dragging at the end of the Hanesboro game, he wanted to get back out there all over again, mix it up with these guys.

A game like this always made you want to get your sneaks back on.

The Vikings should have been having a ball playing in a game this good, the level of play this high, the top seed in the tournament riding on it. But they weren't. Even when one of them, Jack Harty on Da-Rod or Daryll Mullins or the hated Moron Moran, would do something nice and get their team a basket, Mr. Ross would be up almost before the ball was through the net, like he'd been shot up out of a James Bond–type ejector seat, telling them where to go on defense, what to do next.

They all seemed like they were afraid to enjoy doing something right, because in the very next moment they might be doing something wrong.

The Vikings gave Piping Rock a run, all the way to when Jack Harty's shot fell off the rim at the end of overtime and Piping Rock won, 49–48.

The Vikings, without Ty, without Andy Mayne still, had lost, but Danny knew they were the better team, especially with Da-Rod in the house now.

They just didn't seem to be having much fun.

How did Will put it?

The Vikings were a no-mirth zone.

"I don't want to be with them anymore," he said to Tess when the game was over. "The Vikings, I mean."

"I can see why," she said.

It had taken almost the entire season, but he finally knew he was with the right team, after all.

The setup for the first round of the tournament was pretty basic, the number-one seed playing number eight, number two playing number seven, and so on. The teams with the better records got to play home games. Seekonk, for example, which had finished in eighth place, had to go to Piping Rock. The Vikings, at number two, also got a home game, at St. Pat's, but home court didn't matter very much to them, because it was going to be Middletown versus Middletown. They were playing the number-seven Warriors, one o'clock, the following Saturday afternoon.

The Warriors' last practice before the play-offs, the Warriors minus Matt Fitzgerald, would be on Tuesday night. Their last full practice, anyway. Danny still planned to get the key guys together at his house the next night.

That included Colby Danes, who was officially one of the guys now, even if Will Stoddard certainly didn't think of her quite that way.

Colby liked Will as much as he liked her,

at least according to Tess. It didn't change the fact that she was the only person Danny knew about who could cause Will's mouth to malfunction on a fairly regular basis.

The fact that he was able to concentrate on basketball when the two of them were playing basketball together was a minor miracle.

Tess would be at the meeting, too. Danny couldn't believe they had even tried having a team without her.

And his mom, who had come up so big, the last few days, especially.

"Point Mom," is what she'd started calling herself.

"*Point* Mom?" Danny said.

"Don't worry," she said, "I've got the lingo down now."

This was on Tuesday, Ali Walker driving Danny over to St. Pat's before going over to the hospital to visit his dad. Mrs. Stoddard had volunteered to be the team mom for tonight while Danny ran practice.

"Truth or dare," he said to his mom from the backseat.

"Truth."

"Can we really do this?"

They were in front of the gym, the engine idling, the heat going full blast. Ali

Walker turned to face him. "It's like I've been telling you your whole life," she said. "You can do just about anything you set your mind to."

"I set my mind on making the Vikings," Danny said. "How'd that work out for me?"

"I never said it was a one hundred percent foolproof plan," she said. "But it's still a darn good one. And you know it."

She faced front, but he could see her smiling, her reflection in the windshield lit by the dashboard lights.

Danny vaguely remembered some old song she liked to sing along to that had "dashboard light" in it. Another one of her oldies but goodies.

"As far as I'm concerned," she said, "this all worked out the way it was supposed to."

Then she told him to scoot, his team was waiting for him.

The next night. Wednesday.

The small team meeting was over, the minipractice in the driveway had ended, the ice cream sundaes had been consumed by the unlikely group of kids and moms in the Walker kitchen.

Tess was the last to leave. Her parents had gone to the movies, then called to ask if it was all right if she stayed there a little longer while they stopped and had a quick bite at Fierro's.

Tess and Danny sat on the two seats in the backyard swing set Ali Walker said she hadn't taken down because she was never taking it down. It was cold out and getting colder by the minute, but neither one of them cared.

"Tonight, I finally figured out why you love it out here so much," she said. "I mean, on your own private court."

Danny said, "I'm just trying to get better, is all."

"It's more than that and you know it,

Daniel Walker," Tess said. "This is your own little basketball world back here, and nobody can screw things up."

"My mom says it's my own private Madison Square Garden."

"More like a *magic* garden, if you ask me."

She reached over and took his hand out of the big front pocket of his hooded sweatshirt, and held it in her own hand. It made Danny feel as if he'd put a glove on.

They stayed that way for a minute and then, because neither one of them seemed to know how long you were supposed to hold hands, she let him go.

They kept rocking.

"It's a *really* nice world back here," Tess said.

"You always know what to say," Danny said. "What would you call this? The quiet before the storm?"

"Works for me."

"Whatever happens, we're gonna give Middletown basketball a day it's never going to forget," Danny said.

"Like in your dad's day," she said.

"Not that big a day," Danny said. "Nothing will ever be that big around here ever again."

They went back to rocking in silence.

Danny put his head back and stared at the stars. And suddenly, because Tess Hewitt was always full of surprises, because Danny knew in his heart, even at the age of twelve, that she would be full of surprises as long as the two of them knew each other — which he roughly hoped would be forever — she leaned over and kissed him on the cheek.

"Don't be so sure it won't be that big, little guy," she said.

It was all right for her, calling him little guy.

Because when he was with her like this, Danny felt like the biggest guy in town.

When he heard the Hewitts' car in front, he walked Tess up the driveway, told her he'd see her tomorrow at school, then went back inside.

His mom was holding the phone out for him as soon as he got through the front door.

"Your father," she said.

Danny put his hand over the mouthpiece. "Isn't it a little late for him to be up?"

"He has some trouble sleeping sometimes, at least until the pills kick in."

She pointed toward the phone. "Talk,"

she said. "My two big talkers."

Danny took the phone with him up the stairs, saying, "Yo."

Which he'd never say to his mom.

"Hey, bud."

He went into his room, turned on the light next to his bed, adjusted the shade so it shined up on John Stockton like a spotlight, lay down on his back staring up at it.

Waiting for his dad to say something now, on the other end of the phone.

Some parts of it between them, Danny knew, would never change. Even lately, with so much to talk about, they'd sit there in the hospital room with nothing but air between them.

Sometimes Danny compared the two of them starting a conversation to his mom trying to get her car engine to start up on one of these cold mornings.

"Well," his dad said.

"Well."

"Here you are."

He sounded a little groggy. Danny had been with him a few times when the sleeping pills started to work, and it was like somebody had hit his dad with a knockout punch.

"No," Danny said. "Here *we* are."

"Nice try, bud. But it's all you now."

"I wouldn't even have a game tomorrow if you hadn't come back when you did," Danny said. "And did what you did starting the team."

Another long pause.

"Yeah, yeah, yeah."

Which sounded more to Danny like: Lose the nerdy-weepy crap.

Danny didn't know what to say, so he didn't say anything until his dad said, "Anyway, I was just calling to wish you luck. I told your mom not to stop by tomorrow, they've got a bunch of tests they want to run. And they're going to put a smaller cast on my leg so I can get around a little better. Unless, of course, they decide they want to run me into the chop shop again."

"The Vikings are really good," Danny said, "even without Ty."

"Big . . . frigging deal. You guys are better than ever."

"I don't know."

"Well, guess what? You better damn well know by tomorrow." Coming alive a little bit. Cracking the whip.

"Okay?" his dad said.

"Okay."

"Hey, bud?"

"Yeah?"

"Get after it tomorrow, every minute you're out there," he said. "On account of, you never know which day is gonna be the best day of your whole life."

The next thing Danny heard was a dial tone.

He shut off the phone, looked over at the clock next to his bed. Ten-fifteen.

Talking to his dad had made him want to play a little more before he went to bed.

He didn't have to change, because he still had his sweatshirt on. He figured that if it wasn't okay with his mom, going back out at this time of night, she'd come right outside and tell him once she heard the bounce of the ball.

He grabbed the Infusion ball from under his desk.

Slipped out the back door and switched the lights back on.

Warmed up by shooting a few from the outside.

Made a little tricky-dribble move and then put up the shot he'd missed against Hanesboro in the first game, made at the end of the Kirkland game.

Nothing but net.

Feeling jazzed now, as if the night were just beginning, with all his dreams, and schemes.

Andy Mayne's ankle was all better. He'd be playing tomorrow, at least according to Ty, which meant Danny would be going up against a point guard just as good as he was, and a lot bigger.

Nothing new with the part about bigger.

He thought to himself: Bring it on, Colorado boy.

He was ready to play the game right here, right now.

He stepped back until he was about twenty feet away from the basket, tried the double crossover a couple of times, back and forth, not putting the ball too low, just fooling around with it.

Then he was ready to try it for real, imagining he needed it to split Andy Mayne and another defender in the Vikings' press, get himself into the open court in the last minute of the game.

Or even the last ten seconds.

Left hand, right hand.

Then the same move again, just slower this time.

Ready to make his move, right out of the last dribble, his body nearly as low to the ground as the ball.

He made his move, between the imaginary defenders, exploding at the basket like a toy rocket taking off.

And slipped as he did.

Slipped on the patch of black ice he didn't know was there, his feet going straight out from under him like he'd slipped on a banana peel in a comic strip, flying backward through the air without even a dope like Teddy Moran around to break his fall.

He didn't tell his mom about his shoulder in the morning. He wasn't going to tell anybody about his shoulder, as sore as it was. He didn't like tennis too much, it wasn't his favorite, but sometimes when one of the big tournaments was on, he liked to listen to John McEnroe. And one time during the U.S. Open, he'd heard McEnroe talking about what some old Australian guy had told him about injuries when McEnroe was a junior player.

"If you're hurt," McEnroe said, "you don't play. If you play, you're not hurt."

He was playing, case closed.

Even though he did want to call his dad and ask him if they made junior pain pills, preferably chewable.

He took a longer shower than usual, letting the hot water beat on his shoulder as long as possible. When he came downstairs, his mom was in the living room.

There was a big box in the middle of the floor.

"Whatcha got?" he said.

"Take a look for yourself."

They were white basketball jerseys, packed in a zipped-up plastic bag. He unzippered the bag, and pulled one out.

"Middletown" was in blue letters on the back, above the numbers.

"From your father's team," she said.

"No *way!*"

"Way."

"Was this Dad's idea?"

"Nah," she said, "this one came from the old point mom."

The second jersey Danny pulled out of the plastic bag was Richie Walker's Number 3.

Danny tried it on, careful pulling it over his head, knowing that if his face showed any pain, his mom would pounce; he tried not to even think about the shoulder, worried about her mutant mind-reading powers.

His dad's Number 3 fit him as if he'd special-ordered it out of a little-guy catalogue. He didn't have to tuck half of it into the sweats he was wearing right now, didn't lose half of the "3" in the front.

Didn't feel like Stuart Little.

It fit him like a dream.

He looked at his mom. "How . . . ?"

"From Mrs. Hayes. After Mr. Hayes died."

There hadn't been a dad coaching Middletown travel when Richie Walker's team had won the national championship. Their coach had been a local basketball legend named Morgan Hayes, who'd coached basketball at Middletown High until being forced to retire at the age of seventy.

Danny said, "Dad always said Coach Hayes knew more about basketball than any coach he ever had after that."

"I think the only reason Coach Hayes ever agreed to come out of retirement," Ali Walker said, "I mean back then, was because he knew how special your father was, and he was a little sad he wasn't going to be able to coach him in high school."

His mom went on to say that after Mr. Hayes died three years ago, his wife found this box in their basement. In those days, his mom said, the kids didn't get to keep the uniforms when the season was over, they went back to Middletown Basketball. But they'd allowed Morgan Hayes to keep these uniforms because his Vikings had won the title.

"Of course your father had left . . . town by then," his mom said. "But somehow I couldn't bring myself to throw these uniforms away. There wasn't any Middletown Basketball Hall of Fame I could give them to. So I just kept them in the basement."

She looked at Danny. "I think you should wear them today," she said.

He went over and put out his fist. She put on a face that had some attitude in it, like she was saying *uh-huh,* and tapped it with her own.

"*Very* cool idea," he said to his mom. "You think they have any magic in them?"

"The Vikings won't know what these uniforms mean. But you guys will."

They took the rest of the uniforms out of the box and folded them neatly. Danny said they could pass them out when everybody was at St. Pat's. When they finished their folding, the two of them were still kneeling on the floor, facing each other. His mom took his hands.

Don't pull too hard, he thought. *Please.*

"What started out with the worst day of your whole life is going to end up with the best," she said.

"Promise?"

"Cross my heart."

"Everything's all right with the league?"

"We sent over the new and improved Daniel Walker Play-off Roster yesterday."

The doorbell rang then. Danny knew who it was.

More perfect timing between them.

Same as on the court.

He ran over and opened the front door for Ty and Mrs. Ross.

"Wait till you see what my mom has," Danny said, not even bothering with hello or good morning. "The uniforms my dad's team wore!" Danny caught himself. "And your dad's team, too."

Ty said, "Cool."

"Well," Ali Walker said from behind Danny. "Good morning to the newest member of the Warriors."

" 'Morning, Mrs. Walker," Ty Ross said.

Lily Ross said to Ali, "He wanted to go to the game with Danny."

Ali said, "Things any better at home?"

Lily Ross shrugged. "I told my husband at breakfast what I've been telling him all week: It's just a basketball game. And it's a game that was never supposed to be about him in the first place." She pointed toward Danny and Ty, already moving into the living room, Danny asking Ty what number he wanted to wear. "It's about them."

Danny and Ty raced for the uniforms

then, Ty telling him he wanted to see if Number 1 would fit him.

The whole thing had been Ty's idea.

He had IM'd Danny the night after Mr. Ross called him out in front of the gym after the Kirkland game. It was the last message Danny had gotten before he went to bed.

TYBREAK1: I want to play with you guys.

Always a man of few words.
Like Richie Walker.

Danny remembered sitting there at his desk and laughing his head off, just at the craziness of it.

CROSSOVER2: You CANNOT be serious!

Another McEnroe line.

TYBREAK1: I wouldn't be quitting something. You can't quit something you never started.
CROSSOVER2: Can you? Play with us, I mean.
TYBREAK1: My mom says yes.

Moms rule, Danny thought.

Trying to slow down his brain from going a hundred miles an hour.

CROSSOVER2: Don't tell anybody yet.
TYBREAK1: That include Tess?

Danny smiled to himself that night. Everybody knew who the real boss was.

CROSSOVER2: First I want to talk to my mom. Then have her talk to your mom.
TYBREAK1: Deal.
CROSSOVER2: Dude?
TYBREAK1: Yeah?
CROSSOVER2: We are gonna rock their world.

He'd had to keep it a secret for more than a week, from Will and Tess and everybody, the longest he'd ever kept a secret his whole life. Because once the moms got involved — the conspiracy of moms, is what Ali Walker called it — they wanted Danny and Ty to take some time, think things through.

Danny knew that Ty and Mrs. Ross had finally told Mr. Ross the Tuesday night before the play-offs, while the Warriors were practicing at St. Pat's. Ty said on the phone that night that his dad had hit the roof, got as mad as he'd ever seen him, which pretty much meant as mad as anybody had ever gotten.

But then, he said, something awesome had happened:

Ty's mom had sat there across from him at the kitchen table when all the yelling stopped and then — Ty's words — totally dominated him.

Mrs. Ross hit Mr. Ross with what she called his "little recruiting trip," the one where he'd tried to get Danny to join the Vikings. She hit him with the scene between Mr. Ross and Ty after the Kirkland game.

Mr. Ross had finally looked at Ty and asked how he could turn his back on his own team?

"It was never my team, Dad," Ty had told him. "It was always your team. I didn't feel like I was part of anybody's team till I helped Danny coach."

And that, Ty said, was pretty much that.

Danny thinking to himself: Maybe *Mrs.* Ross was the biggest guy in Middletown now.

The next night, Danny couldn't have gotten their full squad, plus Ty, together even if he'd wanted to. Though he didn't mind very much that he couldn't. Michael Harden had tutoring, the O'Brien twins had to go watch their younger sister's ballet recital, and Oliver Towne had gone to a Knicks game with his neighbors, even though it was a school night. Danny had everybody else in his driveway, walking Ty through the Warriors' basic plays with Colby, Will, and Bren.

Tess even came over, pretending she was the center.

When they went inside for ice cream afterward, Mrs. Ross having shown up by then to pick up Ty, they all agreed to keep Ty joining the team a secret for a couple more days, until they made absolutely sure it was all right with the league, a kid switching teams this way, this late in the season. But both Danny's mom and Ty's mom were confident it was going to be all right, since Ty had never even played a league game for the Vikings.

Even if his dad coached the team.

That night in the kitchen Lily Ross said, "It's funny, I was never interested in being a team mom until it was somebody else's team."

Ali Walker said, "It's about time."

Lily Ross said, "I was watching them from the car before. Our sons should have been together all along."

It was agreed that Danny would tell the rest of the Warriors on Saturday morning. Telling a couple of blabberfaces like the O'Brien twins any sooner would have been like hiring one of those sky-writers you saw flying over the beach in the summer.

Now it was Saturday morning.

Danny wearing Number 3 in white, Ty wearing Number 1.

They looked at each other in the living room, then both of them rolled their eyes.

Ty said, "This is nuts."

Like, *sick*, Danny told him.

They went upstairs to send out an instant-message to the rest of the Warriors, telling them that they'd added a pretty decent player for the big game.

Danny took them into his mom's class-room and passed out the uniforms there, once everybody was done high-fiving Ty and pounding him on the back as if he'd made his first three shots of the game.

The guys thought the old-school uni-forms were even cooler than some of the old-school NBA uniforms their parents could order for them online. Tess was the only one frowning, saying she wasn't thrilled that the blue trim on the jerseys really didn't match up with the blue of the Warriors' shorts.

Danny looked at her as if she'd grown another perfect nose.

"I'm just making a fashion statement, is all," she said.

Danny said, "I'll take the hit on the blue thing."

Colby went outside to change into her Number 4. When she came back in, she twirled around and said, "How do I look?"

"Let's ask Will," Danny said, feeling good enough about the day to bust his best friend a little on Colby.

Will playfully gave him a slap on the back, catching Danny right where he'd landed on the ice. Danny couldn't help himself, he bent over as if Will had hit him from behind with an aluminum baseball bat.

They were off to the side from everybody else, so only Will noticed how much pain Danny was in.

"Dude," Will said, "what's *that* about?"

"I fell last night in the driveway," Danny whispered. "But don't say anything to anybody, okay?"

"I'd say I've got your back," Will said, "but that doesn't seem like such a hot idea." Now he managed a whisper. "Can you really play?"

"I never could go to my left, anyway."

Will said, "You go to your left better than any right-hander in town."

"What is this," Danny said, "a practice debate in Miss Kimmet's class?"

There was still a lot of loud, excited chatter in the room when Danny tried — in vain — to get their attention, the way he had at practice that first night. When he couldn't get anybody's attention, he caught Tess's eye, shook his head in resignation, and put two fingers to his lips.

She did her whistle thing, and the room quieted like it did when any teacher walked into any classroom. Even Mrs. Ross and Mrs. Stoddard stopped gabbing over in the corner.

Danny said, "They're gonna want to wipe the floor with us, you all know that, right?"

There were nods all around. "You got that right," somebody said.

"They would've wanted to do that even before Ty joined up with us, because they don't think we're even supposed to be *on* the same floor with them. But now it's gonna be like the Civil War of Middletown or something."

He saw Will take a step forward, start to say something, then stop when Tess and

Mrs. Stoddard both threatened him with pinching motions at the same time.

Danny said, "You guys all know how much I hate making speeches. So I'm just gonna say this: Let's do what my dad told us we might be able to do back at the beginning."

They were all staring at him.

"Even though it's only the first round of the play-offs," he said, "let's see if we can win the championship of all guys like us who ever got told they weren't good enough."

They charged out of Mrs. Walker's classroom and down the hall, running as hard as you did on the last day of school, just running this time toward the first round of the play-offs.

Running, really, at the top of their lungs.

When the Vikings took the court, Danny was positive they'd grown somehow since last Saturday. Da-Rod Rodriguez in particular looked even taller on the court than he had from the top row of the bleachers.

Andy Mayne had his right ankle taped up so high you could see the white bandage above his high-top black Iversons, but that didn't catch Danny's eye as much as this:

He seemed to have grown more than the inch that Danny had grown since October.

The Warriors had come through the door next to the stage, so they didn't have to pass the Vikings to start warming up at the stage end of St. Pat's. That meant they didn't have to pass Mr. Ross, either; he was standing under the basket at the opposite end, arms folded, watching the Vikings shoot layups as if that was maybe the most fascinating thing that would ever happen to him.

When the Warriors got into their own layup line, Danny heard the loudest pregame cheer they'd ever gotten, and that's when he noticed how full the bleachers already were. Down at the corner of them, directly across from the Vikings' basket, was a television cameraman, and the guy who did the sports on Channel 14, the local all-news channel.

After all the *hey-little-guy* taunts in his life, he had to admit this was pretty big stuff.

Maybe that's why his heart was beating as fast as it was.

Tess was standing near the row of folding chairs that served as the Warriors' bench. She was staring straight at him, and when she started to bring her hand up,

Danny was terrified she might blow him a kiss. But she did something even better, something that got him revved a little more.

She made a fist with her right hand and pumped it a couple of times.

He went right back at her with a fist-pump of his own.

Mr. Harden, Danny saw now, was right behind her. Michael said he'd been able to fly back from Florida because it was a weekend, but that he planned to sit in the stands and let Danny and Ali Walker and Tess Hewitt just keep doing what they were doing.

Danny got out of the layup line for a second to run over and shake his hand and thank him for coming.

"Just keep on keepin' on," Mr. Harden said to him.

"Huh?"

"Something people used to say —"

"— back in the day?" Danny said.

"One of those," Mr. Harden said.

Before he went back on the court, Danny asked if his mom was anywhere around and Mr. Harden said he hadn't seen her. Mrs. Ross had driven Danny and Will to the game, but Ali Walker had said she'd be right behind them.

"I'm sure she's here somewhere," Michael's dad said, before adding, "take it right to these guys from the jump."

Danny took the Warriors out of the layup line and started the "Carolina" drill they always did before practices and games, two lines under the basket, everybody seeming to move at once, passing, shooting, rebounding, all of them in a pretty neat formation.

When Danny noticed that the clock showed seven minutes and counting until the start of the game, he told the Warriors to get the rest of the balls and just start shooting around.

Will came out near half-court and stood next to him. "This is, like, *ill*, dude," Will said.

Danny said, "I think I'm the one who's going to be sick."

"How's your shoulder?"

"Don't feel a thing," Danny lied.

A ball bounced away from Steven O'Brien and Danny went to retrieve it. He reached down, stood up, and before he could pass it back to Steven found himself face-to-face with Teddy Moran.

"If it isn't Coach Mini-Me," Teddy said, his face looking, as always, like he'd just smelled some rotten milk.

"Teddy," Danny said. He whipped the ball toward Steven and started to walk away and Teddy grabbed his right hand, smiling as he did so. To anyone watching, this didn't look like anything more than a Viking wishing a Warrior luck.

"You didn't steal enough of our players to win the game," Teddy said.

"You have a good game, too," Danny said.

"Tell Ty Ross to watch himself today."

Danny smiled back at him now. "He's right there, tough guy. Why don't you go tell him yourself?"

"Yeah, right," Teddy said.

"You Morans," Danny said. "You sure do have a way with words."

He was walking with his back to the Vikings' basket when he heard the gym go quiet, except for the bounce of all the balls, as if somebody had found a way to turn down just the crowd noise.

He turned around and saw his mom just inside the middle door to the gym.

Next to her, one crutch under his right arm, the left one up in the air a little bit as he tried to balance on his new cast, was Richie Walker.

Danny knew that most of the people in this crowd knew who his dad was, and knew about the accident. Suddenly, they started to applaud.

Danny wanted to run to his dad, right through the Vikings, but caught himself, and started to walk toward him instead.

Richie Walker saw, shook his head, grinned. Then, looking pretty nimble for a guy on crutches, he picked the left crutch all the way off the ground and pointed it at Danny.

Then he mouthed one word: Play.

This time Danny understood him without any words at all.

"He's okay to do this?" Danny said when his mom came over.

They'd set his dad up with two folding chairs at the end of the bleachers, at the stage end. One for him to sit on, one to rest the cast on.

"Just don't go diving for any loose balls over there," his mom said.

"He'd said they were doing more stuff today."

"He lied, except for the part about the new cast, which they put on yesterday," she said. "If the doctors hadn't said okay, I would have had to bust him out."

"He can come over and coach, if he wants."

"He said you're the coach."

The horn had sounded, meaning they were about to start. Danny huddled his teammates up, knelt down in the middle of the circle, took a deep breath, and just started rattling stuff off. Who was going to start. That he was going to bring Ty off the

376

bench sometime in the first quarter, depending on how the game was going. Will and Oliver, almost at the same time, said Ty could start in place of them. Danny started to say something but Ty cut him off, saying they'd decided he should come off the bench, fit in that way.

And, he said, he could be a bench coach when he was on the bench.

Danny said, "I'm all out of pregame speeches. Anybody got any bright ideas?"

Will Stoddard, looking serious for a change, as if he'd left the class clown back in Mrs. Walker's classroom, said, "I do."

He looked down at Danny. "You're the biggest kid here," he said. "I just thought somebody needed to say that."

The Warriors responded to that by jumping up and down and going *woof woof woof,* like somebody'd let the dogs out.

Danny remembered what his dad had said, and decided to steal the line for himself.

"You never know what day might turn out to be the best day of your whole life," he said.

He gave them all a no-biggie shrug.

He said, "How about we make it today?"

The Vikings started Da-Rod, Jack Harty, Teddy Moran, Andy Mayne, and Daryll Mullins. Danny went with himself, Colby, Bren, Will, and Oliver Towne. Right before they had broken the huddle, Ty had said to Danny, "When you make it a triangle-and-two against Da-Rod, tell them to pack the triangle in tight."

Danny smiled. "I was hoping they'd allow us to use a triangle-and-four."

It was 8–4, Vikings, after four minutes.

Danny had made the first basket of the game, sneaking behind Da-Rod Rodriguez and breaking away for a layup. Then Da-Rod, who was already giving Oliver Towne fits — Danny having Oliver try to shadow him — made three straight for the Vikings.

Colby came back with a bomb from the corner, right near where Richie Walker was sitting, that made him pound one of his crutches on the floor.

Daryll Mullins came right back for the Vikings, streaking down the lane and going up so high over Colby that Danny pictured him actually dunking the sucker for a second.

They got a whistle when the ball went skipping through a door that wasn't closed all the way. When they did, Danny motioned for Ty to go to the scorer's table and come in for Oliver.

"You take the big guy," Danny said.

Ty smiled, just because he was back in the game. "My pleasure," he said.

"You get tired, you tell me," Danny said.

Ty said, "I'm rested enough."

They tapped fists.

Ty went over and stood with Will now, while the refs reset the clock, which had kept running when the ball had disappeared through the door.

Danny couldn't help himself, he looked over at Mr. Ross, who was staring across the court to where Ty and Will were, Ty laughing now at something Will had just said.

Danny thought he'd look mad, but he didn't. There was something else on his face, not a smile, just this curious kind of look.

Tony the ref blew his whistle, meaning they were finally ready to go.

Mr. Ross stood up then and said, "Could you wait a second, Tony?"

His voice sounded loud in the gym.

He leaned down and whispered something to Daryll Mullins's dad, Daryll Senior, his assistant coach. Then he reached down next to his chair and handed Daryll Senior his clipboard.

Then he waved for the Vikings to come over real fast, and now he was the one kneeling in a circle of players, talking and pointing.

Now he was smiling. Tony the ref came over and Mr. Ross put a hand on his shoulder and leaned close to his ear.

Then Mr. Ross folded up his folding chair and walked diagonally across the court toward the bleachers. And then Ty's dad did something even more amazing than leaving the bench.

He went over to where Richie Walker was and reached down and shook his hand and unfolded his chair and got ready to watch the rest of the game from over there.

As great as Ty Ross was at basketball, as easy as he'd made it look from the time Danny first played with him in fifth-grade travel, he didn't have superhuman powers. So he looked rusty on offense from the start, missing his first three shots, even turning the ball over a couple of times. He was giving Da-Rod Rodriguez all he wanted at the other end of the court, though, even keeping him off the boards, outsmarting him time after time when the ball was in the air and beating him to the right spot under the basket.

But even if everybody else didn't know how much he was pressing on offense, Danny could see it as clean as day.

It wasn't until the last minute of the first quarter, a fast break, that Ty showed everybody in the gym just who it was they were watching, and reminded Danny — who really didn't need much reminding — why he'd wanted to hoop with Ty Ross in the first place.

Will came up with a long rebound, beating Teddy Moran to the ball because Teddy had stood there waiting for it to come to him. The Vikings, sure Teddy was going to come up with the ball and keep them on offense, relaxed for just a second. By then, Will had passed the ball to Danny.

Ty, who could always see a play happening about five seconds before it happened, took off for the other end of the court.

Jack Harty had gotten back on defense, maybe because he'd never expected Teddy Moran to hustle after a ball.

Danny came from his right with the ball, Ty from Jack's left.

Two-on-one.

Danny didn't want to be coming down the left side of the court. His left shoulder was aching constantly now, the way a toothache ached, and he was afraid that if Jack backed off to cover Ty, Danny might have to shoot a left-handed layup.

He wasn't sure at this point that he could even raise his arm high enough.

If he went with his right hand, he was begging Jack to try to block his shot, even if Jack had to get back on Danny in a flash to do it.

Danny was at full speed as he passed the free throw line. Jack backed off to cover Ty. Or so Danny thought.

Jack Harty had suckered him. He only head-faked toward Ty, waited until Danny went into the air, and then came at him with arms that looked as tall as trees and seemed to be everywhere at once.

Danny had already committed himself, was already in the air. But instead of putting up his shot anyway, instead of even trying to raise his left arm, he under-handed the ball — hard — underneath Jack Harty's arms and off the backboard.

It was a pass, not a shot.

It was a pass that caromed perfectly off the top of the backboard, came right to Ty on the other side of the basket, Ty catching it and shooting it in the same motion, not even using the backboard himself, putting up a soft shot that was nothing but net.

Like this was a move they'd spent their whole lives practicing.

Vikings 12, Warriors 10.

Nobody scored from there to the end of the quarter. When they ran off the court after the horn, Danny said to Ty, "Okay, dude, you're back."

"I still can't shoot."

"They'll start to fall."

"How do you know?"

"I know the way I know we're gonna win this game," Danny said.

He stopped Ty, turned him around so he was facing where Richie Walker and Mr. Ross were sitting, Richie pointing toward the Vikings' basket and talking a mile a minute, Mr. Ross nodding his head.

"If *that's* possible," Danny said, "*anything's* possible."

"Good point, point guard," Ty said.

The good news was that they were still only down a basket at halftime.

The bad news — double dose of it — was this:

1. Teddy (the Moron) Moran had accidentally figured out that Danny was hurting.

2. Ty, despite scoring ten points in the second quarter and looking like his old self, had picked up three fouls along the way.

He had three fouls and so did Bren.

So did Colby.

Danny was going to take Ty out of the game after his second foul, but Ty told him not to worry, he could make it to halftime without picking up his third, there being only ninety seconds left, if they went into a straight zone. But the next time the Warriors had the ball, Ty made a move to the basket against Da-Rod, and Teddy Moran came over to help out. Ty didn't see Teddy coming, and barely brushed him as he spun into his move against Da-Rod, but Teddy threw out his arms and flopped backward as if he'd been sideswiped by a truck.

Tony the ref gave him the call.

Offensive foul on Ty.

Third foul. Ten seconds left in the half.

The Vikings gave the ball right back when Andy Mayne got called for stepping over the line when he was trying to in-bound the ball. So the Warriors would get the last shot of the half. The Vikings put a half-baked press on them, Teddy covering Danny. While they were waiting for Tony to hand the ball to Colby, Teddy slapped Danny on the back. Smiling again, like they were practically best buds.

But Teddy had caught him on the spot back there that hurt the most, the exact place where he'd landed last night. Danny couldn't help himself, he yelled out in pain, even getting the attention of Tony the ref, who turned around to see what the problem was.

Danny waved him off.

Like they were just kidding.

"What have we here?" Teddy Moran said quietly.

Then clipped Danny again for good measure, right before Danny broke away so Colby could pass him the ball.

They went out into the hall for halftime the way they had at the Kirkland game, Danny's first as coach. Richie Walker always said that when you had a good routine going, stay with it. So they all had Fruit Punch red Gatorade again. His mom brought the oranges.

There was even more excitement crackling around them now, one half in the books, than there had been before the game.

Because of this:

Because they'd showed they could play with the Vikings.

Danny hadn't dominated Andy Mayne when Andy had been guarding him, not by a long shot. But Andy, despite having the size on Danny, and the strength, had only scored one basket. Danny, on the other hand, had at least six assists, probably more than that.

It was right before halftime when Daryll Senior had decided to switch Teddy Moran over on Danny for a couple of minutes, which had to mean only one thing — he was worried that trying to stay in front of Danny was wearing Andy out.

In the hallway, Danny said, "Everybody on this team is a coach now. Anybody has anything to say, speak up now. On account of, now's the time."

Ty said, "I should sit at the start of the third."

Danny said, "Maybe the whole third, if we can just hang in there."

"Keep it close," Bren Darcy said, "and then bring the big dog back."

"*Bad* dog," Will said.

Then the guys started with *woof woof woof* all over again, so loud Danny knew the people inside the gym could hear them. Maybe the Vikings, too.

Tess looked at them, shaking her head, this disappointed look on her face. "Boys," she said.

Danny stood up.

"Here's the deal, okay? I saw the Vikings play Piping Rock. Piping Rock may have gotten the top seed, but they aren't better than these guys."

"Your point being?" Will said.

"If we beat these guys, we're going to win this tournament," Danny said. "No question."

Ty pointed to the front of his jersey.

"We're number one," he said.

After warm-ups, Ty took the chair closest to where Tess was sitting at the scorer's table. With Robert O'Brien in Ty's place, Danny moved Will to a forward position in the triangle, asking both him and Oliver Towne — asking them as nicely as possible — to somehow prevent Da-Rod from turning into Tim Duncan while Ty was out of the game.

There was another delay before the start of the quarter while the refs checked the clock again. Ali Walker came back from the ladies' room and waved Danny over when she saw which players were on the court.

"Question," she said.

"Shoot."

"We did all this to get Ty to play for us, and now he's not going to play for us?" she said. "Discuss."

"It's like this whole deal, Mom," Danny said. "Don't worry about how things are at the start. Just at the finish."

"Check," she said. "Now gimme five."

He did.

"Hey," Tess said from behind him.

For the first time since he'd known her, she looked nervous. Scared, almost. Looked extremely un-Tess-like.

"You okay?" he said.

"You didn't tell me sports were this hard," Tess said.

"Are you kidding?" he said. "We're just getting to the good parts."

Said the one-armed boy to the tall girl.

Halfway through the quarter, the Vikings had stretched their lead to ten points. Not good. Danny called his first time-out of the half at 28–18, thought hard about bringing Ty back right there, decided to stick to his guns. Telling himself that fourteen points was the cutoff point, if the lead got that big, Ty was coming back in.

He explained all that when they got to the huddle. When he finished, he looked over at Ty and said, "I'm right. Right?"

"Your call," Ty said.

Danny said, "When you come back in — for good — I want you to play full out. We just need somebody to get hot until then."

Will Stoddard and Colby Danes somehow got hot at the exact same time.

It's a terrible thing, Will had always said, for a guy to be hot and not know it. He meant, to not be getting any shots at all. Daryll Mullins had been shutting him down the whole day in the Vikings' man-to-man, but suddenly Will got open for two jumpers. Then another. The Vikings tried to double-team him a couple of times after that, and when they did, Will swung the ball to Danny like a champ, and he made two passes to Colby.

Great passes to Colby, if he did say so himself.

One was a bounce pass that went right through Teddy Moran's fat legs, because that was the only way to make it. The other one was a no-looker to her in the corner.

Both Andy Mayne and Teddy kept trying to overplay him, make him go left, because they'd figured out that was the side bothering him. But he made the passes to Colby after going to his left. Then Will and Colby were both hot, and all the Vikings started paying more attention to them, trying to shut them down until Ty came back.

Missing the point, the way people did all the time about basketball.

He'd always known that everything started with the pass, because that's how everything had started with his dad.

A good pass never cared how big you were.

Or how much your stinking shoulder hurt.

It came down to this:

Vikings 37, Warriors 33.

Three minutes left.

Ty had come back in at the start of the fourth quarter and as soon as he did, Danny set him up for three straight baskets. On the last one he drew Da-Rod over, floated the ball over him like he was putting a kite up in the air, knowing it probably looked like an air ball to everybody watching.

Danny didn't care. He knew that Ty knew it was a pass.

Ty had read Danny's eyes all the way, caught the ball when it came down over Da-Rod Rodriguez, faked Daryll Junior to the moon, put it up and in.

Now they had to find a way to make up those four points in three minutes.

The Warriors hadn't been in the lead since Danny's first basket had made it 2–0. Bren had fouled out by now, and so had Colby. Will was sucking so much wind Danny could hear him breathing every time there was a stop in play.

The whole game, Danny had been telling himself — and the Warriors — they'd find a way to win.

Now he wasn't so sure.

No matter what they did, they couldn't catch up.

Ty scored off a steal from Teddy Moran, who stood and cried to the ref he'd been fouled instead of chasing after Ty, who got a bunny layup.

They were only down a basket. But Jack Harty muscled his way in and scored for the Vikings. Will answered by throwing up a prayer from the corner after he got double-teamed, then acting as if he knew he had it all along.

He ran by Danny, still wheezing a little, and said, "I still got it."

Danny called his second-to-last time-out with a minute and thirty showing on the clock. He wasn't even trying to hide how much his arm hurt by then; when he came running over to the sideline he must have looked like he was carrying some kind of imaginary load on his left shoulder.

He was also tired enough to take a nap.

He told everybody to get a drink. Then they all stood around him. Nobody spoke. All he could hear now was everybody's breathing in what was suddenly a fairly quiet gym at St. Pat's.

Vikings 39, Warriors 37.

Tess handed Danny a Gatorade. Gave him a quick squeeze on his good shoulder. Smiled one of her best smiles at him, just because she seemed to have an endless supply of those.

Ali Walker said, "Just exactly how bad is that shoulder you failed to mention to your sainted mother before the game?"

"I just need to rub some dirt on it, is all."

Tess said, "Rub some dirt on it?"

"Baseball expression," he said. He was too tired to smile. "I know, I know, one sport at a time."

To the Warriors he said, "Just don't let them get another score." He pointed to the scoreboard and said, "Forty points wins the game."

Then he told them, no screwing around, what they were going to run.

When they broke the huddle, Danny passed by Teddy Moran, heard Teddy say, "You're going down, little man."

Danny stopped.

"Ask you a question, Teddy?" Danny said.

"What, squirt?"

"You ever, like, run out of saliva?"

The Vikings were still in a man-to-man, and Danny and Ty ran a perfect pick-and-roll. Or so it looked until Jack Harty came racing over and jumped in front of Ty, blocking his path to the basket.

Ty didn't hesitate, gave the ball right back to Danny.

Now he was the one with a clear path to the basket.

Until Teddy Moran grabbed him from behind with two arms before Danny could even bring the ball up, knocking Danny down like it was a football tackle, falling on top of him, planting Danny's left shoulder into the floor.

Ty got to him first as Danny rolled from side to side on the ground, Ty probably remembering the fall he'd taken in the scrimmage. Then he pulled Danny carefully up into a sitting position.

"Deep breaths," Ty said.

Danny finally managed to get his

breathing under control, saw his mom start to run out on the court as he did, froze her where she was with a shake of the head, even though his shoulder now felt like Teddy Moran had set fire to it.

Tony the ref had already thrown Teddy out of the game for his flagrant foul. Danny could see Teddy's dad and Teddy yelling at Tony from behind the Vikings' bench. Tony turned and told them that the next thing he was going to do was throw them both out of the gym.

That finally shut up the whole Moran family.

A flagrant foul in their league meant two shots for Danny, and also meant the Warriors got to keep the ball. Tony asked if Danny could shoot his free throws. If not, Danny knew, there was this dumb rule that the Vikings were allowed to pick a shooter off the Warriors' bench. Which would mean one of the O'Brien twins.

NC.

No chance.

"I'm good to go," Danny said.

He stood up, got what he thought might be the loudest cheer he'd ever gotten, took the ball from Tony, went through his little four-bounce routine. Made the first free throw. Missed the second.

Vikings 39, Warriors 38.

Still Warriors' ball.

Jack Harty was waving his arms in front of Oliver Towne when he tried to inbound the ball to Ty. Oliver forgot you couldn't run the baseline after a made free throw the way you could after a made basket. As soon as he took two steps away from Jack, Tony the ref called him for traveling.

Vikings' ball.

They called their last time-out, came out of it, tried to run out the clock. But when they finally swung the ball to Da-Rod in the corner, Danny and Ty ran at him at the same time, trapping him. In desperation, he tried to bounce the ball off Danny's leg. Danny jumped out of the way. Da-Rod threw it out of bounds instead.

Warriors' ball.

One minute left.

Danny called *his* last time-out.

Instead of going back to his bench, he walked all the way across the court to where his dad was.

When he got there, he crouched down in front of him.

"Got a play for me, Coach?" he said.

Richie Walker looked at Mr. Ross, then back at Danny.

"Yeah," he said. "Mine."

His dad started to describe it to him. Danny cut him off, saying he didn't need anybody to draw him a picture on this one.

"I've known this play my whole life," he said.

"They'll be looking for you to pass," Richie said.

"Yeah," Danny said. "Won't they?"

Then he ran back across the court, feeling fresh all of a sudden, and told the Warriors he had a play he thought just might beat the Vikings.

Ty and Michael Harden were on opposite sidelines, just inside the mid-court line, Will and Oliver Towne went to the corners. Danny had the ball at mid-court.

He could hear Daryll Senior yelling at the Vikings to watch Ty.

"He's gonna give it to Ty," Daryll Senior said.

Danny kept it instead.

He dribbled toward the free throw line, straight down the middle of the court;

when Andy Mayne and Daryll Junior double-teamed him, Danny wheeled around at top speed and dribbled right back outside.

Forty seconds left.

Now he dribbled to his left, toward Ty, just as Ty ran toward him. Da-Rod, still covering Ty, seemed sure Danny was about to pass it to him. Except Danny didn't pass, just put the ball through his legs, spun around again, came back to the middle.

Thirty.

He looked over at Michael Harden. Behind Michael, he could see his mom and Tess, standing there, holding hands, like statues. Danny wondered if his mom knew what she was watching: Watching him dribbling out the clock the way his dad had.

The only difference was, Richie Walker's team had been ahead by a point at the end of the big game, not one behind.

With ten seconds left, Will and Oliver ran out of the corners the way they were supposed to. Ty ran down to where Will had been, in the left corner. Daryll Senior yelled at Daryll Junior to stay where he was, forget his man, guard the basket like he was the back guy in a zone.

Danny made his move down the middle.

When he got inside the free throw line, Daryll Junior stepped up to double-team him along with Andy Mayne.

Danny Walker went left hand, right hand, then back again, the ball as low to the ground as dust, splitting the two of them with a perfect double crossover.

Like in the driveway.

He was wide open, but only for an instant.

On account of, here came Da-Rod.

Now Danny passed.

He passed with a left hand that suddenly didn't hurt one single bit, made a perfect bounce pass to Ty Ross without even looking, knowing exactly where Ty would be, just as if he were one of the folding chairs in the driveway. Then Danny turned his head to see Ty make the catch.

And the layup that beat the stinking Vikings.

Everything seemed to happen at fast-forward speed after that, like somebody in the crowd had a remote in his hands.

He saw his dad standing and pumping his arms over his head, crutches forgotten on the floor next to him, looking as happy as Danny had ever seen him.

Then his mom was over there with his dad, an arm around his shoulder, his mom acting like his crutch.

Tess Hewitt came running for Danny then, started to put her arms around him, then pulled back, remembering his shoulder.

"Is a hug allowed?"

He said, yeah, it was allowed, and she ducked her head and leaned down and hugged him and he hugged her back.

When he pulled away from Tess, not sure where to go next, Ty Ross was standing in front of him, grinning this goofy-looking grin from ear to ear.

"Nice pass," he said.

"Nice shot," Danny said.

The two of them shook hands the regular way.

The old-school way.

Then Ty kept holding on to Danny's hand and somehow lifted him up in the air in the same motion. Then Will was there, and Bren, putting Danny up on their shoulders, carrying him around the court, the way the old Vikings had carried his dad once.

Danny looked down on the day and thought:

So this is what everything looks like from up here.

ABOUT THE AUTHOR

Mike Lupica is the author of many novels for sports fans, including *Red Zone, Bump and Run,* and *Wild Pitch.* His columns for the New York Daily News are syndicated nationally, and he is a regular on ESPN's *The Sports Reporters.*

Partial to little guys, Mr. Lupica enjoys coaching youth basketball. He lives in Connecticut with his wife and their four children.